ABRACADABRA

A BUZZARDS BAY MYSTERY

Also by Lawrence Rotch

Gravely Dead: A Midcoast Maine Mystery
Bulletproof: A Midcoast Maine Mystery
Standing Dead: A Midcoast Maine Mystery
Mistletoe and Murder: A Midcoast Maine Mystery
Beware of the Elephant: A Midcoast Maine Mystery

ABRACADABRA

A BUZZARDS BAY MYSTERY

LAWRENCE ROTCH

S⌣P

Shoal Waters Press

This is a work of fiction. Names, characters, places, and incidents are the product of the author's imagination or are used fictitiously. Any resemblance to actual or persons, living or dead, is entirely coincidental.

Abracadabra: a Buzzards Bay Mystery. Copyright © 2018 Lawrence Rotch. All rights reserved. No part of this book may be used or reproduced in any manner whatsoever without written permission, except in the case of brief quotations embedded in critical articles or reviews.

Printed in the United States of America

ISBN: 978-0-9839079-3-0

First Edition: September 1, 2018

Published by
Shoal Waters Press
Liberty, Maine
Shoalwaterspress.com

10 9 8 7 6 5 4 3 2 1

"Reality leaves a lot to the imagination."
John Lennon

Chapter 1

New Bedford, August 3, 1949

Fog had settled over the town of New Bedford during the night, and it still clung stubbornly to the water, suffocating and damp, at dawn the next morning. As a result, much of New Bedford's fishing fleet was still in the harbor.

Tony Silva had mouths to feed and little cash, so he chose to go out in hopes of getting a jump on the laggards, regardless of the weather. He wasn't especially worried about fog anyway. Having spent most of his thirty-eight years fishing out of New Bedford, he knew the waters of Buzzards Bay like the back of his calloused hand.

If he had known what secrets were lurking in the fog's stifling embrace, Tony would never have coaxed *Maria's* ancient six-cylinder engine into a reluctant, smoky life.

Tony worked his way down the harbor channel, moving slowly from buoy to buoy until the reassuring sound of the Brooklyn Rock gong signaled open water. He set a compass course for the low, sandy Elizabeth islands, which formed the seaward side of Buzzards Bay. He knew a good fishing area there and hoped to be one of the first boats to land fish, thereby fetching top dollar.

The wind had been out of the north until midnight, before

a gentle southerly breeze ushered in this morning's fog. As a result, the sea was calm, with a slight swell—a good situation for *Maria's* tender planking and leaky seams.

Tony may not have been particularly worried about the fog, but he did have other concerns. First, he worried about *Maria* herself. She was a 36-foot fishing vessel, laid out like a Maine lobster boat, with a big, open cockpit aft, a small cuddy cabin forward, and a shelter roof extending over the wheel. *Maria* was old and tired; her engine, rescued from a war-surplus truck, had worn bearings that pounded heavily when he opened the throttle; her topsides were dingy and battered; her worn, punky planking leaked badly in the kind of steep chop that was all too common on the bay.

Most of all, though, Tony worried about Al Valero, his homicidal brother-in-law, who was even now muttering while he prowled around the cockpit with a bloody sheath knife in his hand.

Al had taken part in the landing at Anzio in 1944, was shot in the head, spent months the hospital, and had never been the same since. The doctors talked about brain damage from where the bullet split open the back of his skull.

Tony hadn't known much about head injuries until he got a crash course on the subject one hot summer afternoon not long after Al was mustered out on a medical discharge. The two of them had gone into a bar for a few cold beers, and a couple of bar-flies started making fun of Al's funny way of talking—a memento from the bullet that had unzipped his skull. Tony tried to warn the drunks off, but before he could manage it, something in Al's head snapped and his eyes went all wild—kind of like one of those werewolves in a Lon Chaney movie—and he went to work with his knife.

It had taken three of them to drag Al away, and by then one of the drunks was dead, slashed to ribbons. God, the man was quick with a knife.

Al landed in the Bridgewater mental hospital for three years after that.

He'd been sprung just last month, and this was the first time Tony had taken him out fishing, or much of anywhere else for that matter. He would never have brought Al out this morning if Maria hadn't pestered him into it. "Give Al a chance," she said over and over, trying to wear Tony down.

"A chance to do what?" Tony kept replying.

But Maria wouldn't stop reminding him how the shrinks had told them that Al was fine now. All cured. They'd seemed really sure of themselves, too, like they knew what they were talking about.

The trouble was, they hadn't seen their patient screaming and swearing as he hacked and stabbed that poor drunk to death, blood flying in all directions. "Just try to keep him from getting excited," was their advice, for what it was worth.

The problem was that nobody had explained to Tony how to keep a lunatic from getting excited. What did it take to set a madman off, anyway?

Blood was thicker than water though, and Al Valero was his wife's brother. Even so, Tony had his service .45 tucked away in a pocket under his sweatshirt, just in case his brother-in-law got excited.

And speaking of getting excited, how would he explain things to Maria if worse came to worse and he ended up having to bring her brother home full of bullet holes?

Tony knew how to deal with leaky planks and balky engines. Those were things he could understand, things that made sense and he could fix. He couldn't say the same for the twisted darkness and violence that lurked in a person's mind, waiting to leap forth.

Crazy or not, Tony had to admit that Al was a fast worker when it came to cutting up bait instead of people. Hell, Al was a fast worker even when he *was* filleting people. Tony glanced over his shoulder again, where Al had sat down and was cutting up chunks of bait at a dizzying speed.

Maybe he should have cocked the .45 before putting it in his pocket.

They were longlining this morning so there were hundreds of snoods, or branch lines—each with a hook that needed bait—attached to the main line. Al's hands were a blur as he cut up the bait and loaded the hooks. In spite of his speed, Al hadn't once sliced a finger or hooked himself. As near as Tony could tell, Al seemed to enjoy the gory work, babbling happily to himself in his odd, barely-intelligible way.

Maybe things would work out after all.

Still, as Tony stood at the helm, checking the compass, and peering into the fog, he was uncomfortably aware of Al and his knife behind him. He felt something more, too, a vague sense of evil hidden in the murk ahead of them. Not that Tony Silva thought of himself as being superstitious, you understand.

The fog seemed to be lifting a little as the sun went to work, and Tony figured that Wood Island should be coming out of the mist pretty soon, so he throttled back. The pounding of the engine subsided, as though it was thankful for the respite.

"Oook ere! Oook ere!" Al shouted as he pranced around the cockpit stabbing at the fog with his knife.

The man had good eyesight as well as quick hands.

Tony glanced over his shoulder and watched his brother-in-law hopping up and down, and wondered if this qualified as excitement. How would the shrinks at Bridgewater feel about being alone in a small boat with their knife-wielding ex-patient, now?

"It's just Wood Island," Tony said soothingly, as he looked at the shape coming into view. In truth, there was no wood on Wood Island, except for what might wash ashore from somewhere else after a storm. Even the term "island" was an exaggeration for the three-acre patch of mostly sand and beach grass.

But there was more than just sand and grass on Wood Island this morning.

Tony's eagle-eyed companion had spotted a faint smudge on the low, sandy shore. Tony altered course towards the island, his mind a tangle of curiosity, greed, and foreboding. Wreckage often washed ashore here, but there hadn't been any storms lately—just today's fog.

Before long, Tony could make out a sailboat lying in the sand, its hull as black as coal.

Al would never get back to cutting up bait now.

"Oook ere! Oook ere!" Al wouldn't stop yelling, or waving his damn knife around either. It was enough to drive a man to drink.

Maria didn't draw much water, and Tony was able to run her into the shallows close enough to the beach for them to wade ashore with Al carrying a light anchor.

The derelict lay on her side in the flawless sand like a dozing sunbather, her keel in the water, and her mast pointing up to the coarse beach grass that covered most of the tiny, unpopulated sand spit. Tony couldn't see any obvious damage. The mast and spars were intact, there were no loose bits of rigging, the sail was neatly furled, and the cabin hatch was closed. The boat could have been sitting at her mooring. Perhaps she'd been anchored somewhere and just broke loose and drifted ashore.

Al scampered across the damp sand, slashing the air with his knife like a murderous, overgrown child. Tony followed more slowly, one eye on the derelict, the other on his companion, Slasher Al. The weight of the .45 in his pocket felt comforting.

Tony approached the cockpit warily, while Al splashed and whooped in the water, perhaps checking the hull for damage. Or perhaps working himself into some kind of maniacal frenzy.

The tide was coming in, and water was half way up to Tony's knees as he stood by the rail.

The hull had settled as the beach claimed its prize, and the gentle swell was patiently banking sand against the deck, filling the lower corner of the cockpit with golden grains. The boat was motionless in the sand, not lifting with the incoming tide.

The hair rose on the back of Tony's neck.

Al splashed around the stern, his clothes soaked and his face flushed with excitement. "Nole, nole, okay, okay, okay," he chanted, rocking back and forth.

"She must be full of water," Tony replied. "There may be a hole on the under side where we can't see."

Tony slid the hatch open. Al, reeking of fish offal and unwashed flesh, pushed against him eagerly. The fog had lifted just enough to let a ray of watery sunlight slash low across the water, blinding them and casting the interior in darkness. The two men leaned forward, peering into the cabin as they strained to pierce the gloom. It was full of water. And a smell.

And the bloated face of a man. The skin was alabaster white, the mouth, full of water, gaped in a noiseless scream.

The half submerged body floated mere inches from their faces.

Tony jumped back as though his nose had hit a light socket, but Al Valero leaned in, fascinated. "Sweet Mary, Mother of God," he said, perfectly mimicking the plumy tones of Father O'Malley, their parish priest.

"No!" Tony yelled, but he was much too late as Al's knife flashed out.

Chapter 2

Wissonet, August 3

With its waterfront cottages and mansions, its long-time summer residents, its pleasure boats dotting the harbor's sparkling waters, and its beach goers enjoying the warm August water, Wissonet looked like most of the small, sleepy seaside towns that lined Buzzards Bay.

Like its neighbors in 1949, Wissonet stood on the cusp of a post-war building boom that promised a tidal wave of change destined to sweep away many old and treasured traditions.

Bad news travels fast in such towns, especially when that news involves the gruesome murder of one of the idyllic community's wealthiest citizens.

"The Commodore was murdered? Are you sure?" Mary Wendell's lemonade glass rattled on the scarred wood of the kitchen table. In all of her 26 years, Mary couldn't remember a single person in town being killed. Sure, there were plenty of murders in nearby New Bedford, but never here.

"Of course I'm sure." The table creaked under Loretta Clayton's elbows. "His boat washed up over on Wood Island with his body inside it."

"How did you hear that?"

"Half the town knows," Loretta replied, surprised. "The

police have been questioning people since first thing this morning. Where have you been?"

"I've been tending to a rambunctious toddler, where else would I have been?" It was already in the nineties outside, and an aged fan whined ineffectually on the kitchen counter. "When did it happen?"

"All they're saying is that his body was found around dawn this morning. Did you know him well?" Coming from New Bedford, Loretta was new to the ways of small-town life in Wissonet. Mary, on the other hand, could trace her ancestry almost back to the founding of the town in the late 1700's.

"No, not well," Mary said. "He was ten years older, and the Cummings family had a lot more money." It was true that Mary didn't know him well, at least by Wissonet standards. "He got his own boat when he was thirteen." She started to say something more, but added simply, "He sailed by himself a lot."

Mary glanced across the kitchen to where her three-year-old daughter was hunting Nathaniel Herreshoff, better known as Nat-the-Cat, or simply Nat.

"The Cummings don't have anywhere near as much money as they used to," Loretta commented.

Mary looked at her next-door neighbor skeptically. Loretta Clayton wasn't a person to let a lack of information stifle her imagination.

Nat jumped onto a nearby chair and growled at his tormenter.

"Wendy! Leave Nat alone," Mary said. "Where did you hear that?"

"From Ed. According to him, the Commodore didn't have a head for business, and he's been running Cummings Jewelry into the ground ever since he took over after his father died. Dianne is the business woman of that pair, and Ed says there have been some arguments between them on how to run the company."

Mary digested this. Ed Clayton, Loretta's husband, had been in charge of marketing for Cummings Jewelry for the last three or four years, having been hired by the Commodore's father shortly before his death. Mary figured that Ed probably knew what he was talking about.

"You're not seriously thinking that Dianne would kill her own husband because she doesn't agree with the way he was running the business, are you?" Mary said.

"People have killed for less," Loretta countered. "You've just lived here too long to be objective." Loretta lived next door and Mary could see her neighbor's kitchen window from where she sat. The proximity was a mixed blessing.

"Don't pass this around," the town gossip confided, "but lay-offs are coming at Cummings Jewelry, people are getting pink slips, and some of them are going to have a hard time finding work. Somebody might have taken revenge. Ed has already gotten his notice."

"He has? I'm sorry to hear that."

"Oh, he'll find another job easily enough," Loretta said, belatedly realizing the implications of her comment.

Nat made a dash for the kitchen door, much to Wendy's delight.

"All I'm saying is that the Commodore doesn't have a lot of friends in his jewelry company right now." She swept an errant wisp of blonde hair over her shoulder. Mary congratulated herself for having her brunette hair cut short for the sake of coolness. She got up and let the long-suffering feline outdoors.

Loretta had been trying to have a baby for more than a year without success. Frustrated by her childless state, she leaned towards the bereft toddler. "Why don't you come and sit on my lap, Wendy?"

"You'll regret it," Mary warned. "That child is a blast furnace in this heat." She ran a finger down the side of her glass, leaving a streak on the damp surface. "It's going to be hard for Dianne with him gone."

Loretta cocked an eyebrow. "Is it? She'll be running the company her own way now."

"You're just making things up for the fun of it."

"Aren't you the least bit curious about who killed the Commodore?" Loretta said. "He was the biggest wheel in town, after all."

Mary thought her next door neighbor had more curiosity than was good for her and she often marveled that someone like Loretta, who was "from away," could manage to know more about what was happening in town than people who'd lived here all their lives.

"Of course I'm curious. I just don't see why you assume it has to be someone we know."

"Guessing who it might be is half the fun, and where's the fun if it's a stranger? Don't forget: it's almost always the spouse in a murder like this."

"That's the whole point," Mary replied. "We don't know what kind of murder it is."

* * *

A mile away from the Wendell's house, the midday sun beat down on the hard-packed dirt of Barton's Boatyard, where John Wendell and his two companions had taken refuge from the heat in a sliver of shade beside the main building shed. They were a mis-matched trio. There was Sam Barton, owner of the establishment, in his sixties, short, stocky and balding. Next to him stood John, in his late-twenties, tall and slender with curly blond hair. Facing them was Lieutenant Riley, a state police detective. Riley was about the same height as John, but balding, close to a hundred pounds heavier, and a good twenty years older. Riley had shed his jacket and tie in deference to the heat, and the armpits of his white shirt were stained with sweat.

"Murdered? What happened?" John asked. Sam Barton shifted uneasily.

Riley sighed. "I suppose it will be all over the evening papers, anyway. It looks like someone stabbed him to death and tried to sink his boat, with him in it, by pulling out the drain plug, whatever that is. Luckily for us, it washed up on Wood Island across the bay. A couple of fishermen found him in his boat early this morning."

"That's less than a day's sail from here," John commented. "When was he killed?"

Riley seemed to consider the question as though trying to decide how much information to reveal. "It's hard to tell exactly with the body sloshing around in the water, but it was probably sometime Monday afternoon or evening."

"But today's Wednesday. Why did it take so long to find him?" Sam said.

"It's been foggy up that way," John replied. "There probably haven't been many boats out."

"Where's the boat now?" Sam asked.

"You ask a lot of questions," Riley muttered. "It's at the Carver Creek Boatyard in Pocasset. Now if you don't mind, I'd like to ask a few questions of my own. First of all, do either of you know where he was going?"

John shook his head.

"What about you, Mr. Barton?"

"Why would he tell me anything like that?"

"Why wouldn't he?" Riley countered. "Was he alone when he left?"

Barton's Boatyard sat at the foot of one of the decaying granite piers that punctuated Wissonet's waterfront, reminders of the town's shipbuilding heritage during the whaling days of the eighteenth and nineteenth centuries. Sam gazed out over the pier for a moment before replying. "As far as I know he was alone, but I haven't got time to go spying on everybody in town."

Riley looked pained. "I thought you said the boat was tied up to the dock. He must have walked right by the door. Wouldn't you have noticed if anybody was with him?"

"I was too busy to look."

The lawman frowned. "I hear he went cruising every year during the company vacation. Did Mrs. Cummings ever go with him?"

Sam shuffled his feet. "Why don't you ask her? The Commodore didn't poke his nose into my business and I didn't poke my nose into his."

Riley's frown deepened. "I'll do that. How long have you been servicing Cummings's boat?"

"Servicing?"

"Well, taking care of it, or whatever you do with sailboats."

Sam muttered under his breath. "The Commodore's father bought the boat new around 1912, and it's been kept here ever since, up until last fall."

John could see the Lieutenant's antennae going up. "He kept it somewhere else last winter?"

"Isn't that what I just said?" Sam replied irritably.

"Why the change?" Riley said.

"How the hell would I know? What difference does it make, anyway?"

"Do you know *where* he stored the boat last winter?" Riley was obviously not easily put off.

Sam glared at his tormentor. "The Commodore didn't tell me where he stored the boat, why he stored the boat there, or what his favorite flavor of ice cream was."

John took half a step back as the two men glared at each other.

Riley finally turned to John "Do you know anything about where the boat was kept last winter?"

John shook his head. "All I know is the Commodore went up to Maine in early June, picked up the boat, and sailed back here. It took him about a week."

"A week?"

"The wind was against him on the way back, and he probably took his time."

"Okay," Riley said in a resigned voice. "But you've known the Cummings family for quite a while, haven't you?" he asked Sam.

"Sure. He was born here. He ran a jewelry business in New Bedford. The richest man in town. Very successful."

Riley had been making sporadic entries in a pocket-sized notebook. John watched him thumb through the pages. It didn't take very long.

"Okay, that's about it, except for one more thing. I'd like to look at one of these Manchester 17 boats if you have any around here."

"You haven't seen *Abracadabra* yet?" John said.

"The Coast Guard is towing it over to a boatyard in Pocasset now. I'll be looking at it later today."

Pocasset was a small town on the Cape Cod side of Buzzards Bay, and it would be fairly close to Wood Island. "The boat must be reasonably seaworthy if they're towing it that far,"

John commented.

"So I've been told," Riley said coolly.

Sam looked anxious to end the conversation. "Why don't you take the lieutenant out front and show him *Sadie,*" he said to John. "She's right around the side of the shed." He turned to Riley. "John is the person you want. He's a Naval Architect, knows everything there is to know about Manchester 17's." With that fanciful accolade, Sam fled into the recesses of his shop.

The two men walked in silence around the corner of the building to where a handful of boats sat on wooden cradles, baking in the sun.

Riley looked at the jumble of empty cradles littering the yard, mute testimony to the craft now afloat. "What does the '17' stand for?"

"The boats are seventeen-feet-long at the waterline."

"Waterline?"

It was beginning to look like a long morning. "They're actually twenty-six feet long, overall." John glanced at Riley. "From end to end," he added, "but they're seventeen feet long where they sit in the water."

John never tired of admiring the slender, graceful lines of a Manchester 17. Though nearly 40 years old, *Sadie* had held her shape well. Sam Barton took good care of his flock, which made Riley's question a good one. Why had the Commodore stopped having his boat kept here? Did Sam and the Commodore have a falling out? John suspected that Riley was wondering the same thing—and wondering whether the fact was significant.

Riley looked at *Sadie* with something akin to horror. "Jesus, these things are small. Can you really go out very far in one?"

John's eyes swept the curve of the hull. A patch of bare wood and several fresh bungs marked some new fastenings at the transom. "They're really quite seaworthy. Lots of people sail them up and down the coast or even over to Nova Scotia."

Riley looked skeptical. "Okay, where is this drain plug thing?"

John stooped under the hull's curve and pointed to a pencil-sized hole near the keel.

"That's not very big," Riley said. "What is it for—and don't tell me it's to let the water out."

"Well, actually it is. If you pull the plug when you store the boat for the winter, it keeps rainwater from sitting in the bilge. Sometimes people will fill the bilge with water to let the planking swell up for a few days before launching the boat in the spring. The plug is handy for draining it out."

"This thing is made out of wood, right? Why would it sink just because you took the plug out?"

"Some boats wouldn't sink, but these have 1500 pounds of lead in their keels." The keel was bolted to a two-foot-high oak fin, and John tapped the appendage in question with his toe. "A lot of Manchester 17's don't have flotation tanks either, so they'll sink like a stone."

"It sounds like a death trap to me."

"People don't usually take the plug out with the boat in the water, Lieutenant."

"Apparently they do if they've just killed somebody and want to get rid of the body. How long do you suppose it would take for one of these things to sink once you pulled the plug?"

"I'm not sure. Probably a couple of hours. As you say, the hole isn't very big, so she'd just settle lower and lower in the water. I suppose waves would start coming in over the side sooner if the weather was rough."

"A couple of hours? How far do you think it might drift in two hours?"

"It would depend on where it started from," John said patiently.

"According to Mrs. Cummings, he was planning to stay in Onset—something about waiting for the tide."

Onset was a small harbor at the south end of the Cape Cod Canal. "The boat doesn't have a motor," John said, "so he'd have to wait for a favorable tide to sail through the canal. Onset would be a good place for that."

"Okay, suppose the boat was somewhere near Onset when the plug was pulled. Would it make it to Wood Island before it sank?"

"You want a wild guess? Because that's the best I can do."

"Anything will help."

"It depends a lot on when he was killed." John thought for a moment "The wind was blowing from the south until Monday afternoon when a cool front came through and it started to blow from the northwest." The front had been a glorious, but short-lived respite from the heat wave that had gripped the bay for nearly two weeks.

"The wind came around from the south again early Tuesday morning. If he was killed Monday evening in Onset, the boat must have been towed several miles out to the middle of Buzzards Bay before the plug was pulled, for it to end up on Wood island."

"I imagine the killer would want to have it sink in deep water," Riley said, "but wouldn't somebody have seen it drifting around?"

"Maybe in the daytime, but probably not at night. *Abracadabra*'s hull is black, so the boat would be hard to see."

Thanks to *Sadie*'s fin and keel, her deck was head-high above the ground. Luckily, there was a ladder made from a pair of two-by-fours and a few slats, lying nearby. Favoring his bad leg, John climbed the ladder. The limp, a souvenir of the war, was almost gone, but climbing ladders was still a challenge.

John stood in the cockpit and looked around. He was reminded once again of the old adage that yacht design was ninety percent art and ten percent design. The curves of the deck and the cabin were all in harmony. At the same time, each piece of wood was just the right size and strength to do its job. There was no clumsiness here; grace in form was matched by grace in design.

John was shaken out of his reverie by the jarring thud of Riley's brogues as he landed in the cockpit. The term "flatfoot" flitted through his mind.

John slid the hatch forward and removed the three wash boards that closed off the rear end of the opening. Riley stuck his head into the cabin and gaped at the tiny, Spartan interior.

"My god, it's as bare as a pauper's coffin in there, and about the same size. Where do you sit? Where do you cook? Where's the bathroom? Do people really go off and spend the night in one of these things?"

"You might not go around the world in one, but they're perfectly comfortable for a few days. It's like camping out."

"You can go behind a bush when you're camping out, Wendell." Riley shook his head at the eccentricities of sailors. "What I don't understand is why someone as rich as Cummings would have a boat like this if he could afford something better, and something newer. They must have the biggest house in town, right on the main street."

"I think it's a matter of tradition. *Abracadabra* is like a family heirloom. She's a fixture in the harbor."

"Some heirloom," Riley said, as he started back down the ladder.

Once they were on solid ground again, he asked, "In your

opinion, how likely is it the plug could have worked loose by itself?"

John thought about Sam. "Not very. It gets driven in pretty securely for obvious reasons."

"Look, I don't know much about this sailboat business," Riley said, as they headed back to where their cars were parked, "and I was wondering if you'd come to Pocasset with me tomorrow morning and look over the boat. Barton says you used to sail with Cummings, so you might see something that we've missed."

They stood between John's battered Model A Ford beach wagon and Riley's mammoth pre-war Packard sedan, while Sam's rusted pickup sat nearby. The place looked like a vehicular rest home.

"It would only take a half a day and I could arrange to pay you a fee," Riley added.

"I haven't sailed with the Commodore in years, so I'm not sure what help I'd be. I know this is a bad time to ask her, but Dianne would know *Abracadabra* the best."

"The thing is, I want someone who isn't close to the Cummings family. Someone who knows about things like drain plugs, and why boats sink."

Chapter 3

Wissonet, August 3

John watched Riley's Packard waddle and sway across the potholed yard before lumbering off down the road. Was he making a mistake by agreeing to help the police?

On the other hand, what harm could it do? He wasn't really getting involved in anything. Besides, it would only take a few hours and might help find the Commodore's killer. Plus, he'd get paid—an important consideration in view of their shaky finances. Nursing those comforting thoughts, John turned toward Sam Barton's boat shop.

The shop was a cavernous building with a large door at each end, able to accommodate up to a fifty-foot vessel, though most of the boats Sam had been building lately were somewhat smaller due to wartime restrictions, wartime lack of customers, and the difficulty of finding skilled workers.

The shop's roof displayed shingles of various ages and hues, while a chimney protruded sinuously through the multicolored surface. A weathered sign over the big shed door announced "Barton and Son Boat Building, Repair, Storage." The sign was misleading since the Bartons' only son, Jeff, had gone off to war six years ago and never returned.

A nearly completed sloop filled one end of the building.

The boat's lines and raised deck had the unmistakable signature of a Crocker design, and John paused for a moment, looking up at the deck and savoring the fresh look and smell of Sam Barton's handiwork. The contrary individual generally built a boat over the fall and winter, finishing in the late spring. He appeared to be well behind his usual schedule.

A metallic crash filled the space. John leaped back, his eyes wide, his heart pounding with unwanted memories.

"Hello Sonny." Henry Merton's cadaverous face grinned down like a Halloween death mask from his overhead perch in the sloop's cockpit. "I forgot that you don't like loud noises anymore, or I wouldn't have tossed that bucket over the side." Henry's grin faded. "I saw you over by *Sadie*, talking to that cop a few minutes ago."

"Leave the man alone, you vicious old goat," Sam growled from his workbench.

"Stop being so touchy, Sonny," Henry replied. Anyone under the age of sixty-five was Sonny in Henry Merton's opinion. Though nobody knew his exact age, Henry claimed to have childhood memories of Abraham Lincoln, which would make him close to a hundred years old. Sam, who would soon graduate from Sonny status, employed the cantankerous old man part-time for his boat building skill.

John stared out the open shed door at the water while he struggled to get his breathing under control. And his anger. He vowed not to give Henry the victory. "Just trying to help out, Henry." He managed to sound pleasant.

"You'll be a lot better off if you stay away from the police. They're nothing but trouble." With that advice, Henry sank out of sight into the boat's cabin.

A weedy looking youth was making a project out of sweeping up a pile of wood shavings and sawdust at the back of the building. John smiled at the timelessness of the scene, remembering when he had wielded a similar broom, perhaps even the same one, during his teenage summers. Jeff Barton had been there then. A few years older than John, he was a Wissonet native, whereas John's family rented a summer cottage in town. The difference in background had been an obstacle at first, but the natural good nature of both boys, together with their common passion for boats, had eventually bridged the gap.

In both good economic times and bad, Sam had always managed to find enough work to keep the two boys busy cleaning up, painting, and mastering simple boat building skills. His acerbic guidance led them through the intricacies of building simple, flat-bottomed skiffs, for which there always seemed to be a market. The two boys gradually learned more sophisticated boat building skills as the following summers rolled by. John looked around at the stillness. Perhaps the place wasn't timeless after all.

Sam stood at a long workbench that ran along the side wall. "Does that clown think I've got nothing better to do than spend all afternoon answering his dammfool questions? 'How long have I been servicing the Commodore's boat?'" He grunted in disgust. "What am I, an automobile mechanic? A bull?"

"You sound a little touchy, Sam. He's just doing his job."

"Well he can do it somewhere else. I don't like strangers, especially cops, coming in and nosing around. Why should I help him stir up trouble in town? Does he live here? Let him dig up his own dirt."

Sam watched The Kid's lackadaisical progress with the broom for a moment, grimaced, and turned towards the door. "Come on, I'll show you the boat. It's right out front."

"Riley doesn't seem too bad; he's just in over his head when it comes to boats," John commented while they walked.

Sam squinted as they left the building and entered the sunlight. "Then he should swim in shallow water. What the hell is an Irish cop doing in New Bedford anyway?"

"Why shouldn't he be in New Bedford?"

Sam grunted skeptically. "A lieutenant? He's a pretty big cheese to be working on a murder case."

"The Commodore was a pretty big cheese, too." John shrugged. "All I know is that he's willing to pay to have me go over to Pocasset, look at *Abracadabra*, and hold his hand."

Sam stopped in his tracks. "You're going to help that overstuffed, ignorant, ham-fisted, cigar chewing bear?"

John hadn't seen any hint of a cigar, but he let it pass. "Why not? The Commodore was one of the pillars of the community. Besides, I liked the guy. Don't you want to help find out who killed him?"

"Well, sure." Sam kicked at a rock sticking out of the hard-packed dirt. "But why do the cops think somebody from around here killed him? Why doesn't he snoop around somewhere else?"

"They're probably looking in other places too."

"Well I'm sorry you're getting involved in it."

John looked out over the harbor, where Mike Hartwell's motorboat, a fast twenty-five foot inboard, was tied up to the pier. John could see Mike bending over the engine. A sea breeze was picking up, and a Herreshoff 12 bobbed at her mooring near the end of the pier. Further out, the bigger boats hobby-horsed at their tethers amid the whitecaps. At least the breeze made this side of the building cooler. "Do you suppose the Commodore was alone when he left?"

Sam turned abruptly. "I don't suppose anything. Like I said, I don't like strangers coming in here and asking me to bad mouth my neighbors."

Sam caught himself and placed a callused hand on John's shoulder. His forearm was covered with sawdust and smelled of cedar and sweat. "Look, even if the Commodore did have company when he left, that doesn't mean it was the killer. He probably had enemies everywhere. Maybe some business rival of his did it. Maybe the Rhode Island Mafia is taking over the jewelry business around here, and Cummings got in the way. All I'm saying is to let the cops do their own digging."

Mike Hartwell had abandoned his boat and came sauntering up. In his late twenties, he was about John's age. Despite the bravado, Mike looked nervous.

"Having the cops drop in must remind you of the good old days when you were running booze, right Sam? I figured I'd stay out of the way 'til the coast was clear. Whoever killed the Commodore did the world a favor as far as I'm concerned."

Sam glared at Mike. "Sooner or later the cops will be asking where you've been with that boat of yours."

"Why should they care about me?"

"They're interested in anyone who could have gone over to Onset Monday night," John said.

"Hell, that's a good hour's run from here. I wouldn't dare go that far with the damn engine acting up the way it has lately. I spent most of Monday drifting around the harbor, trying to get the damn thing to run at all."

"If you cleaned out the gas tank once in a while, you wouldn't have so much trouble," Sam retorted.

"Yeah, well I've been too busy to mess with that kind of job. Which reminds me I've got to get back to the store. Can't trust the help nowadays." Mike gave John a sour look. "Say hello to Mary for me, John."

"I'll do that, Mike."

"Great. Well, I gotta get back to work." He turned and

headed towards the road.

"Petty, loud-mouthed, smart-ass, boozing, little weasel," Sam muttered at Mike's retreating back. "There goes a real case of arrested development."

"I don't seem to be one of his favorite people."

"It's not your fault he holds a grudge. I don't like to bad-mouth the kid where he's Henry's grandson, but Mike is headed for trouble if he keeps messing with those small-time crooks and drug dealers in New Bedford."

* * *

With Wendy safely in her crib for the night, John and Mary sat on the porch while the afternoon faded into evening.

"The Commodore might not have been alone when he left."

Mary stared at John. "What makes you say that?"

"Sam was evasive about it when Riley asked, and he almost took my head off when I asked him about it later."

"That doesn't mean anything one way or the other. It would be just like Sam to mislead the police, throwing mud in the water," Mary said.

"Or he's trying to protect somebody."

"You're not suggesting the Commodore had a girlfriend on the side, are you? I can't imagine him taking a chance of being spotted in a compromising situation right here in town."

John thought for a moment. "You're right about that. The thing is that he was stabbed, so he most likely knew his killer. The Commodore was a big man, maybe a bit chubby, but no pushover for anyone trying to force his way onto the boat while it was anchored in Onset harbor."

"I wish you weren't going," Mary said. Her face looked

troubled.

John watched little puffs of wind brushing across the hay below the lawn. A faint land breeze was coming up, sending gentle whispers of warm air down the slope, and keeping the mosquitoes at bay. "It's just this one trip, half a day. Riley will pay and we can use the money."

"We don't need money that much."

"We don't?" John shook his head in frustration. "I hung out my shingle a year ago, and Hibbert's sloop is the first real design job to come in. We'd starve if you weren't working four mornings a week at Cantor Realty, and Sam wasn't tossing me some odds and ends."

"Do you think we should have stayed in Quincy, so you could have kept working for Bill Grey?"

"Of course not. I'm just saying we can't afford to turn down some honest work."

"If it is honest work. You know perfectly well that he'll spend the morning pumping you for information."

"About what?"

"Anything. Goings-on around town, gossip, rumors, who knows?" Mary said, exasperated.

"I'll send him to Loretta for that kind of stuff."

Mary twisted a strand of hair between her fingers. "Suppose you found a clue that implicated Dianne?"

"What kind of a clue?"

"How do I know what kind of clue?" Mary snapped. "Just suppose you did. Then what? The Cummings have a lot of clout in town. Do you want to get on the wrong side of them?"

"Dianne is the only Cummings left in town," John pointed out.

"You know perfectly well what I mean."

"You sound like Sam. I don't plan to get on the wrong side

of anybody, but the Commodore was murdered. Doesn't that count for something?"

She gave an irritated sigh. "Of course it does, but this is a small town; it's not like Quincy where you grew up. I don't want you to get into trouble here."

"Why is everyone more worried about protecting the town's reputation than helping catch the killer?"

"You don't have to make it sound like that. Of course people want to catch the killer, but why does it have to be someone from here? You make it sound as though the whole town is full of murderers. Let the police figure it out."

"That's more or less what Sam said this afternoon."

Mary watched the last of the sun painting the maple tops with a luminous green. "What about this boat Sam wanted you to look at?"

"He's putting a bigger engine in an old Elco power cruiser. I'll have to check the weight distribution and figure out where to put in some reinforcing. Sam is just throwing a little more business my way. I told him he didn't need my help."

"Losing Jeff was an awful blow to the Bartons," she said. "Especially where they married late and he was their only child."

"I suppose Sam was too busy dodging the revenue agents in his younger days."

"Everybody smuggled liquor in those days, and he made good money building rum-runners." Mary shrugged. "I think he looks on you as kind of a second son, especially where you and Jeff were such good friends."

"Do you think that could be making him overly protective?"

"So, I'm being overly protective?"

"I shall be cautious, take good care of myself, and above all, defend the honor of Wissonet," he promised solemnly.

Chapter 4

Wissonet, August 4

The Wendell's house was a modest, L-shaped Victorian. The long end of the L stood perpendicular to the street and contained the pantry, the kitchen, and the dining room. The livingroom occupied the short, water-facing side. The front door was inside the L, as was the driveway, which was just long enough to contain two cars.

"John!" The urgency in Mary's voice brought him to the front hall at a run.

"What's wrong?"

She stood in the open doorway and pointed to clots of blood staining the gray-enameled doorstep. Most of the edges had already dried to a rusty brown, while the rest was still red and sticky looking. It must have happened just before dawn.

"What the hell is all that?"

"I found this on the hall floor." Mary held out her closed fist.

"What is it?"

She looked at her hand and realized the fingers were still clenched. She opened them.

"A rabbit's foot key chain?"

"It was lying on the floor just inside the screen door. I

thought someone might have dropped it," Mary said, "until I saw the door."

John followed her gaze. An inverted cross had been drawn in blood on the front door.

"Look under the car," Mary said in a small voice.

A bundle of fur lay under the Ford's bumper. John stepped carefully over the door sill. "Where's Nat?"

"How would Nat open the screen door?"

John reached under the car. "It's a dead rabbit," he said, removing the carcass. Someone had slit it open.

"How many feet does it have?"

"Three, but those key chains are everywhere. Len has a rack of them at the market. Someone must have butchered the rabbit on the doorstep to paint the cross," he said. "Looks like it was done with a brush of some kind. Or the rabbit's missing foot."

Mary gingerly placed the key chain on the hall table.

"What a mess," John growled. "Should we call the police?"

"Danny Wilson? He'll just say it was some kids having fun—a practical joke," Mary said.

"Maybe he'd be right. Too many kids in town have weird ideas of fun."

"Maybe he'd be wrong. Maybe it's a warning."

"A warning? What for?"

"You know perfectly well what for," Mary said angrily. "You're going with the police to look at the Commodore's boat this morning."

John waved his hand at the scene. "This seems like an overreaction. Besides, Sam is the only one I told about helping the police." He paused. "And maybe Henry, if his hearing is good. He was working inside the Crocker sloop they're building while Sam and I were talking, and he saw me with Riley earlier."

"It doesn't matter about Henry's hearing, for heaven's sake!

Don't you see? By now, half the town knows you're going over there with the police."

John frowned and turned towards the Clayton's house. "Do you suppose Loretta is up yet?"

"She's a late sleeper. You have half an hour to clean up this mess before she comes over to see what's going on." Mary glared at her husband. "I don't want Wendy to see all this."

Fuming at John's apparent inability to understand the depth of ill-will his involvement with the police could produce among certain people in town, Mary went off to get Wendy out of bed. She wondered if the stains would come out of the porch steps. She also wondered about something else that was gnawing at the back of her consciousness.

* * *

The nave of Wissonet's imposing First Congregational Church was light and airy, thanks to a high ceiling, a rank of oversized windows, and countless gallons of white paint. People trickled in steadily despite the early hour and the promise of another fine beach day. Big windows and high ceiling notwithstanding, the church's interior was already becoming uncomfortably hot, and Mary hoped the service would be short.

She and John had a good view from their vantage point near the back, where, between friends, neighbors, and the idly curious, a good part of town had turned out to pay their respects and trade rumors about Wissonet's richest family.

Dianne Cummings, the grieving widow, sat in the first pew. Tall and in her late thirties, with her long brunette hair hidden under a large-brimmed black hat, Dianne had the regal air of a wealthy woman who was comfortable in her position of affluence and prestige. She was flanked by her friends, Edith

Whitten and Mildred Leary. Edith, about Dianne's age, also wore a large black hat over her dark blonde hair, while Mildred, almost ten years younger, was bareheaded, her shoulder-length brown hair in a pony-tail. Nobody else had chosen to sit in the front row, which made the trio all the more conspicuous.

Watching Dianne's two friends, Mary's mind wandered onto the subject of rabbits. Were they part of a witch's repertoire? Their feet were supposed to bring good luck, but their blood on a doorstep? She wondered how the modern church felt about witches drawing bloody, upside-down crosses on doors. Or attending a service for that matter. Mary shook herself. There were no witches, she scolded. John was right; the rabbit was probably just some kids with a warped sense of fun.

Mary's mother, Janet Gooden, was seated next to her, and she was also looking over the crowd with interest.

Further observation led Mary to conclude that churches did have a beneficial effect on people, especially as far as their clothing was concerned. Edith, for example, had put aside her multi-colored togas and serapes for the first time in recent memory and was wearing a simple, black dress. Even Mildred had discarded her work clothes and heavy boots, while Sam Barton squirmed in an unaccustomed suit.

A group of strangers, probably employees of Cummings Jewelry, sat in a group behind the Bartons.

Diagonally in front of her, Mary saw Henry Merton sitting next to the Oglivys, his tall, scrawny frame towering over Fred Oglivy's rotund figure. The town's two historians made quite a pair. Henry was unusually elegant in a black three-piece suit that emphasized the paleness of his face.

"Henry looks awfully old today," she whispered in John's ear.

"He didn't look too good yesterday either," John said. "All

this upset on top of the hot weather must be hard on him."

Mary's boss was right across the aisle. Phil Cantor, in his early thirties, and already showing a receding hairline, had thumb-tacked a "Back at Eleven" sign on his Real Estate office door in order to come and pay his respects, and perhaps lust quietly after the Cummings land on Marsh Point—a prime piece of waterfront if there ever was one. With the Cummings mansion located in town, the sixteen acres out on the point consisted of nothing but scraggly woods and mountains of catbrier, vacant except for the boarded-up remains of Ruth Cummings's old house. The property had been in the Cummings family since the town was founded, and Mary supposed that the Commodore had hung onto the land for sentimental reasons. She wondered if Dianne felt the same way about Marsh Point, and the land was worth a small fortune. Not that the Commodore's widow really needed more money.

Loretta arrived and took a seat in front of the Wendells. Mary leaned forward. "Where's Ed?" she whispered in Loretta's ear.

"He had to work, a meeting of some kind." Her neighbor's tone of voice reinforced the fact that there was no love lost between Ed and his former employer.

Loretta turned over the back of her pew to face Mary. "Dianne isn't wasting any time having the funeral, is she?"

Mary grunted non-committally. Why wait? They were doing an autopsy on the Commodore, and there was no way of knowing when the body would be released, so why not have a memorial service and get it over with? Mary's mother came to the rescue, leaning towards Loretta's eager ear. "Dianne is leaving this evening to visit her brother in New Hampshire for a few days. He's the only family the poor woman has left now."

"But why have the funeral at the ungodly hour of 9 o'clock

in the morning?"

"I think having it early is a good idea," Janet said. "Just imagine how hot it will be in here by midday."

"Actually, I'm glad it's early," Mary said. "I'm meeting a client later this morning to talk about selling her house, and this way I don't have to find two sitters for Wendy."

"The Waller place?" Janet said.

Mary nodded. Loretta would undoubtably pick up on this bit of news and interrogate her later.

Loretta wasn't through grousing about the funeral arrangements, however. "Why doesn't Dianne's brother come here? Why make her—" Loretta, already facing the back of the church, stopped abruptly. "Who is that in the back pew by the door?"

John could guess who it was, but he turned to look anyway. "That's Lieutenant Riley, probably looking for suspects." He noticed that a number of other heads had turned towards Riley as well.

"The man looks like an overaged football player who has gone to seed," Mary commented.

John glanced over his shoulder again. "He'll make himself unpopular if he isn't careful."

Riley was already unpopular with Mary. Why couldn't he leave the town alone to mourn in peace?

Chapter 5

Wissonet, August 4

"I didn't expect Riley to follow us home from church," John grumbled as they drove up High Street to the house.

"I didn't expect him to be in church, either," Mary muttered.

The Wendell's driveway was short enough and Riley's Packard was long enough so the car's rear end reached to the sidewalk when Riley parked behind the Ford. Riley and his vehicle loomed there for all to see while John changed his clothes. It was hard to imagine how anybody in town wouldn't know that John was helping the police, after this.

Riley glanced at the battered Ford as John settled into the Packard's deep velour seat a few minutes later. "Don't see many of those old Fords around anymore," Riley commented. "Tough little buggies. Me, I'm like the Cummings with that big limo of theirs; you can't beat a car with plenty of heft to it." Riley nodded to himself comfortably. "When I get a new car, it'll be a Cadillac like theirs. You can carry a lot of stuff in a vehicle like that."

The Packard's gigantic twelve-cylinder engine rumbled to life as Riley hit the starter. "This is a '38," he said proudly. "With the jump seats, you can get six people in back."

"Do you have a big family, Lieutenant?"

"God, no. But so what? I figure it's better to have the space when you need it then to be caught short. The Cummings could get a lot of people in the back of that Caddy of theirs, and they don't have any family at all."

"Do you always drive your own car for business?"

"Instead of a state vehicle? Hell, yes. Nothing like a roomy car."

"Isn't it a little conspicuous?"

"Conspicuous can be a good thing, Wendell; it depends on where you are." Riley glanced at John. "Do you think being conspicuous is bad?"

John wondered if Riley was toying with him. Certainly the Lieutenant must know that parking his Packard in the Wendell's driveway would be noticed and commented on by many in town. Was he trying to stir the pot?

John didn't reply to Riley's question.

They glided down High Street, turned onto North, and waited for Wissonet's only traffic light at the intersection of Route 6, the main road to Cape Cod. John thought about the effortless quiet of the Packard, with its wood-grain dashboard, and comfortable seats. He thought about the Model A's throaty roar, vibration, and trail of oil smoke. Perhaps he was in the wrong line of work.

Riley turned towards John. "Did you grow up here in town?"

"Well, yes and no. I really grew up in Quincy, but we always rented a cottage here for the summer. My mother brought us down, because she thought the summer air was healthier. I think she worried about polio. My father would come down for the weekends and his vacation."

"Quincy? We were almost neighbors. I grew up in South

Boston. We never went away for the air, though. Couldn't afford it. When did you move here full-time?"

"Last year. I worked for a yacht design firm in Boston after the war, but Mary and I fell in love with the house when it came on the market, and Mary's mother lives here, so we packed up and moved. I'd planned to strike out on my own anyway, and this seemed like a good time to do it, before houses got too expensive." The Wendell's house had been a financial stretch as it was, and only the fact that Mary had a part-time job, and her family had roots in town persuaded the local bank to accept the mortgage.

There wasn't much traffic at eleven o'clock on a weekday morning, and they were soon passing the low sand and marsh grass that marked the Weweantic River.

"Are you really some kind of expert on these Manchester 17's? Did you have anything to do with designing them?"

"No. They were way before my time, in the early 1900's."

"I thought Barton said you were an expert."

"I think he was just trying to impress you."

Riley scowled. "Barton's got a bad attitude when it comes to the police. I gather he used to run booze during prohibition, but that would have been before your time, too."

The Lieutenant had obviously done his homework as far as Sam Barton was concerned. Did Sam's checkered past make him a suspect, or was it just the crusty boatbuilder's bad attitude? Who else had Riley checked on? "I thought everybody smuggled booze during prohibition," John said, "but as you say, that was a long time ago, and it doesn't mean that he had anything to do with the Commodore's murder."

"I didn't get a straight answer from him about why Cummings stopped storing his boat in Barton's yard. Did they have a falling out? It seemed like there could have been hard feelings there."

"Do you really think Sam is a suspect just because the Commodore didn't store his boat there?" John replied incredulously.

"Everybody is a suspect until I rule them out," Riley said.

John began to wonder where he stood on the Lieutenant's suspect list. They drove through the town of Marion in silence. Route 6 was getting more commercialized, with tourist cabins, gas stations, and souvenir shops popping up like tacky weeds.

"Look," Riley said, after a while, "I need your help on more than just the boat. I need someone who's willing to fill me in on some of the people in town, and I've hit a brick wall on that so far. I know what it can be like to live in a small town, so you don't need to worry that anyone will find out what you tell me."

John watched the scrub pine sweep by as the big Packard ate up the miles. Mary had been right; he was obviously going to be questioned about Wissonet and its people all morning. Not that it made any difference whether he aired some of the town's dirty linen or not. It didn't matter what Riley said, or didn't say, about their conversation. The town would assume the worst either way.

John sighed. "Have you ever noticed that some towns seem to have personalities, like people?"

"Towns don't kill people, Wendell." Riley spent a moment scratching at something invisible on the steering wheel with his thumbnail.

"Don't they?" John replied.

Riley nodded, perhaps conceding John's point, or perhaps not.

"Okay, what kind of personality does Wissonet have?" Riley said dubiously.

"Are you superstitious?"

He shot an irritated glance at John. "Not all Irishmen believe in the Little People, Wendell. So the place is superstitious. What does that have to do with Cummings's murder?"

"It has to do with the way people in town think about his murder. This isn't in the history books, and I don't know how much of it is true, but there's a story, a legend, I suppose, that goes back to the roots of the town. Summer people, outsiders, aren't usually told the details, but I heard it from Sam Barton's son when we were working at the boatyard as kids.

"Around 1790, Elijah Cummings and his wife Ruth bought a piece of land on Marsh Point. Elijah was a ship's captain, and he did well after the Revolution, so they were able to build a little cottage out there. Eventually, they had two kids, Jonathan and Prudence.

"Then the war of 1812 came along and the economy was devastated by the British blockade. Life got hard for the Cummings family. Elijah fitted out his ship as a privateer, ran the blockade, and had the bad luck to be caught by the British off Nantucket. His ship was sunk, most of the crew was pressed into service with the British Navy, and Elijah was killed.

"Elijah's son, Jonathan, followed in his father's footsteps, shipping out aboard another privateer at the age of eighteen. This time they got caught off Block Island and the British shot them to pieces. Jonathan disappeared.

"That left Ruth and Prudence on their own. Somehow they managed to survive by taking in sewing, putting up the occasional boarder, and living off what little they could grow in that sandy soil. Things were pretty hard.

"Then Prudence married John Merton and the situation improved for a while—"

"Was he related to the Merton I talked to at Barton's

boatyard?" Riley interrupted.

"Henry is John Merton's grandson."

"The guy must be older than hell."

"He likes to tell people that he can remember Abraham Lincoln." John shrugged. "Anyway, Prudence died giving birth to a son, Amos Merton, who was Henry's father, and John Merton remarried shortly afterwards, leaving Ruth all alone again.

"Ruth was destitute, starving, and embittered. She might have sold the house and moved into something less isolated in town, but rumors were going around that she was a witch, so the townspeople wouldn't allow it—at least according to the legend. In any case, she kept to herself on Marsh Point.

"Then rumors began to circulate about bloodcurdling screams being heard out there in the night. Strange lights were seen on Marsh Point. There were whispers that travelers passing by Marsh Point after dark were disappearing—"

"Wait a minute," Riley interrupted again. "Are you saying that people knew something was going on out there and they ignored it?"

"I doubt if law enforcement was the same back then, Lieutenant, and apparently Ruth was a very intimidating person. Anyway, she began to act more and more strangely as time went on, often wandering around town and muttering to herself. This went on for five or six years, until one day Ruth herself disappeared. It was almost a week before the local parson led a group of townspeople out to Marsh Point.

"He knocked on the door, but there was no answer. Finally, he went inside, holding a lantern and a crucifix in front of him. Nobody would follow. He found the old woman lying dead on her bed in the back room, just a closet really, with no windows. From the twisted position of the corpse, she had died in agony.

Nobody knows what happened next, but the parson came running out of the building, incoherent with terror, his face streaming blood from four scratches on his cheek.

"As soon as he regained his composure he had the house boarded up. The parson became ill and died a few days later. It didn't take long for the town to decide the place was haunted, especially when people reported strange noises coming from Marsh Point at night, even after Ruth's death."

John paused to look at the view as they swept over the Bourne bridge, crossed the canal, and entered Cape Cod.

"Two years later, Jonathan Cummings returned to Wissonet. Apparently he'd spent the war in a British prison and it took him six years to make his way home, making a small fortune on the way. He built the great pile of a house in town that the family lives in now, rather than moving out to Marsh Point, though he kept the property. He never explained where all his money came from.

"The strange noises on Marsh Point stopped after Jonathan's return, and the town came to view him as a sort of savior, protecting them from harm. The Cummings family has been a presence in Wissonet ever since."

For what seemed like the first time that morning, Riley had turned to face front and concentrate on the road. "That's a great ghost story, Wendell. I'll save it for next Halloween. That's just the kind of thing kids would enjoy." He slapped the steering wheel in frustration. "This is 1949, the twentieth century, for crying out loud. What the hell does that foolishness have to do with the murder?"

John bristled. "The point is that some people take the story seriously. And it's more than just idle superstition. Look at the names of the stores in town: the Triple Hex Esso station, the Black Cat restaurant, the Witches' Brew bar and grill, The

Sorceress movie theater. The legend is a bit of a tourist attraction for the town as well, like the Salem witches."

"They burned their witches in Salem, didn't they?" Riley said. "They didn't worship them. And why leave Ruth Cummings's body to rot in her bed? Why didn't the benighted parson burn the place down instead of boarding it up with a body inside? Think of the health code violations."

John struggled with his irritation. "I'm just telling you that you'll get a lot further when you talk to people in town if you understand their legend and take it more seriously. Don't forget that Wissonet still has its witches."

"Wisssonet still has witches?" Riley echoed incredulously. "Like who?"

"Like Edith Whitten, Mildred Leary, and maybe Dianne Cummings."

"The three of them were sitting together at the funeral," Riley commented, "and they all happen to work at Cummings Jewelry." He scowled at John. "What do these witches of yours do, exactly: boil bats, cast spells, call down the moon, have pagan rituals?"

"I have no idea what the town witches do," John said coolly. "Maybe they study books on witchcraft and learn spells. They probably just have coffee and spread gossip, for all I know. Edith and Mildred are both widows, and they probably enjoy each other's company."

"And you're saying I need to take this witch business more seriously?"

"I'm telling you that the town likes having its witches. They're a symbol, sort of like the way the British like their royalty—they're part of a tradition that makes the town feel special."

"How do you get to be a witch, anyway? Is there a test of

some kind? Do you need to be a widow to be a witch? Because Dianne Cummings is a widow, now."

"Are you pulling my leg?" John demanded.

"How can I take this witch business seriously when I don't know how it works, or what they do? How did your two witches become widows in the first place?"

"Not everyone who dies was murdered."

"It's a lucky thing for me that some people are murdered, or I'd be out of a job." Riley shrugged. "What about Edith Whitten's husband?"

"Harry Whitten died of shellfish poisoning," John said with barely disguised impatience.

"Shellfish poisoning? That's not usually fatal."

"He had a bad heart, otherwise he probably would have been okay."

"Maybe somebody knew about his bad ticker."

John rolled his eyes.

"Anything is possible," Riley added serenely. "What about Mildred Leary's husband?"

"Ralph Leary was a fisherman in town. He was out fishing alone one evening, fell off his boat and drowned." John glanced at Riley. "It's not that unusual an accident. Someone gets careless, loses his balance, falls over the side, and can't get back on board. Ralph's boat was found the next day, washed ashore. Mildred still has it and still uses it for fishing."

"Was Ralph Leary a careless type of person?"

"Everybody is careless once in a while."

"Maybe he wasn't alone out there," Riley said. "Maybe he was pushed." He turned to John. "This is why it's important to have all the facts before we can be sure of the truth." Riley nodded comfortably. "Yes indeed, thoroughness is the hallmark of good detective work, Wendell."

Traffic picked up as they neared the Cape Cod Canal.

Riley glanced at John. "You were in the Navy, right? The Pacific?" It was a statement rather than a question.

"Yes."

"Tough out there. Kamikazes," Riley murmured.

So Riley hadn't stopped with Sam. The Lieutenant had looked into his past as well. A past that still haunted him.

Chapter 6

Wissonet, August 4

While John and Lieutenant Riley were heading to Cape Cod and their rendezvous with *Abracadabra*, Mary piloted the Wendell's Model A down the back streets of Wissonet, turning left onto Willow Road, a quiet neighborhood of older homes nestled behind the Congregational Church.

She rattled to a stop in front of a well-kept, white Cape that had once belonged to Glen and Sally Waller, a couple who spent their entire earthly existence living, and ultimately dying, in Wissonet. Glen had passed away from a heart attack many years ago, while Sally had stayed in the house, living alone, until this spring when a neighbor found her dead of a stroke.

Mary alighted with her camera and notebook, and closed in on the house while snapping pictures from different angles.

As she made her way up the walk, the door opened to reveal Louise O'Brien, the Wallers' only offspring. The pair walked through the house while Mary jotted down notes and traded reminiscences. Louise, a year ahead of Mary in high school, had left town to stay with her aunt in Boston the day she graduated, and ended up going to Boston University. She had returned only for the briefest of visits afterwards.

Still trading childhood memories, they gravitated to the

kitchen. "I've got coffee hot on the stove, and a few cookies," Louise offered.

Between the dead rabbit on the doorstep and the Commodore's funeral, it had been a long morning and it was getting on towards noon, so Mary descended on the cookies eagerly. They talked for a while about the process of listing and selling the house.

Later, with the necessary papers signed, Mary rummaged through her purse. "Damn," she said, "I forgot to bring any flashbulbs and I want to get some pictures of the living room."

"Why the living room?"

"The wood paneling in there is unusually good, especially the wainscoting. That sort of thing really helps to sell a house."

Louise smiled. "Remember when we were kids, and we used to hunt for secret panels in the woodwork around the fireplace?"

"Those were our *Nancy Drew* Days," Mary replied, smiling, "though we did find a secret panel."

Louise laughed. "Except it turned out to be the door to the wood box."

"It made a good hide-and-seek place, even so, especially since there wasn't any firewood in it."

"We had a lot of fun back then," Louise replied. "Well, you'll have the keys, and the house will be empty, so you can come and take all the pictures you like. Do you think it will take long to sell the place?"

"I wouldn't think so with the real estate market the way it is right now, but you never know for sure. It's a perfect size for a young couple like you and Harry; it's been well kept, and this is a nice neighborhood."

"The neighbors are quiet all right," Louise smiled as she glanced out the window to where the cemetery wall edged the back yard. "I spent a lot of time playing over there as a kid." Her expression turned serious. "Was there a big turnout for the Commodore's service?"

"It was a pretty good crowd," Mary replied. Louise could have seen the parked cars from the kitchen window, and could have walked two blocks to attend the service, but she obviously didn't.

"I suppose I should have gone, just to see some of my old friends," she said, echoing Mary's thoughts.

"You could always move back here. It would be a wonderful place for you and your family."

A shadow flitted across Louise's face, and she took a long sip of coffee. "It's nothing personal," she said at last. "There are some really nice people here, and I had some really good friends, like you. It's just that when I got out of high school I swore I'd never live here again." Her brow furrowed. "That sounds awful doesn't it? I don't really mean it that way."

"You did seem pretty anxious to leave. Small town life isn't for everybody."

The cup hovered at Louise's lips as her brown eyes studied Mary's face. "I suppose this business with the Commodore reminded me, but it still seems like Wissonet is living in a world of its own, with its little secrets—just stuck in the past."

Mary thought about Louise's comment. It was probably just her friend's distaste for the town's witchcraft fixation, though it was a mystery to Mary why anybody would take a piece of local folklore like that seriously enough to leave home. "It's a small town," she said defensively. "Things change slowly."

"Yes, but Wissonet seems to hang on to things without even knowing why. People make up these stories and live them as though they were real."

Mary remembered that the Wallers had never seemed to

quite fit in. Yes, they got along with everybody all right, but they never really embraced the town, preferring to remain on the fringes. Mary's mother had often referred to the Wallers as being "standoffish." Apparently, Louise had inherited her parents' attitude, only more so.

Louise sipped some more coffee before going on. "I came down yesterday afternoon to clean up the house a little, and bumped into Henry Merton in the Flying Broom Hardware. He must be Wissonet's biggest fan—a one man chamber of commerce. I don't think he likes me very much."

"I can't believe that. What makes you think he doesn't like you?"

"Maybe because I left, or maybe because I don't take his Wissonet stories seriously. Oh, he was friendly enough; we talked for quite a while. He ended up telling me one of his tall tales—something about a local ship's captain being attacked by pirates back in the 1700's. I stopped paying much attention to his stories years ago, and I don't remember all of this one, but the gist of it was that somehow the ship's captain managed to turn the tables and sink the pirates' boat. I don't quite know why, but the story sounded almost like a threat the way he told it." Louise was holding her cup in both hands as though it might escape.

"I don't think Henry really means to threaten anybody. It's just his way of talking. You know how important the town is to him, and he's bound to be upset by the Commodore's murder."

Louise's head twitched in what could have been a nod or a shake. "I suppose so," she said dubiously. "I know Henry probably doesn't mean any harm, but he scares me a little even so—he always has. On the other hand, I suspect that I scare him more than he scares me. He's too much like the town, and he knows I know it."

Mary realized her mouth was open and she snapped it shut. She'd forgotten about Louise's tendency to come up with these strange ideas.

Chapter 7

Wissonet, August 4

Mary pulled into her mother's driveway around noon to pick up Wendy, and found Edith Whitten's car parked there. Although Edith was a good ten years younger than Janet, they'd become good friends since Harry Whitten's death two years ago.

The two women were sitting with Wendy on the livingroom floor amid a pile of toys. Edith's dog, a rangy German shepherd named Rufus, lay nearby, panting in the heat as he watched the trio playing.

Edith's shoulder-length dark blonde hair, streaked with gray, was worn loose to make room for a red and white striped turban, the ends of which were long enough to drag on the ground when she stood up. Centered on the front of the turban sat a brooch whose imitation ruby would dazzle an Oriental potentate. A loose fitting, lime green blouse, combined with a floor-length blue skirt, completed the fashion statement.

Mary gave her pupils a moment to contract and tried to imagine Edith getting all that material through a revolving door. "That's a very colorful outfit, Edith," she said.

Edith beamed, adding to the dazzle. "Thank you. I made most of it myself, and I think the ruby is especially striking," she said proudly. "I'm glad that somebody appreciates my design efforts."

"I'm sure a lot of people admire your designs," Janet said soothingly.

"You'd be amazed how hard it is for an artist to work in a company that's filled with tasteless Philistines," Edith said bitterly. "The snickering, snide remarks, and ignorant criticism can have a crushing effect on one's creative spirit."

"An artist's life can be difficult, I'm sure," Janet said.

"Difficult is an understatement." Edith caught herself. "But enough of that. It was a pleasant surprise to drop in and find Wendy here. Grab a cup and sit down, Mary. The mad rabbit is about to serve us tea. The mad rabbit, a well-worn stuffed creature better known as "Bunny," leaned drunkenly against a doll-sized teapot.

Mary suspected that Edith was really there to fish for gossip, and her suspicion was confirmed when they gathered at the kitchen table for an impromptu lunch.

"I hear John is helping the police look over Dianne's boat," Edith said. "Next thing we know he'll be starting a new career fighting crime."

"He will *not* be starting a new career fighting crime. It's just a one-time thing. They needed someone who was familiar with the boat to go over it, and they persuaded John to help."

"I think it was very civic minded of him to help," Janet said in a tone of voice that suggested grave doubts about the wisdom of becoming involved in murder investigations.

"Of course it was, and we all want to help, but there's such a thing as getting too involved," Edith said, with a glance at Mary.

"Driving over Pocasset to look at *Abracadabra* is not getting too involved by any stretch of the imagination," Janet retorted.

Edith frowned and changed the subject. "Surely the boat must have been damaged, washing ashore like that."

"Actually, there wasn't much harm done at all, according to what Lieutenant Riley told John. Wood Island is mostly sand."

"I wonder when Dianne will get *Abracadabra* back?" Edith said. "The police will probably keep it for a while to look for clues, or evidence, or whatever." She raised an inquisitive eyebrow in Mary's direction.

"I have no idea about that, but I got the impression that they need all the clues they can find."

"Well, I do hope you and John stay out of it, for your sakes. I worry about you."

It was interesting, Mary thought, to hear Edith echoing her own concerns. She tried to change the subject. "I hope the Commodore's funeral didn't disrupt your vacation too much."

"The funeral only took a day, and I wanted to be there for Dianne's sake." Edith brightened. "Actually, I'm leaving for Boston later this afternoon to meet a friend of mine, so we can pick up where we left off. We're planning to spend a week exploring the Berkshires. I still feel a little guilty about doing so much driving after all those years of gas rationing, but it will be fun to do some traveling again."

Edith left shortly afterwards, and Janet sighed with relief. "She's right about staying clear of the murder investigation, you know."

"I couldn't stop John from going off with Lieutenant Riley if I tried—which I did."

"I know perfectly well how stubborn your husband can be, but that's not what's bothering me."

"Then what is?"

"Edith was talking about you before you got here."

"Edith was talking about me, and not John?"

"Aunt Edith," Wendy corrected.

"Edith Whitten is *not* your aunt," Mary said, more sharply than she'd intended.

"She says she is," Wendy replied rebelliously.

"For heaven's sake, it's just a manner of speech," Janet scolded her daughter.

"Fine," Mary snapped. "What did Edith say about me?"

Janet sipped some iced tea—a delaying tactic, Mary thought, peevishly.

"You always were a headstrong child," Janet said finally, "A lot like your daughter. Not to mention your husband."

"Are you going to tell me what Edith said, or not?"

"Aunt Edith," Wendy chimed in.

"You seem a bit irritable today, dear. Is the heat bothering you?" Janet said, pouring fuel on her simmering daughter.

"I'll be fine once you stop hemming and hawing."

"Patience, is a virtue, dear. All she said was that you were different—'special' is the word she used—even as a child. Apparently, she first noticed it when you were a teenager, or so she said."

"What in the world did she mean by that?"

"Nothing, really. She mentioned the high-jinks the four of you kids used to get into back then."

"What high-jinks?"

Janet answered reluctantly. "She mentioned the time you kids broke into Ruth Cummings's cottage, but—"

"It was raining and we were cold, for heaven's sake! It's not as though we vandalized the place."

"Of course not, and I don't think she meant anything particular. You know the way Edith is: a drama queen, lots of theatrics. Foolishness. I shouldn't have mentioned it."

"Then why did you mention it?"

"Because you told me to," Janet retorted. "I just want you and John to be careful. It's not just about John helping the police. Things are different now, with the Commodore gone."

* * *

Mary paced around her kitchen later that afternoon, feeling out of sorts. What had he mother, or more correctly Edith, meant? Was it some kind of warning, and if so, what did it mean? Edith had noticed something about Mary when she was a teenager, but what? Did it mean anything that Edith mentioned it now, after the Commodore's death? If so, why would his murder change things? What things?

She had to do something to take her mind off Edith's cryptic words. Some entertaining distraction that would get her and Wendy out of the house.

Mary loaded Wendy into the car and went off to her favorite raspberry patch. She turned onto Marsh Point Road and parked where the paving turned to dirt.

In their wisdom, Wissonet's selectmen had chosen to pave only the first half-mile of Marsh Point Road, ending the blacktop fifty yards short of the only residents' driveway.

The Oglivys, a couple in their late seventies, had refurbished a run down Cape some fifteen years ago. The idea of an elderly pair of strangers choosing to live alone on Marsh Point, so close to the old Cummings place, had scandalized a number of townspeople at first, but the Oglivys seemed to be happy there. Indeed, Mary had found them to be a delightful couple, and Fred was an amateur historian whose enthusiasm for Wissonet's past won him many friends in town. It also won him the presidency of the Wissonet Historical Society after Henry Merton, who had held the position for more years than anybody could remember, retired.

Beyond the Oglivys' driveway, the dirt road degenerated still further into a sandy, grass-choked track that led out to the point itself. Mary hadn't been further down the road than the Oglivys' place in years, and she didn't plan on doing so today, because the best raspberries were found among an impenetrable thicket of catbrier, brush, and berry canes that lined the roadside next to the car. The road made a cool, shady tunnel through the tangled jungle with its overhanging trees. Birds darting through the branches broke the silence with song, while a light breeze rustled in the tree tops.

Mary lifted Wendy out of the car and reached into the back to fish out a bowl. A hint of movement caught the corner of her eye. Startled, she looked around to see Fred Oglivy, with his dog in tow, emerging from their driveway. Mary waved, wondering if he would recognize her at this distance. Fred gave a nearsighted flip of the hand in return and headed down the road to Marsh Point. Mary smiled to herself. The elderly gentleman's eyesight and hearing weren't what they used to be.

When she turned around, Wendy was gone.

An unreasoning fear gripped Mary as she circled the car calling her wayward daughter's name, to no avail. Where could she have gone? The prickly walls of foliage were thick enough to discourage even a small child, yet this one had vanished in a matter of seconds.

The answer lay a few feet behind the car where she found a low opening in the underbrush. Probably a game trail. She stooped and called Wendy's name into the shadows. The hole was waist high, much too big for a rabbit, but of course there were the neighborhood dogs. The path looped around a tree and disappeared into a forest of catbriers so thick it was impossible to see more than a few feet. Irritation crept into

Mary's voice as she called out again.

The underbrush shook as something much larger than Wendy made its way through the dense foliage.

"Is this who you're looking for?" Mildred Leary appeared from behind the tree with Wendy firmly in tow. Mary backed out onto the road, straightening up as she emerged from the tunnel. Mildred was in her early thirties, a bit shorter and huskier than Mary, though most of her extra bulk was muscle. Her brown hair sat atop her head in a bun, exposing a round, well-tanned face and brown eyes.

"I found Aunt Mildred in the hidey-hole," Wendy said happily.

"I'm not really your aunt, but you can call me that if you like, Wendy." She turned to Mary. "I'm surprised to see you here."

Was there apprehension in Mildred's voice? "I'm just glad you were in there to catch Wendy."

"Oh, it's a regular maze of game trails all through here. I explore them some, but one has to be careful. There are dogs in town. Big dogs. They may be friendly enough during the day, but some of them go wild at night and hunt these trails. I've seen what they can do to a deer, and it's not a pretty sight." She paused dramatically. "You should be careful. A youngster like Wendy can run around in there a lot more easily than an adult, especially someone who isn't properly dressed." She held out her arm, clothed in a long-sleeved denim shirt that matched her jeans. Mary wondered how Mildred avoided heat stroke in such heavy clothing.

"And there are people who come down here at night," Mildred went on, "playing at things they don't understand." Mildred peered at Mary. "Some people are going around telling tales out of school, too. You need to be careful, now. Powers that are best left alone have been turned loose."

Powers? That made two warnings in less that two hours. The Commodore's death was certainly upsetting Wisonet's coven. But why? She wondered if Mildred knew anything about the rabbit. In any case, Mary doubted that she'd get anything useful out of the woman on that score. Besides, she had no desire to be drawn into a discussion of Powers, whatever they might be.

Mary had hoped for a peaceful hour of berry picking and a chance to forget the town's turmoil, but that was clearly not to be. "Thanks for the warning," Mary said tersely, turning to pick up her empty bowl. She hoped Mildred would take the hint and leave them to pick berries in peace and quiet.

Unfortunately, Mildred wanted to talk. "Your husband shouldn't have gone with the police to look over *Abracadabra*. It's not wise for him to get involved in the Commodore's death."

The woman certainly was a scold. "He was only trying to help," Mary said curtly.

"I suppose *Abracadabra* was badly damaged, being sunk like that," Mildred said in a more conciliatory tone of voice.

There obviously was going to be no escape. "The boat was in pretty good shape, from what Lieutenant Riley told John."

"I'm sure Dianne will be pleased to hear that. I know she wants the boat back soon, though I don't know what she'll do with it."

Mary fiddled pointedly with the bowl. "Dianne can always sell it," she replied coolly.

Mildred looked shocked. "I can't see her doing that, either. After all, *Abracadabra* is a landmark in town."

"The Commodore was a landmark, too, and he's gone," Mary said impatiently.

"I'm not sure that you're taking the importance of landmarks seriously enough," Mildred said sternly. "Landmarks anchor us to the past." She took a step closer, and Mary instinctively reached for Wendy's hand, uncomfortably aware of Mildred's physical strength and bulk.

"And without the past," Mildred went on, looming over Mary and Wendy, "our present is meaningless, and our future is doomed."

Chapter 8

Cape Cod, August 4

The Carver Creek Boatyard sat in a clearing at the end of a rough dirt road. A large, tarpapered storage building, its water-facing end adorned with a huge metal Texaco gasoline star, dominated the clearing. The whole place had a look of unweathered newness. A pier, built of wooden pilings, sheltered a handful of boats.

A marine railway stretched from the shed to the water. Some ingenious mechanic had cut the front end off a Model A Ford just behind the dashboard and attached it to a war surplus Navy winch. A heavy cable ran from the winch to the railway's cradle, on which *Abracadabra* sat, high and dry, baking in the hot sun.

"The Coast Guard suggested this place because it's quiet and out of the way, but not too far from town," Riley said as they got out of the car. "It sure doesn't look like much."

The location made sense. A larger yard would have been full of sightseers hoping to satisfy their ghoulish curiosity, while this place looked almost deserted. A well-muscled man in his late twenties, sporting a crew-cut and wearing a sweat-stained tee shirt, bluejeans, and an impatient expression, bore down on them.

"It's about time you got back."

"We're here to look over the boat again," Riley said.

The man looked at them quizzically. "Okay, but I need to get it off my railway. You're gumming up my whole operation."

"We can make a determination as to what should be done next after our marine expert has a chance to look over the crime scene," Riley bristled officiously.

The man shook his head. "A 'marine expert?' That's just what I need." He turned to John with a grin. "So, how are you doing John? Is this some new racket you've gotten into, or what?"

"Just helping out, Jack."

"You two know each other?" Riley said.

"Sure," John replied. "We served in the Pacific together."

"He was in a tin can, and I was in a PT boat," Jack added.

"Well that's really nice," Riley grumbled with a scowl. "You two can trade war stories after we look at the damn boat."

"Go to it, marine expert," Jack said as he walked away, a grin on his face.

"Why didn't you tell me you knew this guy?" Riley muttered as he and John walked over to *Abracadabra*.

"You didn't ask," John replied, feeling like Sam Barton and enjoying it.

"Don't be a smart-ass, Wendell." Riley looked at his watch. "Look at the damn time. Half the day is gone already. We should have stopped for lunch on the way over."

A local policeman, his face a picture of boredom, slouched in the shade of *Abracadabra's* hull. John walked around the boat, but couldn't see much damage, other than some scuffed paint where the hull had lain in the sand. Once again, *Abracadabra* had shown her legendary good luck by surviving her grounding on Wood Island virtually unscathed. "She looks in surprisingly good shape," John said.

"The Coast Guard went over it pretty carefully to make sure the thing wouldn't sink while they were towing it over here. They spent most of the morning pumping the water out and getting it off the beach, even with the two fishermen helping." Riley paused. "Those fishermen seemed awfully anxious to lend a hand."

"Morbid curiosity?"

"Maybe, but I have a feeling about those two. It seemed to me they were hiding something, god knows what. Anyhow, I don't think they were telling me everything they knew."

John rolled his eyes. "Do you believe *anything* people tell you?"

Riley muttered something under his breath, and turned to a soggy pile of odds-and-ends lying on the ground. Some lengths of rope, supported by a collection of saw horses and oil drums, marked off the area where the pile lay beside the boat.

"That's everything there was on board. Mostly it was just floating around in the cabin." Riley looked at the sodden mess, and poked at a dripping heap of mosquito netting with his shoe. "Our people gave it a once-over already, but I thought you could look at it again before they take the stuff away to go over it some more. Maybe you can see something here that looks out of place, or something that should be here and isn't."

John looked over the various items like a disillusioned flea market shopper. "He had some warm clothing: sweater, heavy jacket, and cold-weather sleeping bag." A stream of water dripped from the sleeping bag as he lifted a corner. "I assume your people checked to make sure nothing was wrapped up inside."

"They went over it all with a fine tooth comb." Riley poked gloomily at a heavy woolen sweater. "I wonder where he was planning to go after he left Onset."

"I assume you've asked around to see if anybody saw him in Onset."

"Nobody in town saw anything," Riley grumbled. "Welcome to my world, Wendell."

"That's not surprising. He probably anchored in the outer harbor, which is pretty big, and if he was killed after dark and the boat was towed away..." John let the sentence hang.

"He must have been headed north with all this heavy clothing." Riley opened up a painted tin box containing a handline and an assortment of fishing lures. "He had charts for the whole east coast, right up into Nova Scotia."

"That doesn't mean much. The Commodore always carried a full set of charts for just about everywhere. He liked to be prepared for anything."

"Prepared for anything except being killed," Riley said. "There's a lot of food here," he added.

John studied the unappetizing collection. "It looks like enough for another three or four days. Assuming he was alone."

Riley eyed John speculatively. "That's the question, isn't it? There was only one sleeping bag, though he could have shared it with a friend of the opposite sex."

"It's been too hot to use a sleeping bag," John pointed out.

"What's that board?" Riley pointed to the object in question.

"Part of the cabin sole. Whoever tried to sink the boat would have had to pull it up to get at the drain plug."

"That's part of the cabin's soul? Is this more of your superstitious mumbo jumbo?"

S-O-L-E, Lieutenant." John spelled it out.

"Sole, like the fish?"

"Right, except in this case 'sole' means floor." John's

explanation wasn't well received.

"Why the hell can't you just call it a floor board, if that's what it is? Why do you have to name it after a fish? And why do people call Cummings 'Commodore'? Why don't people call him Frank, or Ralph, or Ignatius? The trouble with you boating people is you can't call a spade a spade. You can't call a floor a floor. What the hell made him a Commodore, anyway?"

"He was the Commodore of the Wissonet Yacht club before the war and people just kept on calling him that."

"They call him Commodore because of the yacht club?" Riley shook his head in despair.

They found nothing else of interest on the ground, so they found a makeshift ladder and climbed aboard *Abracadabra*.

John stuck his head in the cabin and was assailed by the smell of dampness and death. "Nothing in here," he said as he pulled his head out of the hatch and gulped in a breath of fresh air.

The sail had been unfurled, and then sloppily retied. "Did you find it this way?" John asked.

"No it was all tied up. Nice and neat. We undid it to make sure nothing was hidden in there. Like a knife."

"Did you find anything?"

Riley ignored the question.

John took a grip on his patience. "Because if the sail was still furled, then the boat must have been anchored somewhere when the Commodore was killed. Assuming he was murdered on the boat."

"We don't know where he was killed, for sure."

"One of the anchors is missing." John looked over the side at the collection arrayed on the ground. "And one anchor line."

"There was more than one anchor?"

"He always carried two."

"So the boat was anchored, and somebody arrived in a power boat, killed him, dropped the anchor line overboard, towed the boat out to sea, and pulled the plug. What could be simpler than that?"

They found nothing else out of the ordinary on board, and finally they clambered down to the ground. Riley stepped back. "This boat looks in better shape than the other one you showed me."

John admired the shiny black hull. The seams were smooth and tight, while the varnished woodwork was flawless. "The Commodore didn't pinch any pennies when it came to caring for his boat."

Jack had been hovering in the background and he came over. "So what's the verdict? Do we touch a match to the old basket and give her a proper Norse funeral?"

Riley glared at the young man.

Jack sighed. "Look, your boat has tied up my railway since yesterday afternoon, and I need to know what you want to do with the damn thing so I can get back to work."

"This is a crime scene, and nobody touches anything until we're through investigating." It was well past Riley's lunch hour by now and the strain was beginning to show.

"Hey Chief, see the boat out there?" Jack pointed to a new-looking Concordia yawl tied up at the pier. A man was pacing restlessly near it. "That guy ran aground this morning and sprang a leak. He wants his boat hauled *now*, and if he doesn't get what he wants, *I'll* turn into a crime scene. I can put your boat back in the water, or store it in the yard. It will cost you more to store it though."

"How much more?" Riley rumbled ominously.

"A fair amount, since I don't have a cradle that will fit her, where she's so narrow and her fin keel is so deep." Jack stared out over the water, lost in thought. "I do have a cradle out back that I can fiddle with to make it fit."

"How much more?" Riley repeated, even more ominously.

"It's a question of time, too," Jack glanced meaningfully at the Concordia's impatient owner, "and time is money, as they say." Jack put on a pious face. "Naturally, I want to do my civic duty, help the police, and all that razzmatazz, but I'd have to write up a legal contract to store the boat in the yard—" he glanced at Riley's face. "Anyway, what's your preference, Commissioner?"

A few more minutes and the peckish lieutenant would be elevated to Commander-in-chief. John noted the bulge of Riley's jaw muscles, and concluded that another field promotion would not be helpful. "*Abracadabra* would probably be safer out on an empty mooring," John suggested. "She'd be out of the way and Jack could keep an eye on her."

"People are less likely to bother it out there, too," Jack agreed.

It was probably hunger rather than the merits of John's suggestion that convinced Riley, but in the end they arranged for *Abracadabra* to be moored in front of the boatyard, along with her soggy contents.

"Great idea! Consider it done," Jack said enthusiastically. "Don't worry about a thing; she'll be safe as a church."

Jack was wrong, of course.

Chapter 9

Wissonet, August 4

Mary was lurking in the front hall when Riley dropped John off that afternoon.

"Let's sit on the front porch where it's cooler, and you can tell me what you were up to with *Abracadabra* this morning," she said.

Mary, John, and Wendy went to front porch and found a shady spot where a sea breeze made the afternoon heat almost bearable.

Wendy rooted Nat out of his napping place in a shady corner, and stalked the luckless feline up and down the porch while the adults talked. Mary watched the cat-toddler interaction while she listened to John, and felt a kinship with Nat. Why were Wissonet's witches hounding her?

"It doesn't sound as though Riley has got any real suspects," Mary said when John had finished.

"He doesn't even have a motive, though he mentioned a crime of passion, but I think that was just based on the number of stab wounds."

"I suppose he spent the morning pumping you for all the town gossip." Mary's voice had an edge to it.

"I don't know all the town gossip. He needs to talk to

Loretta about that."

"Don't be coy with me. What did he want to know?"

John sighed. "He asked about Dianne, of course. And we talked about Edith and Mildred."

"Why them?"

"Why not them? They were sitting next to Dianne at the funeral. I told him they were the town witches—at least Edith and Mildred are. I don't know about Dianne."

Mary frowned. "Why mention the witch business, for heaven's sake?" she demanded. Wendy abandoned Nat and clambered onto her lap.

"Why not tell him? All I said was that they're part of Wissonet's local color and are harmless oddballs who spend their time spreading gossip and playing cards."

"It's too hot for you to be on my lap, dear," Mary said as she put her daughter on the floor. "Go climb on your daddy," she added perversely. "You didn't tell Riley about Ruth Cummings, did you?"

John shot Mary an unreadable look as he picked Wendy up. "What's wrong with telling him about Ruth Cummings? It's hardly a secret. Everybody knows the fool legend; they may not take it seriously, but they know it."

"That's the whole point! You don't know that nobody takes it seriously!"

John and Wendy looked startled by the outburst.

"Edith and Mildred have both warned me to be careful," Mary added quietly.

"Why in the world would they warn you? I'm the trouble-maker it town."

"How would I know?" Mary snapped. She paused. "I suppose the Commodore's murder has everybody on edge, including me. That and the heat."

"Riley is checking around town to see who might have taken a motorboat out Monday night," John said.

"Does he know how many motorboats there are in the harbor?" Mary said. "Does he know the bluefish are running? Mildred has been out in her boat almost every day. Riley has a lot of work ahead of him."

"Fortunately, it's not my problem." John got to his feet. "Anyway, I've got to get some drawings ready for Ralph Hibbert by the day after tomorrow."

* * *

John's office occupied one of the two upstairs rooms on the water side of the house, the other front chamber serving as the master bedroom. He was just sitting down at his drafting table when the doorbell rang, and Mary's frantic whisper up the stairs announced the arrival of Dianne Cummings. John grumbled to himself. All he needed was another ten or twelve hours of work and he'd have enough done to get a quote, but a perverse fate seemed determined to make that goal impossible.

A twinge of apprehension escorted John downstairs, where Mary was already offering condolences.

"I'm terribly sorry about the Commodore," John said, adding his bit to Mary's.

A few more expressions of sympathy took them into the living room, where John surreptitiously studied their guest as she sat drinking more of the Wendell's rapidly diminishing stock of lemonade. Dianne Cummings was tall, with long brunette hair worn up in a meticulously coifed French twist. Impeccably dressed as always, she was a good looking woman. Yet, even in her grief, Dianne had the air of some wild force lurking below the surface. Unbidden, his mind turned to witchcraft and slaughtered rabbits. Could Dianne be a witch after all?

"It's a tragedy in more ways than one," Dianne said. "It's the end of the family, the last of the line." She stopped, dabbing her eyes. "I worry about Wissonet without any Cummings to protect it. A lot of people don't understand how much he did, and how dangerous it can be without him to watch over us."

"You're right, it will be difficult," John agreed, having no idea what Dianne was talking about. Mary shot him a warning look.

"Oh, I'll do my best," Dianne went on, "but it will be hard. There is so much evil out there." She stared intently at the Wendells through red-rimmed eyes. "So much evil."

"There certainly is." John could only hope that he was making a suitable response.

Mary squirmed in her chair. "I think this hot weather is evil. It certainly is bad for people's tempers."

To John's relief, Dianne rose to the bait like a trophy salmon. "It's the atom bomb testing, of course. The trouble with the world today is that people keep meddling in things they don't understand." She peered into her hosts' faces again. "They're going to ruin the climate if they aren't careful."

"The weather has been unusually hot this summer," Mary said, taking firm hold of this promising new topic and dragging it towards solid ground. "We'll have another hurricane if it doesn't cool off soon. It certainly feels like hurricane weather, don't you think?"

At that point Dianne remembered her agenda, so they remained ignorant of her thoughts on the hurricane season. "I'm going off to stay with friends for the rest of the company vacation. I just need to get away from Wissonet for a while. But before I leave, I wanted to thank you for going to look at *Abracadabra,* and helping the police try to find the

Commodore's killer." Dianne heaved a shaky sigh. "Sam told me you'd offered to help. I know he's worried about *Abracadabra* being all right. Sam is such a sweet lamb."

To John's way of thinking, the words "sweet" and "Sam" didn't belong together. "Old goat" would be more accurate.

"How is poor *Abracadabra*?" Dianne said. "Is she badly hurt? The police said everything was fine, but what do they know?"

"There didn't seem to be much damage at all. Wood Island is mostly sand, and she must have dodged any rocks, so everything looked in good shape."

"Well that's good news." Dianne looked genuinely relieved. "It doesn't feel right, not seeing the dear old boat on her mooring. The Commodore loved her so much." She took out a handkerchief and blew her nose. "The police said she's moored over at some yard in Pocasset. The Carver Creek boatyard, Lieutenant Riley said. Do you think they'll take good care of her?"

"I know the man who runs the yard, and I'm sure she'll be well taken care of until the police let you have her back," he said, wondering what Dianne would do with the boat when she got it. Before he could think of a tactful way to ask, however, there was a loud crash and a bellow of childish glee.

"Wendy must have treed the cat in the pantry again," Mary said, rising.

"Well, I won't keep you any longer," Dianne said hurriedly.

Mary, listening to an ominous series of noises and exclamations, sidled towards the door. Dianne stopped her. "I do feel as though we should all get to know each other better, especially now that you two are so nicely settled here in town. We'll have to have more of these little visits."

* * *

Mary glanced at her watch after she'd extricated Wendy from the pantry, where the child had managed to trap Nat among the canned goods, many of which were now on the floor. "Damn! I forgot we've been invited to the Claytons for ice tea," she said. "I'll have just enough time to get Wendy tidied up."

John grumbled. "A command performance, I suppose. Do you think we can make it a short visit, so I can get some work done before supper?"

"Don't mutter at me, John Wendell. You're the one who went off and spent the day with the cops. Obviously, we're being invited so Loretta can interrogate you about your trip to Carver Creek."

They were heading for the door a few minutes later when the phone rang. It hung on the wall just inside the livingroom door, and John reached out and caught it on the second ring.

"Hey, you're mighty quick with the horn there, Sherlock."

"I just happened to be here when it rang, Jack. Did you get that Concordia hauled out?"

"Yeah, nothing serious—a little chewing gum, some tire tape, and she's as good as new. Thanks for persuading that stiff-necked Irishman to let me clear my railway. I don't think he liked me very much."

"I can't imagine why."

"Neither can I. Anyway, seeing as how you're a detective now, and it's your boat, I thought I'd pass this on."

"I am *not* a detective, and it's *not* my boat, so you'll have to talk to the stiff-necked Irishman."

Jack ignored the advice. "The thing is that Tony Silva came by this afternoon, looking for an engine for his boat—"

"Who is Tony Silva?"

"He's the fisherman from New Bedford."

"And why are you telling me about a fisherman from New Bedford?"

"Don't you gumshoes read the newspaper? Where do you get your clues from?"

"Look," John said, "I had to clean up a slaughtered rabbit before breakfast, go to the Commodore's funeral service, drive out to your god forsaken boatyard, and entertain a grieving widow. I haven't had time to read the newspaper."

"Lordy, I had no idea that fighting crime could be so much fun. You wouldn't like to hire an assistant, would you?"

"Who the hell is Tony Silva?"

"He's one of the fishermen who found your boat, of course. Like I say, he came over asking if I could get him an engine. I sold him a used one out of a war-surplus Dodge four-by-four a few years back—"

John nodded as Mary pointed at her watch.

"Why would he drive all the way out from New Bedford to your place just to get a new engine?" John prompted.

"I wondered that, too. The thing is, I don't think he really cared that much about having me get him an engine."

"Then what did this Silva character want?"

"Well, it seemed like he was more interested in your boat than a new engine."

"How did he know the boat was there?"

"He helped the Coasties refloat her, and they must have told him where she was headed. Anyway, I had her out on a mooring by then, and he looked mighty disappointed to see it in the water. He even asked if everything was on the boat."

Wendy spotted the rabbit's foot on the hall table. Mary snatched it from her fingers.

"Was everything on the boat?" John said.

"Hell yes. I had the stuff draped all over it to dry. The boat looks like a gypsy caravan out there—makes the whole place into a dump. I'll have to put all that junk below, dry or not, pretty quick or it'll scare off the clientele."

"Why are you telling me all this?"

"The thing is," Jack explained, "I asked if he'd lost his watch in the boat. You know, like a joke. You would have thought I'd dropped a red-hot rivet down his drawers. He jumped a mile."

"I didn't see anything he might have lost when we went through the stuff."

"The cops might have found something yesterday afternoon and taken it away with them, I suppose," Jack said.

Mary made impatient noises, and John breathed into the phone.

"I've got to go, Jack."

"The thing is," Jack said, undeterred, "he's a nice guy and I don't want to get him in trouble, so I'm just passing this along to you on the Q.T., for what it's worth."

"You need to tell Riley about that. He'll definitely want to know."

"Forget it. I'm not ratting Tony out to the cops. Besides, you're the assistant—"

"I'm not Riley's assistant, or your patsy, but I am going to hang up the phone."

Chapter 10

Wissonet, August 4

The Clayton's house was a Victorian, like the Wendell's place, but more than twice the size. A basketball court of a verandah, built in the grand Victorian manner, stretched across the water-facing side of the building, and the Claytons made frequent use of the space to entertain.

Loretta seated her guests in green-painted wicker chairs, observed the necessary amenities, and swooped down on her victim.

"Now John, tell us all about your day with the police and *Abracadabra*," she said, almost quivering with anticipation.

Mary gave him an I-told-you-so look.

"You don't miss much, Loretta," John replied, wondering if he'd ever get back to Hibbert's drawings.

"How could anyone miss detective whats-his-name driving around in that great hearse of a car. And speaking of not missing much, I saw Dianne hustling over to pump you for information a little while ago. She must have been lurking right around the corner like a vulture waiting for you to get back."

"A vulture?" John was bemused. "I thought they only preyed on—"

Mary coughed loudly.

"How was *Abracadabra*?" Loretta went on, ignoring John's aborted comment. "I hear the boat is at the Carver Creek boatyard in Pocasset, and you know the man who runs the place. Did Dianne say anything about what she was going to do with *Abracadabra*?"

"Where in the world do you get all your information?" Mary marveled.

"*Abracadabra* was fine, and I didn't get a chance to ask Dianne what she might do with the boat," John replied tersely.

"You're a big disappointment," Loretta complained.

"I doubt if he's allowed to say anything about the investigation, dear," Ed said, coming to John's rescue.

"I wonder what Dianne is going to do with the company, now that the Commodore is gone," Mary said, completing Loretta's derailment.

"She can't be any worse at running Cummings Jewelry than the Commodore was," Ed said. "His problem was that he insisted on operating the place like a family business when it's much too big for that. It needs more structure, and more knowledgeable management." Ed's voice was slurred, and John suspected their host had gotten a head start on happy hour. "It's only taken him two years to run the company into the ground—"

"Two and a half years, dear," Loretta corrected. "Frank Cummings died in the winter of 1946."

"I've heard they weren't doing well," John commented.

Ed nodded in agreement. "In general, jewelry manufacturing is an excellent business to be in right now. With the war over and all the troops coming home and getting married, the demand for wedding rings alone has been tremendous, not to mention all the other jewelry that newlyweds tend to accumulate.

"Over two million couples were married in 1946," Ed added. John, one of those two million, thought he caught a glint of avarice flashing in his neighbor's eyes. "But it's a tricky business too, and a lot of people don't understand all the subtleties. They tend to think of it in terms of an artisan hunched over a workbench, hand-crafting little baubles, one at a time. Firms like Cummings Jewelry are really more like factories turning out thousands of items—think about those millions of wedding rings, for example. It's a manufacturing plant as much as anything and pricing can be a challenge, especially with all the competition that's out there. And it's not just the manufacturing; it's the raw materials as well. Gems and precious metals all need to be obtained in quantity at a reasonable price, and that can be a problem with the European financial markets still in turmoil after the war. Government restrictions on gold purchases are a big headache, too—lots of red tape. And diamonds can be hard to obtain, as well. It's a challenge for Mildred to keep up with the procurement issues."

"So that's what Mildred does," John said.

"At the moment it is, but that could change with Dianne taking over. The Commodore was already turning the company upside down, trying to cut back the staff. He was having Edith take over production, on top her being the head designer—not that she knows anything about production. Plus, he had Dianne taking over from me to run the marketing side of things."

"Not that she knows anything about marketing," Loretta put in.

"Even with all the challenges, it's hard to imagine how a jewelry company could be doing so badly in today's world," Ed said. "The man was hopelessly incompetent. Look at the crazy line of 'Witch Jewelry' he introduced this spring. The stuff is too expensive to sell as paste and too cheap to sell in higher class shops. Not only that, they have strictly local appeal in the Wissonet area. But that's typical of the half-baked, get-rich-quick schemes he kept coming up with."

"The witches are a bit risque, too," Loretta commented.

"That's another problem," Ed said. "A lot of women don't want to wear anatomically correct nudes for broaches and pendants, not even if the nudes are sitting on crescent moons."

"Anatomically correct?" John murmured.

"Why not on broomsticks?" Loretta suggested.

Ed frowned at his wife. "It was probably a mistake for me to make fun of Edith's crazy witchcraft jewelry. She's very sensitive to any criticism of her 'art,' and she and Mildred had too much influence over the Commodore."

Loretta eyed her tipsy husband. "Too much influence? How so? Are you saying he was romantically involved with one of them?"

Ed gave his wife a haunted look. "That's not what I meant. For heaven's sake don't spread that around," he said in a monument to futility.

They talked for a while longer, until Wendy became restless, a convenient excuse in John's mind. Ed took him aside as they were getting ready to leave. "Come down to the cellar for a minute. I need some advice."

The dirt-floored basement was refreshingly cool, though somewhat musty. Ed pointed to a slow drip falling from a water pipe. A puddle had formed in the dirt beneath the leak. "You're a boat designer—an expert on water, leaks, and all that stuff—what do you think?"

John examined the pipe. "I think you need a plumber."

"I was afraid you'd say that."

"Naval architects are seldom wrong about water leaks, Ed."

"I don't doubt it for a second, but we just spent a fortune

having the place repainted. More than we expected. A whole bunch of rotten wood had to be replaced, and money's kind of tight right now. Anyway, I thought I might fix it by tightening up this coupling here. Considering what plumbers charge, I figure it's worth a try."

"It looks pretty rusted," John said dubiously, "but I suppose if you can get a wrench on there and are careful, it might tighten up."

"Well, I'm game to try, but I don't have a big enough wrench. Do you still have that big, two-foot monkey wrench in the back of your car?"

"Darn right. I wouldn't leave home without Crusher."

"Crusher?"

"That's Mary's nickname for the wrench, heaven knows why. Come on over and I'll get it for you. You can put Crusher back when you're done."

Chapter 11

Cape Cod, August 4

The two teenagers had driven all the way to Hyannis, where they figured nobody was likely to recognize them. He'd parked his parent's Chevy in front of one of the larger drug stores, and she waited in the car while he went inside.

It seemed like a long time before he returned, flushed but triumphant.

"What took so long?" she asked.

He explained that an elderly woman had been talking to the druggist, and taking almost forever, while he stood around the magazine rack, trying to look busy. The old lady finally walked away and he was able to talk to the druggist.

"Did you know there was more than one kind of these things?" he asked the girl.

As it happened, the girl did know that, but she laughed sympathetically anyway because he was sweet and funny, and she liked him a lot.

It was well after dark by the time they got to the secluded, sandy beach at the mouth of Carver Creek. Guided by a full moon, the pair made their way down a narrow path through the scrub pine and beach grass, finally spreading a beach towel on a patch of smooth, dry sand well above the high-tide line. It was an idyllic spot, overlooking the mouth of Carver Creek with nothing but sand and beach grass as far as the eye could see.

She suggested making a game of undressing each other, and they lay on the towel a little later while he struggled with clumsy haste to open the foil packet without destroying its contents. She wondered if he was a virgin. She suppressed a giggle as she watched his fumbling, and felt a sudden wave of fondness. He really was cute. She wisely rejected the idea of offering to help with the recalcitrant condom, contenting herself instead with gently stroking his thigh, an activity that did nothing to improve the boy's composure.

She was lying on her back a little later when a sailboat came into view just beyond the boy's thrusting rump. The boat glided down the channel only a hundred feet or so away, its sail shining white in the moonlight.

She tensed for a moment, her instinct telling her to run and hide, but as quickly as it came, her fear was replaced by a wanton bravado. What could anybody see from the boat? Two anonymous lovers entwined on the sand? "Watch all you want," she thought with a sudden thrill. She ran her hands up and down the shifting muscles of the boy's back and moaned softly, losing herself in the primal dance of life, while the silent boat ghosted past their feet, leaving behind the faint, sweet smell of death.

* * *

It was cooling off outside, but the Wendell's bedroom was still hot, even at 10 o'clock in the evening. They lay naked on the bed while the fan struggled to draw cooler air in through the open window.

"We might as well turn out the light and try to get some

sleep," Mary said.

"Yes. I still have to get up early and do some more work on Hibbert's drawings before I can take them over to Sam for a quote."

"Do you want me to leave the fan on?"

She knew perfectly well the treachery that lay in her seemingly harmless question. He looked at the fan as it sat on the window sill. Its spinning blades shimmered in the light from the bedside lamp, while it made a faint, high-pitched metallic whine.

There was only one rational answer to Mary's question, of course. And yet the flashing blades were so much like an airplane propeller...

John tore his eyes away from the deadly fan, hoping it wouldn't follow him into sleep, hoping it wouldn't wake him in terror.

"Better leave it on," he said. "We'll fry if we don't." A jolt ran through him. Why did he use that word, when he'd seen so many men fry already?

* * *

The Zero's .30 caliber machine guns made a sharp rattle above the ship's AA fire as the plane flew closer, its propeller flashing in the sunlight. Closer and closer it came, its engine screaming, the muzzle flash of its guns twinkling like deadly stars on a summer's night—

"John!" Mary's voice shook him awake. He jerked upright in the bed, his heart pounding, panting for breath, and soaked with sweat.

"Are you all right?" she asked.

"I'm fine," he gasped. It was a lie, of course.

"There was a noise under our window."

"A noise?"

"Like firecrackers. Do you want me to go and check?"

"I'll do it," John said getting shakily to his feet.

"You're sure? I can go down."

"I said I'd do it!" There was no staying in bed, now, anyway. He started to get dressed.

It looked like several strings of firecrackers. Lady Fingers, John guessed. The remains still smouldered in the grass, and he stamped them out, oblivious to the tiny embers stinging the soles of his bare feet.

He stormed into the kitchen a few minutes later, where Mary handed him a glass of water. His hands were shaking as he slumped into a chair.

"Firecrackers," he said.

"I don't know about these kids nowadays," Mary replied.

A drop of sweat fell, unnoticed, from the tip of John's nose. "Kids? Are you nuts? Somebody did that on purpose! Somebody who knew what it would do! It's a joke, like Henry throwing that empty bucket on the floor yesterday, just for the fun of seeing me jump."

"You don't seriously think that Henry, at his age, would go wandering around our backyard, setting off firecrackers."

"You want to know what I think? I think there's a killer out there who is trying to play with my mind. And your mind too."

"John, don't—"

He went on, relentless. "Don't you see? Your nice, peaceful little town is full of vicious people, and at least one of them is a killer."

Chapter 12

Wissonet, August 5

John watched Lieutenant Riley look around his office. A drafting table and stool, together with a pair of worn, overstuffed chairs dominated the space. One chair was littered with an assortment of children's toys, papers, and crayons, indicating Wendy's frequent presence.

"Nice view," Riley said as he gazed out the window and down the hillside to where the waters of Wissonet Harbor could be seen over the rooftops. Mary had said the same thing when they first looked at the house.

"Look Lieutenant, I didn't get much sleep last night, and I really have to get some work done this morning."

"Okay, here's the story. Your smart-mouthed pal over at Carver Creek called the local police at dawn to report that *Abracadabra* was missing. They asked around and learned the boat was seen leaving Carver Creek around ten o'clock last night. The witness was pretty sure there was just one person, but all she could see was a silhouette."

"So there could have been somebody out of sight in the cabin?"

"It's possible, but who knows? You can't always tell about witnesses, especially when they don't know they're witnessing something important." Riley paused. "And they aren't paying too much attention."

John was perched on a stool in front of the drafting table, and he looked wistfully at his drawings.

"One of the fishermen who found the boat was nosing around there yesterday, too," Riley said. "I'll have to talk to him again."

So Jack did talk to the "stiff-necked Irishman" after all. Good for Jack, bad for the fisherman. "How reliable is this witness?"

"It was the police chief's daughter. She and a friend were sitting on the beach when they saw the boat, but of course they didn't think anything of it until this morning when all hell broke loose."

All hell being in the form of Lieutenant Joe Riley. John could imagine Riley's descent upon the sleepy town of Pocasset. The police chief's daughter had a lot of courage to speak up.

"Was *Abracadabra* towing a dinghy last night?" John figured it would take four or five more hours to finish the preliminary drawings.

Riley sat down in one of the comfortable chairs. "No. Whoever took the boat used one of the boatyard skiffs to get out to it."

"There's bus service to Pocasset, and it's an easy walk from there to the boat yard, so one person could have done it."

Riley looked at John coolly. "You're the one who suggested leaving it on a mooring where somebody could snatch it."

"Why didn't you have a cop guarding the boat in the first place?"

"The police department isn't made of money, Wendell."

"Just remember that I didn't ask to be involved in this mess. You're the one who talked me into going with you."

"You agreed to go," Riley countered. "The trouble is that I can't see why anyone would steal the boat at this point, just to sink it."

"Agreed. Besides, if somebody did want to sink it, then they would have needed a boat to get away afterwards, or an accomplice with a boat."

Riley got up and paced around the room before standing over the drawing board. He gazed at the maze of lines that represented Hibbert's boat, and picked up a fist-sized object that resembled a stylized whale with an L-shaped prong sticking out of its nose. "What's this? It's heavy."

"It's called a duck and it's made of lead," John said curtly. He glanced at Riley's irritated look and added, "Officially, they're called spline weights."

"Of course they are," the detective muttered. "Make a nice weapon, though."

"When I'm not stealing boats, or hitting people on the head with one of my ducks, I use them like this." John took a long, flexible piece of wood. "This is called a spline, or a batten. I bend it to the curve I want to draw, and use the prongs on a row of ducks to hold it in place while I draw the line." John demonstrated with a piece of scrap paper.

"Lots of curves in a boat."

"It's not like a house. With a boat, you have to draw a three-dimensional curved object on a two-dimensional piece of paper. The curved part is tricky."

"So that's what all these lines are for?" Riley nodded at a blueprint pinned to the wall.

"Yes," John said, warming to his subject. "If you think of a boat as a loaf of bread, and you trace the outline of each slice on a piece of paper, you'd have what are called sections, like these lines here." He pointed to the blueprint.

"Yeah, that makes sense."

"But that's not enough to draw a boat accurately, so we add the waterlines, like slicing our loaf of bread horizontally."

"Like a torte?"

"Right." John pointed to another part of the drawing. "Then we slice the bread lengthwise vertically, to make what are called the buttock lines. Last of all, we slice the bread lengthwise diagonally, to make the diagonal lines."

"Sounds more like making croutons than making a boat."

"The thing is that all four views have to agree. Everything has to fit together; if one is wrong, they're all wrong."

Riley looked at the drawing for a moment. "It sounds like your job and mine aren't all that different." He picked up one of John's ruling pens and examined it. "Who else would know how to sail the boat besides the Commodore, Dianne, and you?"

"It's a pretty simple boat to sail. Almost anybody could do it."

"You're not making my life any easier. I wonder about Dianne."

"Ah, the spouse. She visited here yesterday afternoon, around three o'clock."

"So, she would have had just enough time to get to Carver Creek afterwards."

"Do you think she killed the Commodore?"

"Probably not, but I like to tie up loose ends—you know, buttocks and diagonals." Riley picked up a bottle of India ink and fingered the stopper absentmindedly. "I looked up 'Abracadabra' in the dictionary yesterday."

John, who was hastily sliding a sheet of tracing paper under any possible drips, looked up. This was a side of Lieutenant Riley that he'd never imagined. "What did it say?"

"It's a mystical word that you put on an amulet to ward off disease. They called it a 'pretended spell' and 'jargon.'"

"Jargon?"

"Yes, jargon." Riley gave John a dark look. "I keep hearing a hell of a lot of jargon in this case, like your lead ducks. Whoever thought up a name like that?" He put down the ink bottle, much to John's relief. "Do you normally see much of Dianne Cummings?"

"Not usually. As I say, she dropped by yesterday afternoon, but she hasn't visited more than twice since we moved here about a year ago."

"Was it a 'thank you for looking at my boat' kind of visit?"

"Pretty much. She wanted to know what kind of condition *Abracadabra* was in. She did say that she hoped to get her back soon."

"So Dianne could have left here, taken a bus to Carver Creek yesterday evening, and stolen her own boat," Riley said. "Assuming that somebody like you had told her the boat was seaworthy."

"Or, she could have called the boatyard and found out for herself. It's hardly a secret, after all. But why would she go to the trouble of stealing her own boat if she was going to get it back in a few days, anyway?" John paused. "Maybe somebody else stole it to keep Dianne from getting the boat back at all."

Riley stared out the window at the harbor. "How far do you think the damn boat could have gotten since last night?"

"In roughly ten hours? Manchester 17's were designed for racing and they're fairly fast, even by today's standards. Of course it would depend on the wind direction."

"Meaning?"

"By now, *Abracadabra* could have covered forty, maybe even fifty miles in this wind, assuming a northerly course. A lot less, heading to the south, into the wind." John pulled out a chart and drew a lopsided circle around Carver Creek.

"That's a big area to search."

"And getting bigger all the time."

Riley eyed John balefully. "Unless you figure the boat went straight down."

Chapter 13

Wissonet, August 5

The 38-foot Elco power boat was over 20-years old, long and sleek, with an impressive expanse of varnished mahogany cabin. With her squared-off deckhouse, the Elco looked both fast and elegant, which she was in both regards.

After all, what pleasanter, more opulent way for a roaring-twenties millionaire to spend time on the water visiting east coast yacht clubs than by an Elco Cruiser? Sadly, this Elco's cruising days were over, at least until her worn-out engine was replaced, which was precisely why it sat in Sam's yard, broiling in the morning sun.

It wasn't even noon yet, but the Elco's cramped engine compartment was already like a proverbial oven, with barely enough room for John and Henry Merton. The old man put away his folding rule. "I hope you know what you're doing with all these damnfool measurements, because I'm not crawling back into this hell-hole if I can help it."

"That should be enough do the calculations," John replied, looking at his notes. He wasn't getting much done on Hibbert's boat this morning, but at least he was making money.

"Calculations, hell," Henry grumbled. "Humbug is closer. Sam wouldn't need to mess with all that arithmetic just to put in a new engine."

Henry was right, of course. John had no illusions that his theoretical approach was any better than Sam's seat-of-the-pants way of doing things. Experience mattered. John just hoped his results would be as good.

Henry wormed his way back to the hatch opening and turned to face John. "Why didn't you let Dianne go and look over *Abracadabra*? She knows the boat a lot better than you do."

John badly wanted to get back into the open where at least the ninety-five degree air was moving, but Henry was blocking the way. "Don't you think it would be hard for her to go right from the funeral to look at the boat her husband was just killed in?"

Henry, undeterred by John's comment, veered off to one of his maddening irrelevancies. "Did I ever tell you about Barnley Grindle?" Henry's fund of stories about the town's past was inexhaustible, and all too often, unescapable.

"Could we get out of here first?"

The top part of Henry was already sticking above the hatch, thereby benefitting from what little breeze there was.

Feigning deafness, Henry settled his bony rear on the hatch combing. "Barnley was a Wissonet man, went to sea on a freighter during the Great War. As luck would have it, the freighter got torpedoed in the North Atlantic, and he was the only survivor—a miracle he lived."

"Dammit, Henry—"

"Well, he went back to sea on another freighter a couple of months later, and sure enough, the same thing happened, and again he was the only survivor. After that, Barnley figured he could take a hint, so he decided to stop going to sea and stay ashore where it was safe. You know what happened to him?" Henry didn't wait for an answer. "A couple of months later, he slipped and fell in his bathtub—knocked himself out cold. Poor man drowned in the tub, in less than a foot of water."

"Is there a point to all this?"

"Damn right there is. There's no such thing as cheating fate, Sonny. Destiny's dues will be paid. You know where the saying, 'three on a match' comes from?"

John mopped his brow. "Doesn't everybody?"

Henry forged on, regardless. "It comes from the trenches during the Great War. You're sitting in your trench one night and decide to light up a cigarette. A German sniper sees the glow from your match, but he doesn't have time get a bead on you before you put it out. But matches are scarce in the trenches, so your friend asks for a light too, and you fire up his cigarette. By now, the sniper is lining up his shot, but the match goes out just before he can pull the trigger. You know what happens if second friend wants a light off your match? Bang! Three on a match."

"For crying out loud, move it, Henry!"

"The point is that cats may have nine lives, but people only have three. Three strikes and you're out," Henry warned, shamelessly mixing his metaphors. "You're playing with fire, getting involved in the Cummings business, and you'll pay the dues."

"I'm going to throw you over the side if you don't move out of the damn hatch," John growled.

Just then, Sam began pounding on the outside of the hull. "Come on you two, quit the gab and get back to work."

* * *

Sam turned to Henry after John had left. "What are you pestering him for? What did he do to you that you've got to keep tormenting him?"

"That kid is going around talking to the cops about half the people in town."

"How the hell do you know that?" They were standing in a tiny patch of shade under the Elco's bow. Henry, like most of the Merton family, was tall, and he towered a good three inches over Sam's compact frame. The extra height left Henry's balding skull to bake in the sun as he squinted down at his companion.

"I know a lot more than you think, Sonny, and that kid is heading for trouble if he keeps on like this."

"He liked the Commodore," Sam said. "You can't blame him for wanting to help the cops find out who did it. He probably won't be the only one talking to them, either."

Henry scowled, adding extra wrinkles to his squint. "I'm not sorry to see the last of Cummings. Why should anyone else be? Good riddance to him as far as I'm concerned."

"Why in the world do you say that? What about your precious town legend? Have you forgotten that he's the last direct descendent of Ruth Cummings, your favorite witch?"

"It's not a legend; it's history, and the past won't change just because Cummings was killed."

"You think it's that easy? There's going to be big trouble over this, whether Wendell talks to the police or not, and you damn well know it."

"People have been killed in town before, and people in town will be killed again," Henry said darkly. "Wendell knows just enough to get himself murdered if he's not careful."

It was Sam's turn to scowl. "Commodore Cummings was a big wheel in town, whatever he thought of your fairy tale, and the cops are going to ask around, whether you like it or not."

"I don't like that kid talking to the cops. He could give the town a bad name."

"Give the town a bad name? Have you been painting the bilge with the hatches closed again? What makes you think anyone would give a damn about all that crap? It's ancient history, for crying out loud."

"It's not crap, and you need to show more respect for your elders, Sonny."

"When the hell are you going to stop calling me Sonny?"

"Do *you* remember Abraham Lincoln?"

"And when are you going to stop handing me that Abraham Lincoln malarkey," Sam demanded.

"No respect," Henry groused. "That's the trouble with the younger generation—no respect for the past."

"I've half a mind to toss you off the end of the pier, you superstitious old loon. Your trouble is that you've been working in the hot sun too long." Sam turned on his heel and stamped off.

* * *

While John was baking in the Elco's innards, Mary was putting Wendy to bed for her afternoon nap. She came downstairs just in time to hear the familiar rumble of Paul Labonte's ice truck as it ground to a halt in front of the house. Not too many decades ago, when the luxuries of electricity were rarer in Wissonet's kitchens, Paul Labonte had delivered ice to most of the residents. He was a blatant anachronism now, along with Mary's varnished oak icebox and its nickel-plated trim.

The steady invasion of electric refrigerators had gradually eaten away at Paul's business until only a handful of customers remained. The old man didn't seem worried about the future of his livelihood, however, and Mary assumed he was planning a gradual retirement around the wheels of progress.

"Morning Mrs. W." Paul's muscular frame dwarfed his quarry as it crouched by the pantry door. A block of ice was suspended from a pair of tongs in one hand while an ice pick was sheathed at the old man's belt.

"Good morning Paul. Another hot day."

Mary remembered other hot summer days as a child, when she and her friends would run behind the truck, waiting for Paul to stop, lift the heavy canvas flap that covered the rear end of the big vehicle, and let them stand in the cool dimness.

"Don't touch them picks," he'd warn, pointing to the needle-sharp ice picks holstered to the inside of the truck by a leather strap. They were never allowed to stay long among the blocks of ice, however, because Paul Labonte was a busy man, and ice melted fast on a summer day. With dizzying speed, his pick sounding like an over-sized sewing machine stitching a line in the ice, he'd cut a perfectly sized block from one of the huge slabs, giving each of the kids a sliver to take with them.

Paul opened the top of the icebox, moved the remains of the old ice out of the way with his free hand, and put in the new block.

"I gave you a little extra today to make up for this heat." He took the ice pick from his belt, deftly cut the remains of the old ice in half to fit. His oft-repeated ritual complete, Paul closed the lid with a flourish.

Mary looked at the wickedly sharp pick and shuddered. It was disconcerting how previously innocent things suddenly reminded her of the Commodore's murder.

Paul seemed to read Mary's mind. "Terrible thing about the Commodore. I delivered ice there for years."

He'd delivered ice to everybody for years, including Mary's parents. He seemed to have been coming into the kitchen to perform his icebox ritual since the beginning of time, as ageless and unchanging as the granite piers that dotted the waterfront. Though he looked young for his age, Mary realized that Paul must be close to eighty. A narrow fringe of tightly curled gray hair clung to the sides of a head that glistened in the heat like polished mahogany. The muscular arms and torso remained, but he took noticeably longer to climb the battered, portable wooden steps into the back of his truck.

"Yes. It must be hard on Dianne," Mary said.

"I wouldn't know about her. The Cummings got electric as soon as they were married. Seems like Mrs. C liked her comforts and she could afford them." Paul looked fondly at Mary's ice box. "Not many people in town have ice boxes any more. Just a few folks, like you, who stick with tradition."

Odd, Mary mused, but she'd never thought of herself as being bound by tradition.

"Yes, ma'am," Paul went on, "going electric suited Mrs. C right down to the ground, but I think Mr. C would've been happier with his old ice box, rich as he was." Paul cleared his throat, as though embarrassed at revealing this secret.

Of course the Commodore would have embraced the local icebox cult. Maybe it was the Commodore's death or seeing Louise again after all those years, but somehow her thinking had changed. For the first time, she was noticing the little ways that so many people in Wissonet clung to the past, like the iceboxes, and the crank telephones with their party lines and special rings. The town wasn't really that isolated anymore—not with New Bedford less than an hour away. It occurred to Mary that she might not have noticed Wissonet's tenacious anachronisms even now if it wasn't for the time she and John had lived in Quincy among all the modern wonders of the mid-twentieth century.

"You must feel like you live here with all the houses you stop at," Mary blurted out, to her surprise.

Paul had spent a lot of time in different houses over the years and must know a great many town secrets, Mary thought. He gazed benignly at her for a moment. "No, I don't feel like I live here at all. I just come and deliver ice to folks like you who don't have 'fridges yet, but I don't live here at all." The old man paused. "It's a nice place to come to, but I guess this just isn't my kind of town for living in."

He sounded almost like Louise. Or did he? The Wallers had lived in town for generations, while Paul was just a visitor. "Are people unfriendly here?"

Paul looked at her, or perhaps through her, Mary thought.

"I can remember like it was only yesterday when you reached up to about my knee," Paul said with a smile. "You were always one of the first to come running out looking for a piece of ice." He paused for a moment. "No, people here are friendly enough, but sometimes it feels like they're scared of visitors, so I just come in with my ice and move on."

Mary wondered about the time, perhaps not far off, when Paul Labonte wouldn't be delivering ice to them anymore. Yacht designers were seldom rich, but someday John's career would grow to the point where they could indulge themselves with a refrigerator of their own. The thought of having ice cream whenever she wanted it filled her with a sudden yearning.

Once again, the mind-reading trick. "Let me know if you ever want to buy a 'fridge. I'll give you a good price on a nice used GE."

Paul Labonte selling refrigerators? This was a new, and somehow traitorous, concept. "I don't think we'll be doing that any time soon, Paul."

"Well, just say the word when you do. I'm here every

week," he said. "And if Mr. W ever wants to get rid of that A Model out there, I'll buy it off him."

"It's not much of a car to drive."

"Oh Lord, I wouldn't think of driving it," Paul said with horror, "but I've got a big old shed out back, and I'd put that buggy under a tarp and store it away. It'll be worth good money in a few years when I retire."

"But Model A Fords are a dime a dozen."

"Not those beach wagons Mrs. W. Mister Ford didn't make a lot of beach wagons, and people like old things, especially if there aren't too many of them around. Just look at all the junk they have in these antique stores nowadays, and most of it's stuff we threw away when I was young," Paul smiled. "It's funny the way people like those old things enough to pay for them today. Yes ma'am, I think an antique store would be a good way to make a living, once the ice business dries up."

Chapter 14

Wissonet, August 5

With Wendy safely in bed, John and Mary sat in their favorite spot on the porch, enjoying the quiet of the evening. John supposed it was the aftereffect of yesterday's visit to the Claytons, but the porch's worn and peeling paint looked shabbier than usual.

"I suppose we'll either have to paint the house soon, or only come out here at night," he said.

"The Claytons spent a lot of money this spring, fixing the place up," Mary said. "Of course, that was before Ed got laid off from Cummings Jewelry."

"Which is probably why he has such a low opinion of the Commodore's business skills."

"People have killed for less than being laid off," she murmured.

John was quiet for a while, moving gently in his rocking chair. Finally, he said, "I'm sorry for blowing up last night about the firecrackers."

Mary was unconsciously rocking in sync with John, and she put her hand on his. "Another nightmare?"

"They are getting better then they were," he replied, defiantly.

Mary looked at her husband incredulously. How could he say they were getting better after last night? She took her hand away.

"I just assumed the worst about the firecrackers when I shouldn't have," John went on. "You're probably right and it was just kids."

"Yes," Mary agreed, knowing that her answer was taking the easy way out. "Did you know that Paul Labonte sells refrigerators?"

John shifted mental gears. "We could probably get a used one pretty cheap."

"You mean one of those ugly things with the coil on top?"

"Well, something newer than that."

"You won't get a newer one in Wissonet," Mary retorted. "Nobody around here would sell their refrigerator until it was ancient." She sighed. "Besides, I'm not sure I want one. I like Paul's ice. It has character."

She finished the last of her lemonade "Have you noticed how short the stoplight is on North Street? It's as though the town didn't want to let anyone in or out."

John was beginning to have trouble keeping up. "Maybe Wissonet is just trying to protect its character."

There was a rapidly melting chip of Paul Labonte's ice in the bottom of Mary's glass. She swirled it around idly. "Do you really like living here, or are you just doing it to please me?"

"Yes, I do like it here. Sure, the town is peculiar the way it hangs onto things, but I kind of like that. And it's not as though I didn't know what to expect; I spent my summers growing up here, after all."

Mary shattered the ice between her teeth. "I'm not sure things are the same now, with the Commodore gone. I'm beginning to think that Dianne is right about that."

"You aren't taking her 'so much evil' talk seriously, are you?"

"Of course not. That's just more of her theatrics."

"I wish this wasn't all so personal for you,." he said.

She stared up at the evening sky. "I can't help it. I feel like I'm being torn in half, drawn into something, and I don't know what it is."

"But none of this really has anything to do with us."

"Who was it that said, 'no man is a island?'"

He felt a chill. "John Donne."

Mary shook her head, saying nothing, and after a while the telephone rang.

* * *

Bill Gray's unexpected call and bigger-than-life voice broke the gloom and brought back welcome memories, not the least of which was the security of a regular pay check.

Gray quickly dispensed with the small talk. "Do you remember that big sloop you did for George Finley?" he asked.

It was the last design John had done before leaving the firm, and he remembered both the boat and the man vividly. Finley was in his seventies, wealthy and opinionated, and he'd wanted a fifty-foot sloop for himself and his wife to go cruising, "with a little bit of racing on the side," he'd added. Worried about the couple's safety, John and Bill had tried unsuccessfully to persuade their client to accept a more manageable yawl rig. "What about Finley and his boat?"

"Well, it seem that he and his wife got caught in a storm off Nova Scotia. Scared them half to death. Luckily, they got the boat into Yarmouth, and Finley has been on the phone ever since, yelling that we should have warned him about handling a sloop that big in a storm and demanding to have someone go up there and fix the damn boat. You can bet I had a few words to say to him.

"The thing is, he's lined up a yard in Yarmouth who can do the work to re-rig her as a yawl. I pulled out the sail plan you did when we were trying to get Finley to rig her as a yawl in the first place, so all you have to do is go to the yard up there, make sure they know what to do, and hold Finley's hand a bit. It shouldn't take more than a couple of days. I warned him it would cost a bundle for someone to go up there, so don't pinch the pennies."

John thought about Hibbert's drawings still waiting on his drafting table. Everything seemed to be feast or famine. The minute Hibbert appeared with a worthwhile commission, people like Riley and Gray turned up with these pesky little distractions. Why couldn't they have waited until he had more time?

The famine part was convincing, however.

"Okay, Bill. I guess I can spare a couple of days. But I'll have to burn the midnight oil to make up for it, so you can be sure it'll cost Finley. When do you want me up there?"

"The yard can't start the work until Monday, but if you came up here first thing Saturday to pick up the plans, you could fly into Yarmouth and be there by afternoon in time to talk to the yard up there Sunday. Luckily, Ray Phillips happened to be in Yarmouth with his boat, so the pair of them can entertain themselves until Monday."

"You mean leave tomorrow morning?"

"First thing. That'll get you to Yarmouth early Saturday afternoon."

John groaned.

"Look, I'm sorry about the short notice, but you can

imagine how Finley would be in a rush, seeing as how his wife has gone home and he's cooling his heels up there waiting for his boat to be fixed. Besides, he's willing to fly you up to Yarmouth, which is a helluva lot quicker than spending a day on the steamer. And don't forget the guy knows a lot of people, so he could throw a little work your way if you treat him right. Anyway, I'll buy you an early lunch when you get here."

Bill had hired John a year before Pearl Harbor, kept the position open for him during the war, and helped him mend, physically and mentally in the three years after he got out. It hadn't been easy for either of them.

John figured he owed his former boss. Hibbert's drawings would have to wait.

They arranged the details and Bill added, "Look John, things are getting busy up here, so I could throw a little freelance work your way when you have some extra time." He paused for half a beat. "I know what you're thinking, you pig-headed bastard, but you're wrong. I'm not just throwing out bread crumbs because I feel sorry for you. You were one of my best men—at least once you got your head on straight—and I'm selfish enough to want to take advantage of your services as much as I can.

"Anyway, we can talk about it tomorrow. It's only a two-hour drive up to Boston." There was another pause. "I suppose you're still driving that old rattletrap around."

"It's an antique, not a rattletrap. In fact I have an eager buyer just waiting to snap it up."

"Take the offer, for god's sake, before they give the guy a lobotomy. In the meantime, you can always take the bus."

Chapter 15

Wissonet, August 6

Mary dropped John off to catch the early morning bus to Boston before driving on to the Waller house, her handbag bulging with a camera and flashbulbs.

She walked through the quiet rooms while childhood memories flitted through her mind. The place was being sold with its furnishings, which added to the vividness of those memories. Mary felt a sudden wave of melancholy and, she realized with surprise, homesickness for the simplicity and security of her youth.

She took several interior shots before ending up in the living room. It was an unusually imposing space for a house of this size, and Mary spent some time choosing good vantage points for her camera. Tan wainscoting circled the room, while the interior wall, with its fireplace, was paneled from floor to ceiling, with two small cabinets framing the mantle. Mary remembered with a smile how delighted she and Louise had been to find the built-in wood box cubbyhole.

Perhaps there were more hiding places, Mary thought. Their childhood searches were, of necessity, limited to the lower parts of the room, though they'd dragged a chair over to the fireplace once in a vain effort to reach higher. Mary ran her fingers over the trim above the mantle admiring the craftsmanship while looking for looseness.

It didn't take long to find. A carved corner block at the top of the paneling shifted in her hand and came away. With a guilty thrill, she stood on tiptoe and reached into the opening. The space was a tight fit for her hand, but her questing fingers closed around seven slender, palm-sized books.

The diaries were bound in black leather, dry and brittle with age. Mary looked at her find uncertainly. Surely Louise must have known about them; the hiding place was much too obvious for an adult to miss.

Another thought occurred to Mary: did Louise *want* her to find the diaries? She'd reminded Mary of their youthful woodwork searches just the other day, after all. But why would Mary's childhood friend want her to find the journals? Did she abandon them as a way of further putting the town behind her?

No, Mary decided, Louise must have just forgotten them. She dropped the volumes into her purse, planning to mail them to Louise so they wouldn't fall into the hands of some stranger.

* * *

John arrived at the Yarmouth airport by early afternoon, feeling ready to sit in one place for a while with his feet up. Unfortunately, his client had other ideas, and John was hustled to McCleod's boatyard just long enough to drop off the drawings, and speak briefly to McCleod himself about the needed modifications before rushing off to the dock where *Lady Slipper*, Ray Phillips's boat, waited.

An hour later, John sat at the helm with the late afternoon sun still warm on his back. He felt the response of the boat to his hand on the wheel, her motion as she cut through the seas, and was filled with a sense of peace for the first time since the Commodore's death.

George Finley, to all appearances both ageless and tireless, sat beside John watching the boat's progress attentively. "What do you think?" he said.

"She's a great little yawl, George, sails like a dream—"

"I mean her speed." A note of impatience crept into George's voice. Ray Phillips, *Lady Slipper's* owner, grinned and took a sip from a tumbler full of gin and tonic. All three of them had similar tumblers, though John's was so far untouched.

"*Temptress* is faster," George said wistfully.

John knew perfectly well where this was going. He picked up his glass and took a sip though he didn't care much for gin and tonic.

"She's faster as a sloop, anyway." George was like a dog with a bone. "Will the yawl rig slow her down much?"

"It will depend a lot on the sailing conditions," John said patiently. They had gone over this a dozen times already. "Both boats are about the same size, so I expect they'll be pretty well matched as yawls."

"For heaven's sake George," Ray said, "if you wanted a racing boat, why didn't you get a racing crew to go with it?"

A tern swooped overhead, inspecting *Lady Slipper* for food. John thought of offering it a drink.

"What's wrong with having a fast cruising boat?"

John eased the wheel a trifle as the bow climbed a swell. "You have a tradeoff between speed and comfort," he said. They surfed down the face of the wave, water hissing along the rail.

"Comfort gets more important as you grow older," Ray added.

John took another sip, noticed his host giving the glass a

speculative look, and hastily put it out of sight.

"Linda and I loved to rough it when we were younger," Ray went on, "but we enjoy having a few extra luxuries now, even if the boat is a little slower. Speed isn't everything, after all."

Far ahead, John could see the sun glinting off a sail at the mouth of Yarmouth harbor. Hunger pangs were setting in, and he looked forward to a good meal at the hotel. Since Finley was buying, he planned to eat well.

"—Even poor Cummings was looking for something more comfortable," Ray was saying.

John snapped to attention. "He was?"

"Can you blame him?" Ray said. "Those little boats are wetter than hell in rough weather. I certainly wouldn't want to camp out in one."

John tried to digest this bit of news. "He's had that boat ever since I can remember. It's been in the family ever since it was built."

"Well, I saw him this spring and he talked about buying something bigger—said he was tired of getting his ass wet all the time sitting on the cockpit floor, and those little boats aren't much good for cruising." Ray shook his head sadly.

"He went cruising in that thing?" George sounded incredulous. "I thought he had it just for racing, though they're a pretty old design to be very competitive."

"They're surprisingly fast, especially off the wind," John said, "And there are still a lot of them around in Massachusetts and Maine."

"And they must be quite seaworthy too," Ray said, "because I saw him up here last summer."

George looked goggle-eyed. "He was way up here?"

"All by himself," Ray added.

So that's why the Commodore had all those charts, John

thought. "I expect he harbor-hopped his way along the Maine coast, and then crossed over to Yarmouth. That's the closest major harbor to the Maine coast."

"I suppose it would be okay, if he watched the weather," Ray commented, shooting a meaningful glance at George, who pursed his lips.

"Did you talk to him?" George asked.

"Just to hail each other and say hello. We were sailing in opposite directions, and he didn't seem anxious to talk much, except to say he was headed east. I think he has relatives up here somewhere."

"It's an awfully long way in that little boat, and all by himself. No wonder he was thinking about getting something bigger," George concluded.

John sat at the helm and wondered if the Commodore sailed this far every summer. How far east did he go? The weather would have to be perfect in order to make it up here and back during the company's two-week vacation.

* * *

Tired out at last, Finley headed for bed right after dinner, but John had somehow gotten his second wind and felt restless, so he decided to take a short walk. The evening air was cooler and dryer than Wissonet, a welcome relief.

Like a homesick frog, he instinctively headed towards the water. Yarmouth was a working harbor and much of the waterfront was devoted to fishing boats.

John walked by Ian McCleod's shop, a worn clapboard shed that perched on pilings at the water's edge like a malformed stork. *Temptress* lay against the dock in front, waiting for the start of her coming surgery Monday.

John had taken a liking to Macleod from the moment they met, especially when the bearded Scot announced that he planned to send Finley off Monday to "run some errands so we can get a bit of work done."

Few people were out in the approaching dusk and John walked unnoticed onto the docks where groups of large wooden barrels, presumably used to carry bait or salted fish, were scattered around the piers. At one time these piers had been home to some of the world's most famous Grand Banks fishing schooners—fast, graceful craft that had lent an air of romance to a hard and dangerous way of life. John let his feet and mind wander aimlessly as he soaked up the atmosphere of the place.

Abracadabra lay tied up to a dock, well separated from the bustle of the harbor. At least John thought it was *Abracadabra*. He stared down at the sleek black hull, wondering what to do next. The tide was high, making the boat's deck almost level with the dock, and John was able to kneel down and read the name on the stern. Indeed, the verdigris-stained brass letters spelled *Abracadabra*.

John stood up and thought about his next step. He'd have to call the local police and tell them he'd found a stolen boat. Riley would be glad to get his crime scene back.

But what was the boat doing here? Could it have been the sail he'd seen earlier from *Lady Slipper*?

"What are you doing with that boat?" Startled, John turned. The man looked to be in his forties, a bit shorter than John but huskier, with sandy, crew cut hair.

"The boat looked familiar, and I was just checking the name."

"This is a private dock and people aren't allowed on it without permission. Things get stolen," the stranger said belligerently...

* * *

John thought he must be a bee in his new incarnation. He could hear the buzzing of another bee nearby, and could feel himself enclosed in one of the hexagonal cells of the hive. Perhaps the other bee had sealed him in to await whatever came next.

Awareness crept over him a piece at a time. The buzzing wasn't from some gigantic bee, but the whine of a truck's gearbox as it labored uphill. He had no idea where he was at first, only that he was uncomfortably curled up in a cramped space that smelled of dead fish—definitely not honey. It took a moment to realize that he'd somehow gotten closed up inside one of the over-size fish barrels that were scattered around the dock.

Normally John would have been reduced to a state of claustrophobic panic, but in this half-real world between consciousness and dreaming he was able to dispassionately observe the situation as though he was somebody else.

A flatbed truck, laden with half a dozen barrels, had been parked near *Abracadabra's* berth, and was probably what he was riding on.

Something was pressing against John's cheek, probably his hand, since there was no sign of anybody else inside his barrel. He wiggled his fingers experimentally and found that it was his right hand, numb from being twisted into an unnatural position between his face and the top of the barrel. He could clearly hear the truck's engine now, and feel the barrel sway with the vehicle's motion. The driver was obviously in a hurry.

He could tell that the air, already thick with the aroma of decayed fish, was running out of oxygen.

His final destination remained to be seen, but his prospects were obviously not good.

Terror swept over him as full consciousness returned. He threw himself as best he could against side of the barrel, and his prison began rocking, which suggested that his attacker hadn't taken the time to lash down the latest addition to the truck's cargo.

Ignoring the waves of pain, he heaved himself from side to side in time with the swaying of the truck. He could feel the barrel shifting from side to side, rocking more and more with each heave.

Then the truck lurched around a corner, the barrel tumbled off the truck bed, hit the road, tumbled down an embankment, and shattered against a tree.

Chapter 16

Yarmouth, August 6

John imagined the telephone's shrill sound filling the living room a world away. He imagined its incessant call echoing up the stairs. He imagined Mary's reluctant return to wakefulness in the wee-small hours. He imagined her tramping down the stairs...

"Hello?"

"Hi. It's me."

"John? Why are you calling at this hour? Are you all right?"

"I had a little...accident. Not serious. Mostly just some bruises and a concussion."

The night nurse sat at her station and glared at him across the counter. She had looked up a few minutes earlier to see him staggering down the corridor, leaning against the wall for support and demanding a telephone. After a heated discussion, she allowed him five minutes on the phone, in return for his agreement to accept a wheelchair.

"What do you mean a little accident? Where are you? What happened?"

"I hit my head...fell...and got a little banged up. I'm in the hospital." John paused, trying to collect his thoughts. Putting together a coherent sentence was nearly impossible. "They want me to stay here for a little bit. For observation. I wanted to call and let you know, before somebody else got you worried over nothing." He chose not to mention the scrapes and bruises he'd sustained during the barrel's trip down the embankment and disintegration against the tree. Every bone in his body hurt.

"Worried over nothing? You sound awful. Is there a doctor I can talk to?"

John looked around vaguely. "I don't think so. It's after midnight here." The simple act of turning his head started the world spinning crazily and made his skull throb as though its contents had grown too large for their container. This was a mild concussion? He'd have to rethink all those Westerns where people were constantly being knocked out, only to wake up a few minutes later with no sign of ill-effects.

"What's the phone number there?" Mary said.

"Phone number?" John thought for a moment and asked the nurse, who pointed to the telephone. He knew it was printed on the white card in the middle of the dial, but staring at the numbers only made them swim around like restless minnows. Besides, there didn't seem to be the right number of digits.

The nurse shook her head and spoke the number with exaggerated slowness while John passed it on.

"I'll call tomorrow and talk to the doctor," Mary said. "I'd better come up. You shouldn't be there all alone, and you'll certainly need somebody to help you travel."

"No need. They said I'll only be in here for twenty-four hours before I can go home, and George Finley has been a big help. He only just left the hospital." Finley might be a mule when it came to his boat, but he was an angel when it came to John's "accident." In fact, he'd risen to the challenge with uncharacteristic sensitivity, pestering the doctors and nurses mercilessly to ensure that John received the best possible care. In the end, he'd perched at the bedside until well after visiting hours like an oversized, featherless mother hen.

"He's offered to stay and escort me home," John reported.

"Oh." Mary didn't sound entirely satisfied. "How in the world did you hit your head?"

"Well," John stalled for time. "I don't think I can explain it all right now. I'm not sure exactly how it all happened." That was true enough. One minute he was staring at *Abracadabra*, a stranger came up, and the next thing he knew he was in a barrel, or, as he was informed by the constable questioning him, a "hogshead." Unfortunately, he felt totally unable to convey all this to Mary with his head about to split open.

The nurse stood up and started making back to bed gestures, thereby saving him further difficulty.

"I've got to go back to my room," he said. "Could you call Lieutenant Riley and tell him I saw *Abracadabra* in the harbor?"

"Call who? You saw what?"

John could tell that he'd just derailed his attempt at reassurance.

"What have you been up to?" Mary demanded.

The nurse was reaching for the phone. "I'll talk to you later. I've really got to go. I love you."

* * *

Constable Walters arrived first thing in the morning and questioned John once again about last night's events. John's head was going like a trip hammer by the time the Mountie left with the promise that the "unfortunate matter would be investigated further."

An hour later, John was allowed to walk—stagger would be

more accurate—out to the nurse's desk to receive a telephone call from Lieutenant Riley.

"What the hell are you doing up there, Wendell? First, your wife calls before I've even had my morning coffee, and then the Canadian police give me some cock-and-bull story about you poking around my crime scene."

"I was not poking around your damn crime scene, for crissake."

Riley was unconvinced. "If you knew the boat was up there, why the hell didn't you tell me instead of going off to play Sam Spade? Do you realize you've probably let the murderer get away?"

John's head felt like it was about to explode. "I was *not* playing Sam Spade, or anybody else! Your goddam crime scene attacked me!"

Riley's voice became more ominous. "This is no joke, Wendell. I've got a bunch of Mounties on my tail, wanting to know who the hell you are. How do I know who you are? For all I know *you're* the killer. For all I know *you* stole the damn boat and sailed it up there yourself. For all I know, you slipped on a dead fish trying to get away and fell into the barrel—"

"Hogshead," John snarled.

"What?"

"The proper term is hogshead, not barrel. A hogshead is twice the capacity of a barrel." Not that the hogshead had seemed all that big when he was crammed into it.

"Sweet Mary-Mother-of-God, don't you ever stop? Hogshead, pig's eye, whatever the hell it was, you're creating a goddamn international incident. I've wasted half the morning trying to straighten this out."

* * *

It was already hot in Mary's kitchen even with the fan running, and a trickle of sweat traveled down her mother's cheek while Mary told Janet what little she knew about John's encounter with *Abracadabra*.

"How do you know it was a coincidence?" Janet asked when Mary had finished. "How do you know whoever stole *Abracadabra* wasn't following John to Yarmouth?"

"That's crazy, mother. If someone wanted to follow him they could have taken the ferry, or a plane. That would be a lot less conspicuous than *Abracadabra*."

"And John had no idea that the boat was in Yarmouth?"

Mary had invited her mother over hoping for somebody to offer sympathy and reassurance, not raise questions and doubts. "Of course not. How could he? I've already told you he went to Yarmouth to do some work for Bill Gray." At least, a tiny voice whispered in her brain, that's what John had told her. Was there more he hadn't told her?

"I'm sorry, dear. It's just such a coincidence for him to find the boat there."

Mary struggled with her temper. "It's not really that big a coincidence, mother. Yarmouth is the closest big port to our east coast. People sail there from the U.S. all the time."

"I'm sure you're right."

"Coincidences happen all the time," Mary repeated, partly to convince herself. Her mother was an excellent sounding board, and Mary knew that if Janet had trouble accepting the coincidence, then the rest of the town would as well. John's strained relationship with Wissonet was bound to get worse after this, through no fault of his own.

"When is John getting back?" Janet asked in an effort to paper over the painful questions.

"Tomorrow afternoon. George Finley has chartered a plane and they're flying into New Bedford." Much as Mary appreciated Finley's solicitousness and generosity, she couldn't stop her irrational feeling of resentment that he'd unwittingly put John in harm's way.

Janet looked troubled. "I wish he wasn't so involved with the murder investigation—"

"Mother—"

"I know it was just a coincidence," Janet hurried on, "but still, it's bound to make people wonder about John being involved with the Commodore's murder."

Mary was thankful that she hadn't told Janet about the dead rabbit, or the firecrackers. "He's doing his best not to get involved." Even as she said the words, Mary wondered if it was even possible for John to stay away from the Commodore's murder, or if it would continue to pursue him like some malevolent ghost.

A thumping noise from upstairs interrupted Mary's gloomy thoughts. Wendy's bad temper had destroyed her normally placid Sunday morning, and the afternoon wasn't looking any better.

"I suppose all this has upset Wendy too," Janet said.

"She's been a monster. It's partly the heat, but John being away makes it a lot worse."

Janet gave her daughter a motherly look, an ominous sign in Mary's experience. "You know that I love having you live here in Wissonet, and this is a marvelous place to raise kids, but I'm worried about both of you."

"Worried?"

"About the expense. At least John had a real job when you two were in Quincy."

Mary bristled. "He has a real job, now."

"Yes, but it's not the same thing as a regular pay check, what with him having to go off and leave you like this, and you having to work at Cantor Realty—"

"I like working there," Mary retorted, with more sharpness than she'd intended.

Janet heaved another sigh. "I'm glad, but I can't help worrying that you two have bitten off more than you can chew, buying a house so soon, before John has settled in and established himself."

Mary glared at her mother and Janet wisely offered a truce. "Let's take Wendy down to the beach and cool off. This heat is making everybody grouchy."

varied collection of poisons, and other assorted facts—all presented in tiny print, sure to confound anybody with less than hawk-like eyesight.

Ezra Waller wrote in a cramped, but generally legible hand. Most of the entries were short and uninformative, consisting of little more than a sentence or two outlining some event of the day like, "Rain. Visited G in p.m." A few days were reported more extensively, however, and Mary thumbed through the pages, stopping at the longer entries. One, for March 12th, 1816, ran onto the next day's space:

"Prudence Hastings died today. A great tragedy. Worse still that she cannot lie in holy ground. I blame Jeremiah Dutton for what happened, but others carry the guilt as well. Those who helped cause Ruth C's troubles have her daughter's blood on their hands."

Mary wondered about the passage. Prudence was Ruth Cummings's only daughter, who had died giving birth to Amos Merton, Henry Merton's father. Everybody knew that Prudence was Henry's grandmother—he seldom missed a chance to remind people of his closeness to the founding family—but why was Prudence denied burial on holy ground? This sounded more like a scandal or a suicide than death during childbirth. Could she have been a witch like her mother? And what would prevent Ruth from living in town, other than witchcraft? Mary skimmed more of the diaries. Ruth's death was reported on August 15th, 1819, with a terse entry:

"Ruth C died today, a gruesome end to tragic life. May God give her rest."

There was no mention of the parson's bizarre fate, as

Chapter 17

Wissonet, August 7

Sunday evening had brought slightly cooler and dryer air, along with a gentle land breeze that wafted the scent of summer and the drone of crickets through the open windows.

John wouldn't be back for two more days, and Mary was feeling restless, impatient, and out of sorts. Partly as a result of this unease, nine o'clock found her in her favorite living room chair, turning Ezra Waller's diaries over in her hands and thinking about how to wrap them for mailing. She also thought about the Waller family in general, and why they'd never quite fitted in.

Truth be told, Mary was caught on the horns of a dilemma, torn between Louise's right to privacy and her own curiosity. Mary reminded herself once again that Louise might have wanted her to find the diaries all along, in which case...

"You're as bad as Loretta," she scolded herself. John would surely thwart her temptation if he was home. Comforted by the notion that it was all her husband's fault for being away, she gave in and opened one of the volumes.

It was for the year of 1816. The first few pages contained the publisher's idea of useful information: a calendar, table of legal holidays, currency exchange rates, antidotes for a widely varied collection of poisons, and other assorted facts—all presented in tiny print, sure to confound anybody with less than hawk-like eyesight.

Ezra Waller wrote in a cramped, but generally legible hand. Most of the entries were short and uninformative, consisting of little more than a sentence or two outlining some event of the day like, "Rain. Visited G in p.m." A few days were reported more extensively, however, and Mary thumbed through the pages, stopping at the longer entries. One, for March 12th, 1816, ran onto the next day's space:

"Prudence Hastings died today. A great tragedy. Worse still that she cannot lie in holy ground. I blame Jeremiah Dutton for what happened, but others carry the guilt as well. Those who helped cause Ruth C's troubles have her daughter's blood on their hands."

Mary wondered about the passage. Prudence was Ruth Cummings's only daughter, who had died giving birth to Amos Merton, Henry Merton's father. Everybody knew that Prudence was Henry's grandmother—he seldom missed a chance to remind people of his closeness to the founding family—but why was Prudence denied burial on holy ground? This sounded more like a scandal or a suicide than death during childbirth. Could she have been a witch like her mother? And what would prevent Ruth from living in town, other than witchcraft? Mary skimmed more of the diaries. Ruth's death was reported on August 15th, 1819, with a terse entry:

"Ruth C died today, a gruesome end to tragic life. May God give her rest."

There was no mention of the parson's bizarre fate, as

described in Wissonet's legend.

Like the impatient reader of a murder mystery, Mary turned to the last diary. It was for the year 1822. April 19th reported the prodigal son's return:

> *"Jonathan Cummings is back! So Ruth C was right to maintain her vigil, tho' she didn't live to see the homecoming. Nobody knows where J has been and what his plans are now, but there are people in town who have reason to fear his return."*

Why would people fear Jonathan's return? It looked like the town legend had left out some key details. She thumbed through a few more pages and found another banner day:

> *"Jeremiah Dutton died today—a shock for us all. It is said he was struck by lightning while working on his barn roof and fell to his death. If so, I imagine Ruth C has exacted her vengeance from the Other Side. If not, I fear Jonathan may be trying to right the wrongs that have been done. Heaven help us all."*

Ezra Waller was certainly doing violence to the Cummings legend. It was almost eleven o'clock when Mary finished browsing through the diaries and set them aside. What did it all mean? She'd never thought of questioning the legend's veracity. Why bother? How could anything that happened all those years ago matter today?

But maybe it did. Everybody in Wissonet knew the legend, and knowledge of the story was a part of belonging, and a part of what made Wissonet a special place. And that was the case, not just for those who accepted the history as true, but those, like her mother, who did lip service to the story without real belief.

The Wallers obviously knew a very different Wissonet—a town that was less than ideal, if not downright homicidal. No doubt that was why the Wallers had made fun of the legend, unlike those who went along, accepting the status quo.

A knock at the door startled her. She made her way to the front hall, reached for the knob, and stopped.

"Who is it?" she said.

"Mike Hartwell. Mary, I've got news about John. I need to talk to you." There was a pause. "It's important."

She opened the door. Mike was standing with his head close to the screen door, half leaning against the jamb. The smell of honeysuckle from the bush by the corner of the house mixed with the reek of alcohol.

"Hi, Mare. Can I come in?"

Mare. His pet nickname carried Mary back to her childhood. A group of them had hung out together when they were in their early teens—"The Four Musketeers" they'd called themselves. As often happens to such friendships, the group had broken up by high school, and she hadn't had much to do with Mike until they rediscovered each other during the spring of her sophomore year.

Mike had been a year older than her, tall, athletic, with dark wavy hair, hazel eyes and a devil-may-care attitude. He had also been a pitching ace for the highschool baseball team, the Wissonet Warlocks. Mary was smitten, and they were together for nearly a year before disillusionment set in and she broke off the relationship. Mike hadn't taken it well.

She met John in the spring of her senior year—a young man who was everything that Mike was not. They married in 1940, living in Quincy for two years until Pearl Harbor swept John and millions of other Americans into the maelstrom.

Mare. In her innocence, it had taken Mary a long time to

realize the word wasn't so much a term of endearment as a tool of persuasion.

"It's late, Mike. Why don't you drop by the Realty office tomorrow morning." She started to close the door.

Mike was too quick. He flipped open the screen door and his hand clamped down on Mary's arm as he pushed her back into the hall and slammed her against the wall with a jarring crash. Dazed by the impact, she found herself pinned there, her arms trapped.

She struggled against shock and disbelief. "Let go! This is crazy. Go home before you make things worse."

"I am home, Mare, right here in Wissonet with my friends."

"You're drunk, Mike. Go home."

"Remember the old days, when the four of us hung out together? Remember that afternoon in Ruth's old house?"

"We were thirteen years old, for heaven's sake! Now go home!"

"Remember sitting in the old rocking chair? Remember what happened? Remember how you scared us half to death?" The alcoholic fog from his breath was making her dizzy.

"No, I don't remember! Now let me go, dammit!"

"Pudge is gone, now, Mare. There's only three of us left. If you're not careful, there'll only be two."

"So help me, God, if you don't let go—"

"Then you spoiled it all by taking up with your precious Johnny and moving away. Thought you were too good for your friends, didn't you? Well Johnny isn't here now, is he? He got his head caved in for poking around where he shouldn't. He'll be in even worse trouble if he keeps sticking his nose where it doesn't belong."

Pressing himself against her, Mike released an arm, reaching for her breast.

The initial shock dissipated, replaced by fury. Mary twisted, planted a shoulder in Mike's chest, and pushed with all her strength. Taken by surprise in his drunken ardor, Mike staggered back.

She needed a weapon. She broke free and raced down the hall, through the darkened diningroom to the kitchen.

"Mareee," Mike's sing-song voice was all that followed her down the hall. He was obviously smart enough not to venture into the unfamiliar darkness.

A faint ray of moonlight gave just enough light for her to move around in the kitchen's familiar space. She reached for a drawer and extracted her rolling pin, just like in the comic strips—only this wasn't funny. Not an original weapon, but sometimes the old ways are the best.

"Don't be a bad girl, Mare. You know I'll have to get little Wendy if you don't come out." She froze for an instant, a sense of dread creeping up her spine. Mike must be at the foot of the stairs.

Mary sprinted through the diningroom.

He was leaning against the wall by the diningroom door as she shot into the hall. She tried to dodge his grasp, but he managed grab her left arm, pulling her off balance—but not before she swung the rolling pin at arm's length in a great sweeping arc.

There was a numbing jolt and the smack of maple against flesh and bone as she connected with the side of Mike's shin.

He let her go, staggered back against the wall, doubling over and nursing his leg amid a torrent of curses. The blow had caught him just above the ankle.

A few quick steps and Mary was beside him. Mike was still doubled over, holding his leg with both hands. She raised the rolling pin high above the back of his unprotected head. Fury dimmed her vision. One blow and it would be over. One blow...

At the last instant the rolling pin fell from her fingers with a crash.

"Get out!" Her voice was a hoarse whisper. One hand on the back of his belt, the other on his left arm, she pushed him down the hall and head-first through the still-closed screen door.

Mary stood against the stair newel, heaving great sobbing breaths, trying to grasp what had almost happened. Wendy was screaming upstairs.

"Mary?" A voice came from the darkness.

Go away, she thought, unsure if she was speaking aloud.

"Mary, are you all right?"

"I've got to take care of Wendy." She turned vaguely towards the stairs.

"Are you all right?" The voice was getting closer.

"Wendy is crying." Mary felt totally drained of energy.

A step on the porch. "Mary, can I come in?"

"No! I've got to get Wendy." Her muscles quivered with the effort to stand.

A face appeared at the ruined screen door. "You want me to call your mother?"

"No!" She turned and fell into Sam Barton's arms.

It was almost an hour before Mary, a scalding cup of Sam's tea in her hand, felt able to talk coherently.

"God, this stuff is awful." She added another load of sugar.

"Strong tea makes strong people." Sam intoned, watching her solemnly from across the kitchen table. After a pause, he added, "You shouldn't stay here alone right now, not without someone to keep you company. I think you should call your mother."

"No. She'd just get upset and want to call the police."

"Don't you think she has a right to be upset after what just happened?"

"Nothing happened."

"Nothing? I know what Mike Hartwell is like when he's drunk. I know your screen door is demolished. I know the plaster in the front hall has a dent the shape of your head in it. I know there's a rolling pin lying in the middle of the front hall, and I know you look like death warmed over."

She looked up.

"I saw his car pulling away from the curb. It'll be a miracle if he makes it home in one piece."

Mary stared into Sam's steaming brew and wondered if the china would be permanently stained. "I almost killed him, Sam. All I could think of was crushing his skull with the rolling pin, splattering his brains on the floor. God, I came so close." She shuddered. "A helpless, staggering drunk and I almost killed him."

"A dangerous drunk, Mary."

"By the time I got through with him he was a helpless, staggering drunk. He made threats. I was so furious. It was like I was possessed, like I'd turned into someone else I had no control over." She cradled her head in her hands.

After a while Sam replied quietly, "But you didn't kill him, Mary. You did what you had to do. You protected yourself and your daughter."

Mary stared into the murky depths. After a while Sam tried again. "When is John getting home?"

"Tuesday, the day after tomorrow." She looked at the wall clock. "Actually, I guess it would be tomorrow, now."

They talked a while longer, and Sam finally persuaded Mary to spend the following night with her mother. It was one o'clock before he left, the remains of the screen door flopping limply under one arm.

Chapter 18

Wissonet, August 8

Mike Hartwell's place of business was a small building located on Second Street, three blocks back from the water. His shop was a soda and hamburger joint, strategically located near Wissonet's high school, and therefore popular with the local teenagers. It was also rumored that Mike sold illicit drugs on the side.

Early morning business was slow, with only a pair of high-school kids sharing a malt in the corner. Fortunately, it was expected to be hot again, which would bring in a crowd, later.

Mike half sat on the bank of ice cream freezers behind the counter, trying to ease the pain of his throbbing leg. He didn't think anything was broken, but the huge swelling had made it hard to get his pants on. He looked up as Sam Barton came through the door.

Mike shuffled to the counter, placed his hands on the surface, and leaned forward to ease the weight on his leg.

"Doing some painting, Sam?" Mike nodded at his visitor's paint-stained bib overalls.

Sam had no time for pleasantries. "You were over at the Wendells' house stirring up trouble last night, Mike Hartwell. I'm here to make sure that never happens again."

"Oh, come on, Sam. I don't know what Mary told you, but John is the one who's stirring up trouble around here. I know he was good friends with your Jeff years ago, but Wendell's been—"

Sam snaked a length of iron pipe out of his overalls and crashed it down on the counter top a hair's breadth from Mike's fingers. He yelped, snatched his hand from the counter, and nearly fell as his leg gave way. His fingers were numb from the near miss, and anger battled fear as he looked at a deep gouge in the splintered counter top. Jesus, he thought, a fraction of an inch closer and my hand would have been pulp.

The two wide-eyed teenagers scuttled out the door.

Sam leaned forward, moving the pipe-end in a small circle under Mike's chin. "Don't ever go near Mary Wendell again."

Mike bit back a defiant response. It was common knowledge that Sam had been involved with some well-dressed Italian gentlemen from Boston during prohibition. Townspeople had called these strangers "magicians" for their ability to make people disappear. Whatever was going on in town, Sam Barton wasn't a man to be trifled with.

"Sure," Mike replied, regaining his composure. "No problem. It was just a little misunderstanding."

Mike watched Sam leave. Why did Mary have to make such a big thing out of a harmless visit? Sure, he was a little tipsy, but why did she have to get Sam Barton, of all people, involved? Did she tell Sam about last night just to get him in trouble? Mike began to wonder how John Wendell might react if she gave him a big song-and-dance about their misunderstanding. That's the trouble with the whole damn town, he concluded bitterly; people took things too damn seriously for their own good.

Mike had to admit that it wasn't just Sam who scared him.

Mary did, too, but for a different reason. Hell, the whole thing was beginning to scare him.

On the bright side, he knew some things about the Commodore's death that would make him good money. Not even Barton and his damn pipe could stop that.

* * *

Meanwhile, at the geographical edge of Wissonet—though some thought of it as the historical heart of town—Fred Oglivy was setting out to walk his dog. One of the drawbacks of being over eighty was that Fred and Martha Oglivy didn't tolerate the hot weather well. They'd slept restlessly on damp sheets in the close, humid air, and Fred rose early to walk their dog before the morning heat grew worse. Boswell was a black, chunky animal of mostly labrador retriever ancestry, and his thickening waistline and graying muzzle suggested canine middle age. He trotted placidly at Fred's side, with an occasional detour to investigate a scent, as they walked slowly down the road to the end of Marsh Point. It was already hot enough to make the old man's wire-rimmed glasses slither aggravatingly down his sweat-slicked nose, and he was glad when the sandy track opened up to the point itself, where the faintest hint of a breeze brought some relief.

A quirk in the local current had produced an arm of sand that wrapped around the end of Marsh Point, forming a tiny cove about the size of a baseball diamond. A narrow, twisting channel led from the cove to the sea. The ancient Cummings house overlooked the cove, and it must have had a spectacular view of the bay beyond, before the trees, brush, and briers grew up. Today, the house's roof was barely visible through a wall of greenery.

The little cove was a pleasant spot in the early morning, and Fred sat on a convenient boulder with a contented sigh. Nearby, a small brook, little more than a trickle this time of year, ran into the cove from inland.

Like most of the people in town, Fred thought idly about the Commodore's death, which led his mind to wander off to the day, shortly after they moved in, when curiosity had caused him to work his way through the prickly jungle in order to look at the old house. He'd wondered at the time if the catbrier had been planted in such vast quantities on purpose. In any case, the task had cost the old man a good part of the morning, numerous scratches to his hands and face, and the near ruination of a perfectly good leather jacket, before he finally got through to the house.

He'd found a small clearing surrounding the two-room cottage. Surprisingly, the structure appeared to be in remarkably good condition. Somebody had obviously been taking care of the place over the years, though how they got through the wall of briers was a mystery to him. He was forced to conclude that there must be a path hidden away somewhere in the woods.

While Fred had been daydreaming, Boswell had been soaking in the water, as labrador retrievers are fond of doing, and he returned to shake himself dry in front of his master.

"No, Bos, you're getting me all wet," the old man said complacently.

It was a ritual, of course. Boswell was good at creating little rituals—like going into the water, getting wet, and coming back to shake at the feet of his master or mistress. The humans played their part as well by scolding him good naturedly with the same words each time. There was something reassuring for both human and dog in these little traditions, an affirmation that all was well with the relationship.

Fred settled into a comfortable reverie and thought about rituals, relationships, and Boswell—the eighteenth century biographer, and the dog's namesake—for Fred had been a high-school English teacher in his younger days.

Deciding that his master wasn't going to need him for a while, Boswell rolled in the sand, making little doggie groans of pleasure, and shambled off to find some entertainment.

Had Fred's hearing been more acute he might have been quicker to notice the odd combination of growl and whine emanating from his canine companion as Boswell dug in the sand.

Thanks to Boswell's keen nose and industrious paws, Fred Oglivy, town historian and retired English teacher, would soon meet Lieutenant Joseph Riley, overworked and irritable state police detective.

Chapter 19

Wissonet, August 8

Mary slept badly and got up late, or as late as Wendy would allow. Her head and shoulders ached where they had hit the wall, her stomach rumbled sullenly from Sam's tea, and it was Monday. She was tempted to call in sick, but a young couple was due in to look at the Waller house at noon.

Mary dropped Wendy off with her mother on the way to work. She kept her visit brief, explaining that she was late for work. This was true enough, though the real reason was to avoid having to tell Janet about Mike's "visit" last night. Perhaps later when she was feeling better...

Mike was just drunk, after all, so it wasn't really an attack. She'd start locking her doors at night when she was alone, though.

It was almost eleven by the time Mary finally arrived at work.

Cantor Realty occupied a one-story converted bungalow on Route 6. The front room held two desks, one of which belonged to Mary, while the other, presently covered with maps, sheets of listings, and miscellaneous papers, anticipated the happy day when the firm could afford a second employee. Phil Cantor's office took up what had once been a tiny bedroom in back.

The first thing Mary saw on entering was Lieutenant Riley looming in the guest chair beside her desk.

"I was sorry to hear about your husband's accident, Mrs. Wendell," he said, "I gather he'll be home tomorrow."

Hypocrite, Mary fumed. "If you're not here to talk about real estate, then get out," she growled. Phil's startled face looked up from his desk.

"Actually, this is sort of about real estate," Riley replied.

"Sort of?" Mary stood beside her desk, thinking about rolling pins and wondering at her new found inclination to mayhem. Everything, even her own emotions, seemed to be spinning out of control. Mary scolded herself. It was all worry over John. And last night, of course. She had the uncomfortable feeling that the two things were related, and to make matters worse, Riley's presence reminded her that she had nearly killed a man in what was, for her, an uncharacteristic fit of rage. Was it the physical attack, or something Mike had said that triggered her fury? Once again, Dianne's 'so much evil' comment flitted through her mind.

Riley broke into her train of thought. "I need someone who can tell me about Marsh Point, so naturally I came to the local Realtor. Mr. Cantor said that you grew up in town and could fill me in on some of its history."

"I see." Mary shot a venomous look at Phil that sent him diving back into his paperwork.

"The problem is, that some human remains were found near the old Cummings house out on Marsh Point this morning."

"Human remains?" Mary felt unsteady on her feet.

"A skeleton. It may be quite old, but we can't be sure until the lab results come in. We're still digging in case there are other bones."

"Where did you find them, exactly?"

"At the edge of the beach, up against the brush and briers."

Mary felt another surge of anger. It wasn't enough for Riley to be stirring up everyone in town. Now he was literally digging up the town's very origins as well. "You're going to have quite a job digging up all that brush. Why bother if the bones are that old?" she demanded.

"We won't bother if the bones are as old as they seem, Mrs. Wendell."

"You probably just dug up an old family burial plot."

"We thought of that, but there weren't any caskets or headstones, just the bones. Anyway, I was hoping you might have some answers. Do you know of an old cemetery being out there?"

"No," she admitted reluctantly.

"Well, there you are," Riley smiled, oozing contentment from every pore. "It's my job to investigate these things, especially if the remains turn out to be more recent. There was a good deal of illegal activity around these parts during prohibition, for example."

Mary resented the not-so-veiled reference to Sam. "Why in the world were you digging out there anyway?"

"Actually, a neighbor, Fred Oglivy, found the bones, or his dog did. He was out walking it early this morning."

"And why would Fred's dog suddenly dig up an old skeleton?"

"Finding the skeleton was more or less accidental. The dog dug up a dead rabbit that happened to be near the skeleton. The rabbit appears to have been slaughtered and buried quite recently."

Mary collapsed into her chair.

"Are you all right, Mrs. Wendell?"

Mary concentrated on breathing for a moment. Another rabbit? This had to be more than a kid's prank. "Yes, I'm fine, just a little shaky today. I caught a bug of some kind last night and didn't sleep too well."

"You do look pale. Maybe I shouldn't bother you right now."

Phil came over. "Why don't you go home and get some rest. I can show the Waller house for you."

But Mary wasn't interested in going home after hearing Riley's news. "I'm okay," she assured Phil, "but if you'll show the Waller place, I'll help Lieutenant Riley and then go home and rest for a while."

"That's the spirit," Phil said, sounding relieved.

Mary handed him the Waller file and turned to Riley.

"What do you want to know, Lieutenant?"

"Mr. Cantor tells me the land where the body was found belonged to Commodore Cummings. Of course the bones may have nothing to do with his murder. I gather the family has owned it for a long time?"

"Since the founding of the town. Elijah Cummings bought it in the late 1700's. It's a good-sized parcel by today's standards, close to sixteen acres." Mary stood up and ran her finger around the area on a large scale map of Wissonet that was thumb-tacked to the wall behind her.

"I understand the old Cummings house out there has been abandoned and boarded up for years. When was it last occupied?"

Mary frowned. What did this have to do with anything? "As far as I know, it's been empty since around 1820, when Ruth Cummings died."

"I'm surprised the place didn't fall down years ago; it seems to be in remarkably good shape. Does somebody go out there and maintain it?"

Of course Riley would have poked around Ruth's old cottage, Mary fumed. "I suppose somebody must, though I don't know why." There was a possible reason to maintain the old house, but she chose not to think about it, and certainly not mention it to Riley.

"I was out there a couple of weeks ago," Phil said from the other room. "It was a helluva a job to get to the shack, but I did catch a glimpse of somebody in the underbrush, couldn't tell who. It gave me quite a fright. Anyway, someone must be keeping an eye on the place."

"What were you doing out there?" Mary asked, thinking about Mildred in the underbrush.

"Cummings was in here a couple of weeks ago, looking for some land to develop, and here he had a prime piece right in his pocket. It got me curious, so naturally I went out to look it over."

"He was looking for land to develop?" Riley said.

"Diversification," Phil replied. "He figured if he could sell engagement and wedding rings to the returning soldiers, why not sell them a house after they got married? One-stop shopping, like these new shopping centers. It's a smart idea.

"I've been trying to get Cummings to sell the Marsh Point property for years," Phil went on, "but he wouldn't budge. I kept telling him that he could clear out all the brush and brambles, pull the shack down, build a really nice modern house with lots of glass, and have a million-dollar view across the bay."

Phil joined the others in the front room, excitement glowing in his eyes. "Why, you could take that little pond where you found the bones and turn it into a salt-water swimming pool—"

"He never would have done it, Phil," Mary said.

"Maybe not, but he could have made a fortune by developing the property, without spending a dime of his own money." Phil shrugged. "Anyway, I figured it was worth looking at the land again. Sentiment is all very well and good, but—"

"Do you think Mrs. Cummings might be willing to sell?" Riley said.

Selling Marsh Point could make Dianne a very wealthy woman, Mary thought, which was undoubtably what Riley was thinking. "What does any of this have to do with the bones you found?" Mary said.

Riley waved a placating hand. "Maybe nothing. You never know what might be connected to what. I understand there's some legend: strange noises and people disappearing, part of the town folklore, apparently. Once in a while these old tales have some basis in fact, so we like to check them out. Do you know anything about that?"

How much had John already told Riley? Mary paused as she searched for an objective reply, uncomfortably aware that being objective about Wissonet's past was becoming harder and harder for her. "Ruth Cummings was supposed to be a witch, but who knows? That was more than a hundred and fifty years ago." She paused and tried to force herself to sound detached before going on. "I suppose a few people may take the story seriously."

"Does the legend mention any investigation of people disappearing?" Riley asked.

"Wouldn't there be police records if that happened?"

"We're checking, but records that old tend to be pretty sketchy."

"Have you talked to Fred Oglivy about Ruth Cummings?" Phil said. "He's the town historian, and he lives right next door, as you know. You could ask Henry Merton, too. He was the town historian for seventy or eighty years before Fred came along."

Riley made an entry in his notebook. "We'll talk to Mr. Merton as soon as we finish looking for other remains out there." He closed his notebook and leaned back in his chair. "Do you think Mrs. Cummings might be interested in developing the property?"

"She's never said, one way or the other," Phil replied. "Anyway, I plan to talk to her about it in a few weeks."

Mary tried to imagine a dozen houses being built on Marsh Point. Phil could be right; Dianne wouldn't have the same attachment to Marsh Point as her dead husband, and the money would be tempting.

She could picture the carnage: most of the scrub oaks would be cut; the land would be stripped and bulldozed; the raspberry bushes and catbrier ripped up; all of it replaced with neat suburban lawns and shrubs. What would Mildred do without the thorny undergrowth to scuttle through? What would Mary do without the raspberries to pick? What would the poor Oglivys do with all those houses on their doorstep? And what would they name the development, anyway? Witch Acres? Skeleton Beach, Sorcery Shores, Cauldron Cove? The possibilities were endless.

Mary shuddered. Suddenly the real estate business took on a darker tone.

Chapter 20

Wissonet, August 9

Yet another day, and the hot weather continued. The heat wave seemed endless, its oppressive, crushing weight inescapable. Fortunately, Tuesday was a day off from Cantor Realty, so Mary had plenty of time to get ready for John's return that afternoon, under Finley's protective wing.

Or so she thought.

She was busy cleaning up the kitchen when Mildred appeared. From her long-billed cap down to her knee-high rubber boots, Mildred looked as though she'd just stepped off her fishing boat. The faint aroma of dead fish accompanied her into the room. Mary sighed. This was all she needed to liven up her morning.

"You look like a train wreck," Mildred informed her host. "Why don't you sit for a while and let me clean things up?"

"Thanks Mildred, but I was just washing the breakfast dishes. There's some coffee left over from breakfast. I'll ice it up if you like."

"Don't be silly. You sit and let me deal with the coffee."

"No you don't," Loretta said, as she hustled through the kitchen door. "I'm the expert on coffee around here. Besides, this is an emergency; I need some now."

Mary had hoped for a more peaceful morning. A visit from Mildred-the-scold was bad enough, but adding Loretta to the mix was almost too much, though it was probably inevitable, since her next door neighbor seemed to have been watching the Wendell's house non-stop all week.

Loretta looked at Mildred, sniffing discreetly. "When are you going to spend some time ashore? You have less than a week of company vacation left, and it doesn't look as though you've gotten much rest so far."

"I've had a very good rest, thank you," Mildred replied stiffly.

"What are you going to do with the rest of your vacation? Why aren't you away like everybody else?" Loretta was not easily put off.

"One doesn't need to go away in order to have a vacation," Mildred informed her, "though I plan to go off for a few days, later."

Loretta nodded skeptically. "So, tell us where you're planning to go, and what you're planning to do."

Mary smiled encouragement at Loretta, thinking that her neighbor might prove to be an asset after all if she deflected the conversation away from John.

Unfortunately, Mildred was not interested in sharing her plans, and Wissonet's leading scandal-monger was only able to elicit the fact that Mildred planned to spend the rest of her vacation visiting with friends in Boston. After that all-too-brief report, Mildred took firm hold of the conversation and turned the spotlight on John. "I want to know how John is doing. I just heard about his accident this morning."

Loretta was omnivorous when it came to gossip, and she joined in happily. "Some accident. Attempted murder is closer. How is John? I understand he's getting back this afternoon.

How is his amnesia? Is he going to get his memory back?"

The speed of Wissonet's grapevine constantly amazed Mary. Was no scrap of privacy sacred? "He doesn't really have amnesia. He just can't remember what happened when he was knocked out," Mary said, "or for a few minutes before," she added.

"But will he remember any of it later?" Loretta asked.

"People often get their memory back in cases like that, with time," Mildred said.

"I doubt if there's much to remember," Mary said irritably.

"I suppose not," Loretta said. "Whoever attacked him probably struck from behind."

"On the other hand, you never know," Mildred said. "He might have caught a glimpse of something or somebody. What in the world was he doing up there anyway?"

"He was doing some work on a boat for Bill Gray."

"It's quite a coincidence that *Abracadabra* should just happen to be there." Loretta's voice was heavy with disbelief. "He didn't happen to see any familiar faces, or anything that might explain how the boat got there?"

Mary ground her teeth. This was getting too much like the third-degree. "Stranger coincidences have happened. Lots of boats visit Yarmouth. It's a common stopover for boats from the states."

"And some events are part of the Spirit World's larger plan," Mildred announced portentously. "Perhaps it was in the cards for John to find *Abracadabra*. One can't defy fate."

Loretta stifled a coughing fit, which earned her a glare from Mildred.

"In any case," Mildred said, "It's very unfortunate for John that things happened as they did. He would be well advised to walk softly for a while until things calm down."

"I wonder what Dianne makes of having her boat turn up in Yarmouth," Loretta said.

"I'd just as soon stay away from Dianne," Mary replied.

"I don't blame you for not wanting to see her," Mildred said. "I'm afraid she may think John is responsible for *Abracadabra* being there."

* * *

George Finley had been as good as his word, not only accompanying John on the plane ride from Nova Scotia, but driving him back to Wissonet as well. He was carefully instructing Mary on the care and feeding of her husband when Loretta, ever hovering at her window, arrived to make an encore appearance. She was no match for George Finley, however. To Mary's delight, Finley took charge, and Loretta was soon thoroughly ruffled and on her way home. It took a sizable lunch, profuse thanks and a bit of nudging to ease John's self-appointed guardian out the door.

* * *

Later that afternoon, John sat brooding on the veranda in one of the high-backed wicker rocking chairs as he sweltered in the heat.

"I hope you're not too upset over Mike," Mary said, having decided that it would be better to tell him about Mike's visit before somebody else—like her next door neighbor—got the chance. It had been hard enough to keep Loretta bottled up on the subject, even with Finley shooing her out the door.

"It really wasn't that bad when you think about it. He was drunk, came in and pushed me, I hit him with the rolling pin, and threw him out. That's all there was to it," Mary concluded.

"I know, but why did he come over in the first place?"

"I guess I never thought much about it beyond that he was drunk. Thinking about it now, it seemed almost as though he was trying to give me some kind of warning, but he was too drunk for it to come out right. He said something about you poking your nose into things you shouldn't."

"So now it's my fault he attacked you?"

"Of course not," Mary replied, irritated, "but if you hadn't been helping the police, you wouldn't have made yourself so unpopular in town, and Mike probably wouldn't have dared to come over here. I warned you that it would cause trouble when you first got involved with Riley."

Scowling, John turned away and glared across the field. "I'm fed up with being blamed for wanting to help find the Commodore's killer. Doesn't anybody care? I'm even more fed up with having everyone assume I knew *Abracadabra* was up there. Even Riley accused me of playing Sam Spade. Is it my fault for stumbling over the damn boat?"

"It's just the coincidence that bothers them."

John sat for a while, thinking. "Why didn't you call the police?"

"The police? This isn't Quincy," Mary retorted. "The police here is Danny Wilson, and he's only part-time. Besides, he and Mike went to school together."

"I was thinking about the state police, for crying out loud. Why not call Riley?"

"Riley? Surely, with the Commodore's murder, he has more important things to worry about than some drunk forcing his way into the house."

"Maybe there's a connection between the two. Besides, there are lots of other state policemen."

Mary sighed. "I don't know why I didn't. I suppose I felt guilty about nearly killing Mike with the rolling pin. He was so drunk."

"Maybe you should have hit him again," John said viciously. "What if he'd sobered up and come back? If he attacked you once, what's to prevent him from doing it again?"

"Don't you think I was tempted to hit him again?!" Mary realized that she was shouting and caught herself. She turned to her husband. "I came so close, it scared me. Something came over me, like suddenly I was a different person." She paused, her voice just above a whisper. "I never believed until last night that I could kill somebody."

"Somebody killed the Commodore."

"Don't you understand?" Mary said with a hint of desperation. "I'm sorry the Commodore is dead, but I don't *want* to know who killed him—not if it means tearing the town apart like this." Mary paused. "Not if it means tearing us apart like this."

Jim Delling had cut the hay below the lawn's edge and carried it off while John was away, and the bare field looked larger now, and the tree-line farther away. The effect was disconcerting after the closeness of the standing hay. They sat and stared out over the patch of stubble in silence.

"I keep feeling as though there's a disease going around town, a disease like polio, that nobody can stop," Mary said. "A disease of mistrust and suspicion. It's like the murder is hunting *us* somehow, and turning us into..." She struggled to control her emotions, and turned to John. "I grew up here and yet all of a sudden it doesn't seem as though I know anybody. I don't know if I can trust anybody." Mary gave her head a quick shake. "I've known Mike all my life. Sure, he drank too much, but I dated him even so. I thought he was a friend. I trusted him, up to a point.

"And Sam. When Riley told me about finding a skeleton out on Marsh Point, all I could think of was that Sam might have killed someone during prohibition. He's like a second father to me, and yet I was ready to think of him as a cold-blooded murderer. And it's not just me. The whole town keeps going around saying that an outsider must have killed the Commodore, but all the time they're saying it they keep looking at each other and wondering. That's why I don't want to know who the killer is."

She stopped, biting her lip. "And the rabbit. Boswell found the bones because someone had buried a slaughtered rabbit out on Marsh Point. How can that not have something to do with our rabbit? Is there some kind of ritual going on out there, some kind of black magic?"

John sat, as though lost in another world. Finally, he said, "I wonder why Sam happened to be in front of our house during Mike's visit."

* * *

Mary was able to fend off her mother until late afternoon. She had hoped to get John upstairs for a nap, but as the prime exhibit, he could hardly escape.

Before inspecting her son-in-law, however, Janet spotted two discrepancies that required explanation.

"What happened to your screen door?" she asked as Mary escorted her into the living room.

"Oh, Sam dropped by the other day and noticed it was broken, so he's making a new one," Mary replied, with the airy confidence of one speaking a well-rehearsed lie.

"That was very nice of him. Funny, it looked all right the

other day."

"Oh, it was just a crack in the frame somewhere. You know what a perfectionist Sam is."

"I'm surprised he didn't offer to fix your wall."

"Wall?" Mary's mind whirred frantically. She'd forgotten about her head and the wall. It was just a small dent. Weren't old people supposed to have trouble seeing things?

"What on earth happened to it?"

"The wall..." Mary wasn't a glib liar by nature, and she stalled for time to think up some kind of story. "Oh the dent in the hall. That was John. He hit it by mistake."

John looked at his wife in horror. "I did? Oh, yes. Just a little accident," he temporized.

"With a bowling ball," Mary added brightly, realizing too late that her fabricated story was swerving into quicksand.

"Yes," John said, joining her in the mire, "I'm thinking about learning how to bowl and I was practicing—"

"His back swing," Mary added.

"And I misjudged," John concluded.

"Just say so if you don't want to talk about it," Janet said tartly. She took a swallow of lemonade. "Did you know we were on the front page of the Boston Herald?"

"We?"

"Not you, silly. Wissonet. I'll read part of it if you like." Mary wouldn't like, but her mother didn't wait for permission. She reached into her purse and pulled out a carefully folded piece of newsprint. "Listen to this:

> *The ancient legend of the Wissonet Witch took on new life today with the discovery of four skeletons in that quiet Buzzards Bay town. Local resident Frederick W. Oglivy made the grisly find when his dog unearthed the remains on Wissonet's isolated Marsh Point yesterday*

morning.

The skeletons appear to date to the early 1800's, a time when Marsh Point, also known locally as Witch Point, was home to Ruth Cummings, the famous Wissonet Witch. Strange noises, mysterious lights, and blood curdling screams have been reported at night almost up to the present. Wissonet's one-man police force scoffs at the idea of ghosts, attributing the odd goings-on to the pranks of local kids. The old bones, however, lend a grim credence to the Witch Point legend.

In a sinister twist, the last direct descendant of the Wissonet Witch, Commodore Cummings, was found murdered in his boat last week when the vessel washed up on Wood Island in Buzzards Bay.'"

There was a moment of silence while they digested the luridly written story.

"Wissonet Witch? It didn't take long for them to pick that one up," John said.

"Newspaper hype, though it has a nice ring to it," Mary said. "Probably irresistible for them."

"Fiddlesticks," Janet retorted. "That's just superstitious nonsense."

"If Ruth wasn't a witch, then what was she?" John growled.

Janet frowned at her son-in-law. "I expect she was nothing more than a lonely, eccentric old woman, abandoned by her children."

John scowled. "With a backyard full of human bones? What about the stories of screams and odd noises out there? How could the town have ignored what was going on?"

For some reason, newsreel images of Nazi death camp survivors flashed through Mary's mind, and she noted the flush of anger on her mother's face, matched by her husband's mulish expression.

"It could just be an old burial ground," Mary suggested.

The two adversaries, sensing the cliff edge, stepped back to safer ground. Yes, they agreed; it was probably just an old Indian burial site.

Chapter 21

Wissonet, August 10

The Zero had dropped its two bombs on the *Dunn*'s aft five-inch gun mount, turning it into a pyre of smoke and flame. The plane, trailing smoke, swung around the doomed destroyer and came in low on the starboard side, flying at bridge level. With no chance of making it back to base, the pilot had obviously chosen to go out in a blaze of glory.

The Bofors on the gun mount below the bridge opened up on the flaming plane, followed a few seconds later by the shorter range guns. The Zero was being chewed to pieces by the ship's guns, yet it still hurtled on, the scream of its engine cutting through the gunfire.

"Down!" the captain yelled as the plane opened fire, filling the space with glass and shrapnel. John and the helmsman dropped to the deck, while the hapless boatswain's mate was cut to pieces.

The Zero was a burning wreck, a flaming missile aimed at the Dunn's bridge as it plunged ahead, closer and closer, its propeller glinting in the sunlight, slicing through the destroyer's defenses, rushing towards him, bigger and bigger until it filled his vision and overwhelmed every corner of his mind—

"John, wake up," Mary shook the thrashing body next to

her. One of his flailing arms caught the side of her head, leaving her momentarily stunned.

With a cry, he woke and sat up, soaked with sweat and gasping for breath.

Mary turned on the light and looked at her husband. He'd had the nightmares before, of course, but they'd been steadily getting fewer and milder the last few years—certainly nothing like tonight.

"It's that goddam fan!" he yelled as he got up, snatched the fan from the window sill and hurled it across the room.

Mary looked at him fearfully. Even at their worst right after the war, the nightmares had never been this bad; there had never been such rage; he'd never lashed out so violently before. She touched the bruise on her ear. Her fingers came away wet with blood.

She turned her head so he wouldn't see the blood trickling down the side of her face. "You need to go back and see the doctor again, John. What happened in Yarmouth has been a setback, but I'm sure—"

"I'm fine! It was just the damn fan!" John looked at her, still breathing hard, his face flushed.

"You're not fine! Look what you did to my ear! My God, I'm not even safe in my own bed with my own husband!"

John collapsed on the bed beside her and stared at the floor. "I'm sorry. It was just the fan that triggered..." His voice trailed off like a Victrola running down.

"It's not just the fan, and you know it," she replied softly. "This is worse than before. I never thought it was dangerous to be with you before."

"It won't happen again."

"Promise you'll go back and see Doctor Edwards."

"It was just—"

"It wasn't just the damn fan!" Mary sat and breathed as she tried to manage her temper. It occurred to her that Wendy now had the only working fan left in the house.

"Wendy and I will have to move out if you don't promise to get help. I don't dare stay here otherwise." She buried her face in her hands.

"Fine," John said in a resigned voice. "I'll see Doc Edwards tomorrow and get some more of his damn pills." John got up and started to dress. "I can't sleep any more now, anyway. I'm going to try and do some work on Hibbert's boat before I get hopelessly behind."

"I'll get up too."

"No! You need your sleep if you're going to work tomorrow," he snapped, and then added more gently, "I'll be fine. I'm just going to work for a little while and get my mind off things."

Mary heard John going into his office while she was in the bathroom, putting a gauze pad on her ear. The bleeding had almost stopped, but the back of her ear was going to be bruised and swollen by morning. She returned to the bedroom, and heard the creak of the stool as John sat down at his drafting table.

A few minutes later, after she was back in bed, she heard him on the stairs, then moving around the living room. After a while the front door creaked shut and all was quiet, except for the patient ticking of the bedside Westclox.

Sleep didn't come to Mary for a long time.

* * *

It was approaching midnight, the witching hour, John thought wryly, and there were no cars driving around Wissonet's picturesque streets, no people walking the uneven brick-paved sidewalks, and not even any broomsticks flying through the air. In Quincy, where he grew up, cars and people wandered around all night, and one was never alone with one's memories, wanted or unwanted.

John knew there wasn't anybody around because he was hyper-vigilant tonight, aware of the slightest suspicious sound, after Yarmouth.

But people had been wandering around Wissonet last Sunday night, though: Mike and Sam, for two.

On the surface, Mike's wanderings made some sense; he got drunk, started thinking fondly about his high-school days, hanging out with Mary, Dianne, and the Commodore. The past is often, though not always, filled with fond memories that call out to be revisited. It would be reasonable for Mike, in his inebriated state, to "visit" Mary for old time's sake.

But why had Sam been outside their house that night? Could he, like John, have been struggling with unwanted memories—killer's remorse, for example—and been trying to walk them off? Had he been following Mike? If so, why? Sam was hiding something about Mike, but what?

Memories are strange things. Some are solid and unforgettable, burned indelibly into the mind; some are fragile and uncertain; some are so dazzling that all others fade in comparison; some are inextricably tied to other people or events. Without warning or fanfare, the last few words John had heard on the night he was attacked slipped out of the darkness into his consciousness.

He had been standing on the dock beside *Abracadabra*, thinking that he should call Lieutenant Riley, when the stranger had confronted him, saying, "What are you doing with that boat?"

"The boat looked familiar, and I was just checking the name," John had replied.

"This is a private dock and people aren't allowed on it without permission. Things get stolen," the stranger had said belligerently.

That was the last thing John remembered, until now.

* * *

"I didn't know I was trespassing, John had replied, "I was just out for an evening walk."

"The damn boat shouldn't have been left here all evening. This is going to be trouble, for sure," the stranger said.

"I'm sorry if I made any trouble," John replied, confused.

"We've got to get rid of him quick. The police will look for him. You'll have to take the boat back until things settle down."

If the evening light had been better, and he hadn't been so tired after his long day, John might have caught the man's shifting eyes and changed expression, and realized in time that somebody was behind him. As it was, he turned too late.

The world gave a jolt, the ground opened up, and John spun into darkness.

* * *

The newly recovered memories made it clear to John that his unexpected arrival had forced a change in plans, and somebody would have to "take the boat back."

Back to where?

John turned around, knowing that Sam Barton held the key, and determined to get it from him.

Chapter 22

Wissonet, August 11

John was waiting when Sam's piebald pickup rattled into the boatyard lot just after dawn.

"You look like hell," Sam commented, as he got out and slammed the truck door.

John wasn't in the mood to bandy words. "Where did the Commodore keep his boat last winter?"

"You came here at this hour to ask me that? Like I told the Irish flatfoot, I have no idea."

"You can lie to the Irish flatfoot all you want, but I want a straight answer. Where did he keep the damn boat?"

"Let go of my arm, you lunatic. What the hell do you want to know for? Hasn't that boat given you enough trouble already? For your sake and Mary's leave it alone."

"I can't leave it alone! The goddamn boat is like a curse, following me around."

Sam heaved a great sigh. "Honest to god, I really don't remember the name of the place. Why should I?" He wiped his brow. Not yet six o'clock and the air was already stifling. "It was something-or-other Cove that began with a 'B.' That's all I can tell you."

"Think," John urged. "You've got to do better that just a

'B.'"

"The hell I do," Sam muttered, apparently deep in thought. "I'm pretty sure it began with a 'B,' though. Yes, it was a 'B,' as in 'barrel.'" Sam brightened. "No, that's not right. Wait, I remember now; it wasn't Cove at all; it was Harbor. 'Hogshead Harbor.'"

"You're a goddamn pain, Barton," John snarled.

"And you're a pig-headed idiot, Wendell. Somebody has tried to kill you once already, and now you're going to make it easy for them to try again. Have you got a death wish of some kind?"

Sam glared at John for a moment. "Fine, if you want to get yourself killed then why should I stand in your way?" He shook his head in disgust. "It really was something like Barrel Cove, though, or maybe Barren Cove, or Bucket Cove, or Barrett Cove." Sam shrugged. "It was something like that. Like I said, Cummings just tossed out the name in passing and I wasn't paying any attention."

Like an omen of doom, Lieutenant Riley's Packard chose that moment to roll into the lot.

* * *

Mary had gotten up early, partly because Wendy had begun crying at dawn, but mostly because John hadn't come back last night. Of course, he might have crept in and left again, which might explain Wendy's restlessness.

She fed Wendy distractedly while she worried about John and his whereabouts. She'd just finished tidying up after her daughter's meal when the phone rang.

"Hello, dear," came the voice on the line.

"Oh, hi mother."

"How is John doing today?"

"Oh, he's fine, just a little restless last night from all the bruises," she lied. At least the restless part was true. "I'm just about to leave and bring Wendy over for the morning on my way to work. Is that still all right for you?"

"Yes, of course." Janet paused before going on. "Actually, I wanted to tell you about Mike Hartwell before you left the house."

"What about him?"

"He was killed last night, dear," Janet said gently.

Mary sat down as what was left of her world collapsed in on itself. "God," was all she could manage.

"I'm sorry. I know you were close years ago and I hated to tell you what with all you're going through, but I thought you should hear it from me rather than..." Janet's voice trailed off into silence.

"What happened?"

"Nobody is saying much right now, but you know that Mike keeps the PX open until ten o'clock at night during the summer, and apparently he often stays there until the wee-small hours after the place closes. God knows what he's doing—working on his drug smuggling schemes, I suppose. Anyway, that's when it happened—sometime in the middle of the night after the place was closed. The ice cream truck driver found him around dawn this morning. They say he was hit on the head." Janet didn't elaborate on the graphic details provided by the local rumor mill. "He'd been drinking a lot lately and mixing with some unsavory types from New Bedford. I expect he got on the wrong side of one of them. The police have been asking around all morning, but nobody is saying much."

"Nobody ever says much," Mary said bitterly.

She sat at the kitchen table for a long time after hanging up the phone. She'd be late for work, but couldn't summon the energy to move. Wendy came over and clambered into her lap, clinging like a gigantic hot-water bottle in the growing heat.

John finally returned, and Wendy hopped off Mary's lap to run and greet him.

"Where have you been all night?" Mary demanded, standing with her hands on her hips. "I've been worried sick—"

The expression on his face stopped her outburst in it's tracks.

"Sam and I have been talking with Riley."

"So you heard about Mike."

John nodded. "Sam and I are Riley's two prime suspects."

"What are you talking about?"

"Two kids saw Sam confront Mike in his soda shop yesterday. Apparently he threatened Mike with a piece of iron pipe for coming here and attacking you. As for me, I'm the outraged husband. That puts both Sam and me on the spot in Riley's book."

"What did Riley ask you?"

"Well, he asked where I was between midnight and four in the morning, when Mike was 'bludgeoned,' as he so delicately put it. It sounds as though they haven't found the murder weapon yet."

"So, where were you?"

John looked vague. "I'm not sure exactly where I was all the time. Mostly, I just walked around. I remember going by Sam's boatyard, and I remember sitting on the beach, and maybe dozing off at some point. But mostly I just wandered around, thinking."

"Thinking? Thinking about what?"

"About the goddam boat, about Yarmouth, about Mike, about us, about everything. What do you think I was thinking?"

Mary rubbed her sweating forehead in frustration.

"He asked if I'd killed Mike," he went on. "I told him that I didn't think so."

"You told him you didn't *think* so? Couldn't you have been more positive than that? You need to do some work on your "thinking," for crying out loud! Surely you'd remember if you'd killed Mike!"

"I'd have blood on my clothes if I'd bludgeoned him, wouldn't I?"

"Blood on your clothes? You'll drive me crazy yet!"

Just then a flash of movement caught Mary's attention. It was Edith's Buick gliding in the driveway. Mary watched it creep perilously close to the side of the house as it tried to ooze by the Wendell's Ford. In the end, Edith abandoned the effort only after her right front tire had flattened a corner of Mary's daylily bed.

"I'm going upstairs to get some work done," John said as he headed for the stairs.

"We aren't done talking about this," Mary said, grabbing his shirt. "And you're not leaving me alone with Edith, either."

Mary cursed under her breath as she watched from the kitchen window. Slithering out of her horticultural Genghis Kahn, Edith turned and reached inside for something on the floor in front of the passenger's seat. Unfortunately, she'd parked too close to the Ford and couldn't open the driver's side door wide enough to stretch across. She straightened, flounced around to the far side, and opened the passenger door, inflicting further carnage among the daylilies.

Mary ground her teeth while Edith rummaged around the front seat. This was all she needed on top of everything else. Couldn't the clumsy fool see she was standing in the middle of the flower bed? Why were Dianne and her crazy friends so thoroughly underfoot all of a sudden? They'd never come around this often before, why now?

Edith emerged at last, carrying a large earthenware bowl that she carried, shimmying and swaying in a tight black skirt, towards the door. A low-cut white blouse of sheer material completed the ensemble. At least it looked cooler than Edith's usual flowing togas and serapes.

Mary had never seen Edith dressed like a streetwalker before, and she had to admire the woman's figure. A golden witch was nestled in her ample cleavage—another nude, Mary saw, this one straddling a crescent moon. Freshly permed hair framed Edith's face in a golden-brown halo. Mary half expected an unseen band to strike up a bump-and-grind burlesque tune.

"Well, what a surprise," Mary said, greeting her visitor at the kitchen door. There were times when it was hard to be a gracious host, and this was one of them.

"I heard about that terrible business up in Canada. You poor thing," Edith said, trapping John before he could make his escape. "You look so peaked, I do hope you're feeling better."

Mary frowned. Edith's way of talking, as well as her clothing, were very uncharacteristic. Had she slipped a cog? Was she drunk? Had she taken some of Mike's illicit drugs?

Edith turned to Mary. "I'm sorry for not coming over sooner, but things have been so busy and I didn't want to bother you two. Anyway, I brought a casserole for your supper so you can have a quiet evening instead of having to cook in this heat."

"Thank you, that's very sweet." Mary took the bowl.

"It's one of my favorite shrimp recipes," Edith said, smiling coquettishly at John. "Eat hearty John. I swear you've lost weight."

* * *

Mary stood in the kitchen after Edith had left and John had escaped upstairs. She looked at the bowl, wondering about her visitor. Edith's rare appearances had never before included bowls of food, and certainly not such scanty clothing. Edith's flirtatiousness would have amused John greatly under normal circumstances, but these were not normal times, and Edith, like others in town, didn't seem to be acting in predictable ways.

Unsure about the glass lid, Mary put it on the counter beside her. The air filled with a seductively mouth-watering aroma. The bowl itself was an inexpensive brown pottery kitchen utensil of the type available in any hardware store, and Mary held it high in front of her before dropping it to the floor.

She didn't want to lie to Edith, after all.

"Damn!" she said theatrically, admiring the shattered crockery and ruined food.

John, summoned from his office by the crash, came through the door and stood beside her, looking impassively at the mess on the floor.

"You dropped it," he said unnecessarily. "Probably wise. Her husband died of shellfish poisoning, after all, and we might know too much."

Mary turned to study his face. Talking about abstract "suspects"—she inserted the quotation marks in her mind—was one thing, but Edith was a real-live person whose uncharacteristic perfume still hung in the air, and whose casserole decorated the floor.

"I can't stand this," she said. "I don't know anybody anymore. I don't know who to trust." She buried her head on John's chest, ignoring the pain of her injured ear as it pressed against his neck, and held him close—even as a tiny corner of her mind wondered if her husband, the man she loved, was a killer.

Nat strolled unnoticed around their legs and began licking hungrily at the spilled food.

Later, Mary noticed Nat's sticky paw prints and an area of freshly licked floor. She searched the house without success. Nat must have gone outside. Finding him out there would be impossible. Mary mopped up the mess, then sat at the kitchen table staring into space, wondering who had created this nightmare, and dreading how it would end.

Chapter 23

Wissonet, August 11

With Mary at work and Wendy at her grandmother's house for the morning, John walked down to the Wissonet Public Library. The small, turn-of-the-century brick structure was adorned with a miniature columned entrance and capped by a tiny cupola. A huge Civil War cannon sat on a concrete base in front of the building, along with a stone monument bearing the names of those who had died in that conflict. The town had belatedly filled the cannon's barrel with concrete after an unfortunate incident where a rock was fired through the house across the street.

A group of wealthy summer residents had donated this charmingly pretentious building to the town, along with an appropriate collection of books, as a gift to the local community.

The library's benefactors had been generous when it came to geographical matters, and John found a more than adequate collection of maps and charts. He pored over them and began to grasp the magnitude of his problem. First and most challenging, he couldn't be absolutely sure of the name. Was Sam leading him on a wild goose chase, and if not, how clearly had Sam heard the words? There were so many possibilities:

Barrack, Barrick, Barret, Barit, Barrel. The list grew by the minute. The cove part helped narrow things down some, but not all that much.

John went to the front desk. "Could I please have a piece of paper, Mabel?"

Mabel Sturtevant, the librarian, was a study in gray. She had gray hair, gray eyes, and a gray dress with a fitted bodice and full skirt in the style of a Victorian-era school teacher. Only her tennis sneakers, invisible beneath the counter, were white. She gave John a gray look.

"This is a library," she said, as though imparting some great piece of wisdom. "We aren't here to provide everyone with writing materials."

"I just need one piece—"

"We aren't like the big city libraries you may be used to back in Boston, that can afford to give away paper and pencils right and left."

"I did bring a pencil, Mabel."

She frowned at his number 2 Ticonderoga through her steel-rimmed glasses.

"You think our little town and all it stands for is a joke, don't you?"

"I don't think it's a joke at all," John said earnestly. Indeed, Wissonet was beginning to look less and less like a joke, and more and more like a nightmare. "I'm just looking for a piece of paper."

Mabel glared for a moment longer, kicked her tennis racquet out of the way, jerked open a drawer, and passed over a sheet of paper.

John returned to his maps. He had to narrow things down somehow, and he started by limiting the search to coves that were no more than a three-day sail from Wissonet. Half an hour later, he had a list of some twenty-three possibilities scattered along the coast between Massachusetts and Maine. Many were tiny, isolated places, and some were on uninhabited islands. Most were in Maine. John totaled up eight Berry Coves, three Barry Coves, two Barrack Coves, and an assortment of similar names. With a sigh, he took his list and left the cloistered peace of the library.

For the first time since the attack, John felt hungry—famished, in fact. He decided to eat an early lunch before working on Hibbert's drawings, and his list of coves.

Even better, the mental fog seemed to have lifted, and his mind seemed clear enough to be capable of logical thought.

But could he really trust his thinking? The amnesia, temporary as is was, had shaken him. Was his memory riddled with other holes, like a moth-eaten blanket? As he had told the ever-suspicious Lieutenant Riley, even last night, when Mike was killed, became vague when he tried to remember exactly what he had been doing. He remembered walking down High Street. He remembered sitting on the town beach. Yet he couldn't be positive that the memories were all connected, tied together with the glue of continuity. Had chunks of time fallen away, unnoticed? Had he dozed off while sitting on the beach? Did he truly remember everything? Could he have attacked Mike and blocked out the event? How far could he trust his own memory, which was already haunted by flashbacks?

Center Street delivered John to the Magic Spell Market, a large, white-clapboard building whose two plate glass windows sported the inevitable Salada Tea sign, plus an assortment of other brand names. Inside, John worked his way down Mary's list.

"Morning Len," John said, piling his groceries onto the worn, wooden counter top. Len, his normally friendly face a blank mask, ignored John's greeting as he rang up the purchases. Apparently, Len had no doubts about who had killed Mike.

The surly shopkeeper collected John's money without comment and began loading the groceries into a bag. The egg carton went first, with a precisely calculated thud just loud enough to bring a cringe without causing actual breakage. The canned goods followed in a manner reminiscent of Len's high-school basketball career.

"Umm, Len..."

Len toiled on, ignoring the growing flush of anger on his customer's face.

Gladys Kirkland, waiting in line behind John, watched Len's efforts with obvious approval.

John gripped the edge of the counter with both hands as he fought the urge to grab Len by the neck and stuff his head in with the groceries.

The last tiny corner was filled with a mashed loaf of Wonder Bread.

Barely able to breathe, John took the bag and its mangled contents and stalked out.

* * *

Nat-the-cat was waiting hungrily at the kitchen door when John came up the street carrying his bag of mutilated groceries under one arm. Obviously, Edith's casserole hadn't been poisoned after all. Did that mean her husband's poisoning really was accidental as everybody believed? In any case, Edith apparently wasn't out to kill them, at least not by poison. Was it intentional that she should feed them the same kind of meal that killed her husband? Was it another example of the twisted, petty cruelty that inspired Henry and his bucket, or the firecracker vandal?

Or, had he and Mary become paranoid about people in town just because somebody had nearly killed him in Yarmouth? On the other hand, the Commodore had been murdered, and so had Mike. Was there some connection, or was Mike's death just a drug deal gone wrong? John brooded over these things as he unloaded the groceries and fixed lunch for Nat and himself.

Most of John's rage had dissipated by the time he finished lunch. Mary, Janet, and Wendy had planned a picnic lunch by the water so he would have some more time to work.

* * *

John rolled up a collection of drawings a few hours later, and headed downstairs. The drawings weren't complete, but they should be enough to get cost estimates. He left a note on the hall table and walked down to Sam Barton's boatyard, hoping he and the town's only boatbuilder were still on speaking terms.

Sam unrolled John's drawings on his cluttered workbench, and glanced briefly at them, before straightening up. "Just between the two of us, I've been meaning to ask if you killed Mike by any chance. I'm only asking because you didn't seem too sure when Riley was here."

"You heard me tell him I didn't do it," John grumbled, unsure if Sam's question was serious.

"Let me pass on a little tip that I've picked up in my years of dealing with the police, Wendell. If a cop asks you whether or not you murdered someone, you tell them absolutely not, and you say it like you mean it, even if you did snuff the guy an hour earlier." Sam glanced at the Crocker sloop, where faint noises from inside the boat's cabin suggested Henry's presence.

"I'm just trying to save you some grief."

"Well, I have a tip for you too, Barton. Don't go threatening someone in public if you're going to kill him a couple of days later."

Sam nodded ruefully. "I should have chased those kids out before I talked to the bastard. Half the town knows what happened in there."

It was John's turn to glance at the half-finished sloop. Was Henry really working in there, or was he trying to eavesdrop? Probably both. "If it's any comfort, the other half of town thinks I killed Mike. What does Henry think?"

"He thinks his great-grandson was mixed up with a tough bunch from New Bedford, and was bound to come to a bad end."

Sam turned back to John's drawings.

"She's a nice looking boat, but to tell you the truth, I've half made up my mind to just do some repair work this winter. Building a boat is getting to be too damn much work at my age. My hands don't work as well as they used to in the cold anymore, and it's a damned hassle to find decent timber nowadays. I have to go over to Providence to get a keel poured, now that Fossett has gone out of business. Beckman doesn't have the bronze fittings I need half the time, and Connolly is too busy sawing house lumber to bother with boat boards. Hell, he's too busy trying to keep up with the building boom to saw anything for me." Sam shrugged. "Anyhow, I'm not planning to do any building for a little while."

"You mean you're not planning to do any building for me." John glared at Sam.

The reluctant boatbuilder's eyes ran up and down John's six-foot frame. "Did they really stuff you into a barrel?"

"I told you it was a hogshead," he replied coldly.

"A Hogshead. Right." Sam glanced at John's drawings again. "Look, what happened in Yarmouth is none of my business, and if you say it was just a coincidence that you found the boat up there, then as far as I'm concerned that's what happened, but there are people in town who don't believe your story, and most of them think you killed Mike. There are some pretty hard feelings being stirred up. Mike may not have been much, but he was born here, after all."

"You think I don't know that?"

Sam shook his head. "You sure as hell act like you don't."

"Don't you care that one of your neighbors could be a multiple murderer?"

"Since you asked, no, I don't give a damn. I have to live with these people, whether they're killers or not. They put food on my table. I need them, and they need me. That's just the way it is around here."

Sam rested his hand on John's shoulder. "Sure, Wissonet has it quirks, like everyplace else, but so what? If people want to think the town was founded by a witch, that's fine with me. If people think the witch legend is the word of God, that's fine with me; if people think Commodore Cummings and a coven of witches are keeping the town free from harm, that's fine with me. I just go along and get along, and you'd be smart to do the same thing. I can't afford to make enemies here, and neither can you. Leave it be. Let the cops stir up trouble on their own."

John felt his face flush. "Do you think I want to be involved in this? It won't let me go."

"That's what you keep saying. What I think is that you need something to distract yourself." Sam turned abruptly and headed for the door. "Come on, I've got just the thing."

He led the way to a weed-infested area behind the shed and stopped in front of a decaying square of canvas draped over an amorphous shape on the ground. After removing a few scraps of lumber anchoring the canvas, he whisked the fabric away like a waiter removing the cover of a pheasant under glass, or a magician revealing a pet duck.

The object in question wasn't either a pheasant or a duck.

The Beetle Cat is an open sail boat about twelve-feet long and six-feet wide, with its mast stepped well up in the bow, and a big, wet bathtub of a cockpit. The inverted specimen lying before them had seen a great many better days. Or years, for that matter. Most of the paint was either peeling or long gone, and several planks had come unfastened from the bow, where they stuck out like broken bones.

"There," Sam announced, "a little paint and she'll be good as new."

John looked incredulously at his companion. "Are you serious? Half the planks are sprung at the stem. I'll bet there's rot—"

"So? What's a loose plank or two? Have you forgotten how to use a screwdriver?"

"We don't have the money for a boat right now, Sam."

"Who's talking about money? It's a worthless piece of junk. I just want to get the damn eyesore out from underfoot. The Kid can clean out the back of the shop where you and Jeff used to make those god-awful skiffs." Sam gave an involuntary shudder at the memory. "You can work there. It'll give The Kid something to do, maybe you can teach him something, and I can keep an eye on the two of you in case you forget which end of a screw goes in first."

John wondered if Sam was trying to apologize for not offering a quote on Hibbert's boat. Maybe he was trying to recapture the old days before the war. Was The Kid a replacement for Sam's dead son?

"This place is as close to paradise as you can get," Sam said, interrupting John's thoughts. "At least for sailing."

He turned towards the water, where the first hint of a sea breeze was making a belated entrance. "Look out there. Another year or two and Wendy will be asking for a real boat. What are you going to do, then? Ruin the poor kid's childhood? You and Mary could join the yacht club and do some racing. Wendy could get into the children's sailing program."

"Ruin her childhood? She's only three, for crying out loud. Besides, we can hardly afford groceries."

"So fix it up and sell it. I don't give a damn. Buy groceries. Buy a real car. Put one of those bedsprings up on the roof, buy one of those television sets and let the kid watch Howdy Doody, for all I care."

"I don't think we're close enough to Providence to get television here."

"For chrissake," Sam growled, "I've never seen anyone flog a gift horse so hard in my life."

Chapter 24

Wissonet, August 11

Mary and Wendy got home later that afternoon and discovered that John had fixed the mangled fan, after a fashion. The wire cage was straightened following its collision with the bedroom wall, and the blades ran more or less true. The high-pitched whine was gone, replaced with a rumbling vibration, and the light glinting off the blades was somewhat wobbly—a bit like their relationship at the moment, she thought.

John assured her that the fan didn't bother him in its present condition. The rumble bothered Mary, but at least it was moving the air as they sat in the living room that evening.

"Do you remember Louise Waller?" Mary said.

"Vaguely."

"She's Louise Stinson now, with a four-year-old boy. Her parents are both dead, so she's planning to sell the place."

"Didn't the Wallers have a reputation for being a little strange?"

"I don't think Louise had many friends. We played together once in a while as kids. It's funny, but she was saying the other day what great friends we were."

"You sound doubtful."

"I never thought of us as great friends. Sometimes I'd go over and we'd run around the cemetery to play hide and seek, or explore the livingroom woodwork once in a while if the weather was bad. Things like that."

"Explore the woodwork?"

"We were sure there must be secret panels in all the fancy trim."

"Were there?"

"All we found at the time was the woodbox. The thing is, I looked again last Sunday, and I did find a little cubbyhole up high with some old Waller family diaries in it."

"And you never found them as kids?"

"We were too short then. The funny thing is, Louise must have known they were there."

"Once she was tall enough to reach? What do they say?"

"Why do you assume I looked?" Mary said, mildly peeved.

"Why should I assume you didn't?"

Mary frowned. "Be all that as it may, they paint a very different picture of Wissonet's early history than what I've always been told."

"Different? How?"

"I don't know how to describe it, but there was just a darker feel to things the way he described it. For instance, there was a hint that Jonathan may have taken revenge on Jeremiah Dutton."

"And you think that's why the Wallers were standoffish?" John said incredulously.

"I never thought Louise was standoffish. It's just that she didn't like it here."

"Why not? Did Len mash *her* groceries?"

"I think she may have wanted me to read the diaries." Mary absentmindedly touched her sore and swollen ear, which had turned an interesting shade of purple. "Maybe we should move back to Quincy..."

John looked at her, shocked. "And leave your mother?" He shook his head. "I'm not going to let a few rumor-mongers chase me out of our house just because I decide to help the police."

"I did warn you about that."

John scowled. "Why should people assume I killed Mike? Why don't they suspect Sam? He actually threatened the guy. Nobody blames him, or mashes his groceries."

"It will blow over."

"When?" John shook his head in frustration. "I can live with people setting off fireworks under our window, Len trashing the groceries, Mabel giving me a hard time at the library, and people crossing the street when they see me coming, but having Sam refuse to even give me a quote to build Hibbert's boat..."

"I was afraid of that," Mary murmured. "But he does have to make a living in town."

"He pointed that out, but it means I'll have to find somebody else."

"There must be lots of other boatbuilders out there."

John watched the fan wobbling on the window sill for a while. "I think I'll go to Maine and check out builders there," he said at last.

"Why Maine of all places? Why so far away?"

"There are several good builders up there, and they're cheaper, plus they have access to better timber. I'll only be away for a few days."

Mary nodded. "That might be a good idea, and maybe the town will cool down while you're away. Who knows, Riley might have solved the murders by the time you get back."

"I doubt it. I don't think he understands Wissonet well

enough to figure out the killer's motives." John paused. "Hell, even I don't understand what makes the town tick."

"If it is somebody in town," Mary said.

"Of course it is," John said curtly.

Mary sighed. "When are you planning to go?"

"I thought I'd leave first thing tomorrow morning."

"Tomorrow? Why the rush?"

John looked irritated. "The longer I wait, the more impatient Hibbert is going to be. I really had assumed that Sam would do the job." He turned to Mary. "Do you think you'll be safe here, alone?"

"Why wouldn't I be safe? I don't have to worry about Mike getting drunk and coming over, and he was easy enough to deal with, anyway. You're the one that people are trying to kill, and it'll be harder to do that with you away somewhere."

"You could stay with your mother for a few days—"

"I am not going to impose on my mother, or ask her to stay here either. Just take your trip, and don't worry about me."

John got the feeling that Mary was relieved to have him going away.

Chapter 25

Wissonet, August 12

John decided to fill the Model A's gas tank in Lakeville rather than stop at Cliff's Triple Hex Esso station in Wissonet.

Early Friday morning traffic was light and John had plenty of time to rehash his plans while the beach wagon rattled and howled along the two-lane roads linking Bridgewater, Brockton, and Boston. He'd pared down the list of coves, rewriting it several times as he eliminated candidates.

First, he'd crossed off any coves on deserted islands or uninhabited areas simply because it would be impossible to explore them all.

He'd ended up with five possible coves: one in Nova Scotia, and four in Maine. He'd explore the ones in Maine first.

* * *

Mary's workday ended at noon, and she stopped at her mother's house for lunch and to pick up Wendy.

"You've done your hair differently," Janet said as they sat over lunch. "I noticed it this morning."

"I'm trying something new."

"It does help cover up the bruise on your ear. What

happened to it?"

Mary grumbled to herself. She had rearranged her hair to hide the purple ear, but obviously not well enough. Why was her mother always so infuriatingly observant? "I banged it against the closet door," she said sullenly.

"The closet door?"

"It was in the dark."

"Does your ear have anything to do with John's trip? Does it have anything to do with the dent I saw in your wall the other day? Are you two fighting?"

"We are not fighting, mother! Can't I bang my head without getting the third-degree?"

"You don't need to yell, dear, you'll upset Wendy."

Mary picked up Wendy and sat the toddler on her lap. "John was thrashing around in his sleep, that's all."

"When?"

"Tuesday night. He's been distracted and…irritable ever since he got back from Yarmouth."

"The night Mike was killed—"

"John didn't kill anybody," Mary protested, almost desperately.

"Of course not," Janet said soothingly, "but I can see how he could be stressed after almost being killed up in Nova Scotia, and then Mike attacking you while he was away."

"Yes," Mary replied, brushing irritably at her hair. If she hadn't cut it short in the spring, her ear would be out of sight and they wouldn't be having this conversation. Life always seemed to be cluttered up with unintended consequences. "He's the way he was when he first got back from the Navy—the nightmares, the anger. I was glad when John said he was going to Maine."

Her mother captured her daughter's hand. "I'd be glad to

come over and stay a few days until he gets back, if you like. Or you and Wendy could stay here."

"No, I'm all right." She glanced at her mother. "I don't think you should tell anyone John is away, though."

"I wish you'd told me right away about Mike forcing his way into the house, instead of letting me find out from the grapevine after his murder," Janet groused.

"I've already said I was sorry. It just never occurred to me at the time that Mike would be killed." Mary could tell her answer wasn't satisfactory.

"Is there anything else you haven't told me?" Is there something more I should know about?"

"Edith came over Wednesday afternoon," Mary said evasively, hoping to put an end to the ear interrogation. "She was dressed up like a street-walker and almost seemed to be making a pass at John. She brought over a shrimp casserole, too. It was strange."

Janet considered this. "A shrimp casserole? That is worrying, though it's close to the anniversary of when her husband died. That sort of thing can be hard. Heaven knows, I still get a little down in the dumps about the time of year your father died, even after all this time."

Another widow. Mary suddenly realized that she was surrounded by widows, their dead husbands lurking in the shadows—hiding just out of reach, like so many other things.

* * *

It was mid-afternoon by the time John arrived at the hamlet of Barry Cove, Maine. There was no sign of *Abracadabra*. In fact, there wasn't really much sign of a town. A handful of battered houses, a decayed pier, and a few lobster boats—the sum and substance of the place—baked in the afternoon sun. John figured that an hour's work with a bulldozer and the whole place could be fitted into a single dump truck. Still, he was here, and perhaps somebody would know something. He headed for what appeared to be a combination of general store, post office, gas station, local gathering place, and private home, all contained within a sagging, weatherbeaten house.

* * *

Mary put Wendy up for a nap when they got home from her mother's, and went out to repair the carnage Edith had inflicted on her daylilies, where a sizable strip along the front edge of the garden was flattened. Mary grumbled as she kneeled and started cleaning up the ruins. They would grow back, after all.

Near the rear of the bed, hidden in the lush growth, Mary spotted Crusher, John's over-sized monkey wrench. Why wasn't it in its usual place in the wooden tool box behind the car seat? She reached for the heavy metal handle. It must have been there for quite a while, she thought, seeing the jaws of the wrench brown with rust.

She looked more closely.

They weren't rust stains. It was dried blood. A gory clump of what looked like hair was caught in a crevice. She slowly put the wrench down and thought as she kneeled amid the battered greenery.

Mostly, she thought about Loretta's eyes boring into the back of her head. Why did the pesky woman's kitchen window have to be on this side of their house? Even now, Loretta might be on her way over to investigate this unusual behavior.

Mary remembered Ed borrowing the wrench, but he'd put it back in the Ford days ago. Of course, he could easily have picked it up later to kill Mike, but why would he want to kill Mike, if that was what the wrench had been used for? His grudge was with the Commodore and Cummings Jewelry. Besides, anyone glancing into the Ford could see the open tool box wedged behind the front seat and might easily take Crusher.

But why would the killer leave the wrench in her flower bed where she was likely to find it? Was it an attempt to frame John? If so, why not leave the wrench in a more public place?

There was another, more terrifying possibility, made all the more real by John's erratic behavior since coming back from Yarmouth. Could he have killed Mike during some sort of psychotic break, dropped the wrench here afterwards, and blocked the murder from his consciousness?

What to do? Should she clean off the blood, return Crusher when she got the chance, and pretend nothing had happened? No, she decided, that would be too much like admitting John's guilt to herself, which she wasn't ready to do, yet. She would give him the benefit of the doubt and confront him when he got back. Perhaps he had an explanation.

She got up, retrieved a paper bag from the pantry drawer and carefully folded Crusher inside. With the bag and its contents safely hidden away in the remotest corner of a seldom used kitchen cabinet, she continued to methodically clean up the mangled flowers, her mind awash with thoughts of murder.

* * *

Barry Cove had produced nothing of interest, no boatyard, and no sign of *Abracadabra*.

His next stop was Berry Cove. Surprisingly, the turnoff sported a weather-beaten sign that marked a little-used dirt road. The first mile or so of deeply rutted track lay in thick woods, and John was thankful for the old Ford's ample ground clearance. The road snaked its way higher until suddenly he came onto a rocky, overgrown blueberry field, which undoubtably gave the cove its name. The way led directly over the field's granite spine and down a steep incline to what must be Berry Cove itself.

There were three abandoned, swaybacked houses, their broken windows staring blindly out over a tiny inlet. There was no sign of life and no indication that boat or human had recently visited the place. John got out and walked over to the rotted remains of a small pier.

Suddenly he felt alone and vulnerable, an intruder with no excuse to be here. What would he do if somebody appeared and demanded an explanation? What could he hope to find here anyway? A chip of black paint? Some recognizable artifact from *Abracadabra*? It took only a few minutes to determine that no such things were to be found. He turned around and headed back to the main road.

It was mid-afternoon by now. He had time for two more stops before finding a place to stay for the night and continuing his search tomorrow.

He arrived at his next stop, Barrack Cove, an hour later. At least the place was inhabited. Perhaps it had even contained a barracks at some time in the distant past, though there was no sign of one now. The handful of houses reflected a modest level of wealth and industry, apparently from fishing. John headed for a small boatyard whose lopsided shed had a forlorn and abandoned look. A disheveled ancient, wearing a grimy bowler hat, sat propped against a shady piece of wall, nursing a half-empty bottle. John wondered whether the old man would notice *Abracadabra* if she fell on him, but one had to start somewhere.

"Good afternoon. I was wondering if you do any custom

building or repair work." John asked.

"Yep, but we're too busy to take on any new jobs."

John refrained from glancing around the cobwebbed interior of the shed. "Have you seen a black sailboat recently?"

"Nope. Don't get many strangers around here."

* * *

The telephone rang just as Mary was getting ready to feed Wendy her supper. Muttering, she hurried to the living room.

"Hello, Mrs. Wendell? Ralph Hibbert here. How are you?"

"I'm fine Mr. Hibbert, but I'm afraid John is still in Maine if you want to talk to him."

"Maine?"

"Yes. He's looking for yards to build your boat." His obvious confusion made Mary feel as though the conversation was wriggling out of her grasp.

There was a pause. "Oh, yes of course. I must have forgotten—I'd hoped Sam Barton might be willing to build the boat."

"I think John was trying to get some other quotes, too."

"Oh, that's all right, then." Hibbert still sounded confused. "When is he getting back?"

"As far as I know, he's planning to be home the day after tomorrow. He's going to call tomorrow when he knows more. I can take a message if you like."

* * *

Mary went to John's office after putting Wendy to bed and stood looking at the drafting table, where the usual jumble of drawings had been arranged into orderly piles.

The uncharacteristic neatness was unnerving. Only a ball of scrap paper laying next to the waste basket marred the tidiness. She picked it up absentmindedly, started to throw it away, and stopped. She felt a twinge of guilt as she flattened the sheet. She wouldn't think of prying into John's business normally, but he hadn't been acting normal lately. Come to think of it, nobody was acting normal.

The paper contained a column of names. It must be a list of the boatyards John was planning to visit in Maine, but why were so many entries crossed out? She started to ball the paper up again and realized something else strange. All the names started with the letter B. Not only that, they were all coves.

Mary stared at the list with growing apprehension, went downstairs, and reached for the telephone.

Chapter 26

Wissonet, August 12

Mary watched Riley as he sat at the kitchen table and examined the bloody wrench that rested on his crisply ironed handkerchief. He seemed remarkably calm, considering that she had probably interrupted his supper. On the other hand, murder weapons probably had higher priority than meals for a homicide detective.

In any case, Mary planned to test the limits of her guest's equanimity.

"Let me get this straight," Riley said. "This is your husband's wrench?"

"Yes."

"And you found it in your flower bed?"

"That's right."

"And you think it was used to attack Mike Hartwell?"

"Don't you? It's got blood on it, and the bits of hair are the same color as Mike's."

"All that remains to be seen, but you could be right. And you think Edith Whitten might have put it there?"

Mary was beginning to get impatient with Riley's plodding interrogation. "All I'm saying is that I wouldn't have noticed the wrench if Edith hadn't parked in my flower bed the day before yesterday, but I didn't actually see her put it in the garden." The memory still raised her blood pressure.

"Why did she park in you flower bed?"

Mary took a deep breath. "I hadn't pulled the Ford in far enough to leave room for her to park behind it, but that's not the point."

Riley gave her an ominous look. "And what is the point?"

"The point is that this wrench belongs to my husband and it was used to kill Mike Hartwell," she said, trying to control her voice.

Riley scowled. "Are you and your husband on the outs or something? Are you trying to frame him for some reason?"

Mary shook her head. "That's not it at all. I just want you to find him before he gets hurt."

"Why would he get hurt?"

Mary couldn't answer the question except for her deep feeling of unease. Her mother had often muttered disapprovingly about Mary's sixth sense, and that sense had filled her with dread as soon as she saw John's list. "Because I think he knows where *Abracadabra* is, and he's gone off to find her, or the people who took her."

Riley swore under his breath. "Why the hell does he keep chasing after that damn boat?"

"How hard are *you* trying to find *Abracadabra*?" Mary demanded, echoing John's frustration.

Riley snorted like an enraged bull. "Why didn't he just call me if he knew where the boat was? Why can't he leave well enough alone?"

"You don't understand. He's not chasing after *Abracadabra;* he's *never* cared about finding the boat. He's hunting the people who tried to kill him—the people who put him the barrel."

"The term is hogshead," Riley said absentmindedly as he

stared at Crusher. "And the truck was headed to a rendering plant," he added.

"The truck was taking him to a rendering plant? They were going to turn my husband into lard?!" Livid, Mary leaned into Riley's face. "And you have the gall to wonder why he's up there looking for revenge!"

"We don't know for sure what they were—"

Mary took a deep breath. Not wanting to wake up Wendy, she lowered her voice. "Listen to me, Lieutenant. My husband is the stubbornest man I know, he's furious, and he will *not* let this go."

Riley heaved a great sigh. "So, you're telling me that your husband used his own wrench to kill Mike Hartwell, which means your husband must have dropped the wrench in your flower bed. Wouldn't it be kind of careless of him to leave the murder weapon in his own backyard?"

"His fingerprints are bound to be on the wrench. Isn't that enough to go on?"

"Of course his prints are on it. It's his wrench. I'm guessing that your's are on there too. Why shouldn't I arrest you?"

"Are you going to find John or not?"

"All this about forcing me to find your husband? Do you really want me to arrest him for murder?"

"I'd rather have him arrested for murder and be alive. He almost got killed last time he saw *Abracadabra*."

"You are one strange lady." Riley shook his head. "Do you have any idea where he might be in Maine? When did you talk to him last?"

"He's supposed to call tomorrow evening."

"Well, tell him to get back here before you frame him for high treason."

"Don't you understand? He's in danger *now*! Surely you

aren't going to just sit around for days hoping your prime murder suspect will turn up, when you have a piece of evidence like that in your hands. Maybe he won't come back at all. Maybe he'll flee the country. You can't take a chance on him escaping."

Riley's eyebrows descended alarmingly. "Are you serious about this? You may not believe it, but I'm not in the business of hunting down wayward husbands."

"You have the evidence; what more do you need?"

"What more do I need? Do you have any idea what will happen if I send out an All-Points-Bulletin for your husband? It will set things in motion that I may not be able to control. You'd better do some explaining before I promise anything."

Mary handed over John's list of coves.

Riley grumbled under his breath while he read the list. "That's a lot of names."

"Most of them have been crossed out."

"There are still a lot left. I assume he's working his way up the coast." He put the list on the table and turned to look at Mary. "Your husband served in the Navy during the war? On a destroyer?"

"The USS *Dunn*. She was sunk in the Leyte Gulf."

Riley watched and waited for more.

"A Japanese plane crashed just behind the bridge and he was trapped in the debris. His left leg was broken in two places. He lay there for a long time, hearing the screams as the rest of the bridge crew burned to death."

"I'm sorry," Riley said softly.

"It left scars. Physical and emotional scars: flashbacks, anger, guilt, depression." Mary turned away, gritting her teeth. "There are certain things," she said softly, "loud sounds, and fire, that can trigger it. Things were getting better until Yarmouth."

"I served in the Great War, Mrs. Wendell." Riley's gaze shifted away. "They called it shell shock back then—from being trapped in the trenches for weeks on end, never knowing if the next artillery barrage was going to land on your head. I saw what it could do to men..." His gaze came back from the past to focus on Mary. "They call it battle fatigue, now. I suppose each war has a different name, but it's all the same thing." Riley sighed. "The concussion he received up in Yarmouth could be affecting his judgement, too."

Riley straightened up. "I'll talk to the state police up there. They can start with this Barry Cove, but it won't be easy to find him. Maine is a big place."

"There can't be all that many Model A Ford beach wagons with Massachusetts plates in Maine."

"Maybe not, but Maine is still a big state."

Mary opened her mouth to speak, but he held up his hand. "Just to be clear, Mrs. Wendell, I'm not doing this because of the wrench, or because I think your husband killed Hartwell, even though he doesn't seem to be all that sure himself."

Riley went on more gently. "Is there somebody in town you can talk to, somebody you can trust?"

Normally, she could have come up with a long list of names, but not now. "My mother. And Doctor Edwards, our family doctor, I suppose."

"Talk to them." Riley levered himself out of the chair, picked up the gruesome souvenir with his handkerchief, and put it back in its paper bag. "Now, if you could show me exactly where you found the wrench."

They went outside, where Riley loomed over the daylily bed. Standing near his Packard in the fading light, the hulking lawman looked like a Mafia goon in the climactic scene of a George Raft movie. At least the bulky vehicle hid them from the ever-alert Loretta.

"Now, exactly where did you find the wrench?"

"In the middle of this clump of daylilies, right there," she said, pointing out the flattened greenery. "I would never have seen it if I hadn't been looking at the damage Edith did with her car and doing a little weeding."

Riley leaned over to examine the lush, knee-high growth. "It's pretty thick in there." He straightened up and looked at the kitchen window. "I suppose she might have put it there without you being able to see. It'll be your word against hers, of course."

Mary bristled. "I'm not accusing her of anything," she said, thinking with a guilty twinge about her reaction to Edith's ill-fated casserole. "Anybody could have put it there."

"Yes, but I don't see why anybody would come here to leave a piece of incriminating evidence on your doorstep where you or your husband are likely to find it. And having planted it, why wouldn't he or she tip off the police that it was here?"

"It's your job to figure that out."

"I wish your husband thought that way," Riley muttered. "On the other hand, if your husband had killed Hartwell, why he would leave his own wrench here, of all places?"

Riley was toying with her, Mary thought bitterly. There was an obvious reason why John might drop the wrench here. It was a reason that had plagued her from the start, and Riley knew what it was: her husband had blocked out his attack on Mike.

* * *

By evening, John had visited Barkley Cove, with no results. This was the fourth cove, and his trip was looking more and more like a waste of time and energy.

He came to another of a seemingly endless series of small,

mostly isolated towns, stopped at a cheap motel, and took a room. He realized too late that his lodgings were located near an intersection with heavy truck traffic. Thanks to the noise and the paper-thin walls, John slept fitfully.

* * *

At the last instant, the Zero's propeller jerked to a stop, flames burst from the engine nacelle, the plane sideslipped aft and impacted just below the chartroom. The explosion burst the bridge deck upwards, turning the space into a shattered, flaming ruin.

John's legs were pinned under a jumble of twisted steel. The chartroom deck had been peeled back, an unrecognizable mass, and a fireball of aircraft fuel engulfed the aft end of the bridge. The screams of the dying bridge crew filled John's ears as he lay trapped, unable to move or help.

After what seemed like an eternity, the screams ended and a damage control crew managed to force their way through the wreckage. Voices filled the space: "Get a hose in here. Knock down the fire. Jeez, everybody is dead."

Everybody except John. The damage control crew had just managed to free him when the first torpedo struck in the aft boiler room, where the two boilers exploded in a tower of shrapnel and steam. Another explosion a few seconds later severed the *Dunn's* keel, and a third hinged the bow upwards.

The entire engagement had only taken a matter of minutes.

John's screams jolted him awake. He lay for a while, soaked with sweat, gasping for breath on the lumpy motel mattress.

He sat on the edge of the bed and wondered, as he had so often before, why he hadn't died along with all the others on the bridge.

For months after the sinking, he would glimpse a face in a crowd, or across the street—a face so much like a dead crew mate that the shock would leave him momentarily paralyzed.

Worst of all was seeing the widows looking at him, the same unspoken question in their eyes that still haunted him: why had he lived and their husbands died?

It was after midnight, but there would be no more sleep tonight. He dressed and went out to wander in the darkness.

Chapter 27

Maine, August 13

John ate an early breakfast of fried eggs, sunny-side up. Not that he felt sunny—exhausted, discouraged, and depressed was closer to the truth. He was beginning to question the reasons for his quixotic quest. He wished Mary was here. His fruitless odyssey was costing time and money he could ill-afford, and Barrick Cove, the next place on the list, was two hours further up the coast. Even worse, it was on an island, which added to the difficulty. John finished breakfast and reached a compromise that partially soothed his guilty conscience. He would drop off a set of plans with a builder he knew in nearby Bristol and ask if there was a boatyard in Barrick Cove. If there was none, he'd give up his fruitless quest and go home.

* * *

Miraculously, Loretta hadn't turned up yet this morning, so Mary had time to wrack her brain in peace.

She wished John were here. She wondered if he'd ever speak to her again after her treachery with Crusher. Yet she couldn't help the feeling that he was in mortal danger. What else could she have done to save him from himself?

ABRACADABRA

She could only hope that the police would arrest John before he got himself killed.

Perhaps, she thought bleakly, he was subconsciously trying to get himself killed. Perhaps the attack in Yarmouth had resurrected the wartime memories and guilt.

Mary stopped herself. She had to get her mind off the wrench, and think about something else.

She was missing something. It lurked in the shadows of her mind, a vague, ominous form. What was it?

A sudden resolve overtook her. If John could go haring off on a senseless hunt for truth, justice, and revenge, surely she could go off on a hunt of her own.

Riley had told John about the two fishermen who found *Abracadabra*. He was suspicious of their story. Of course Riley seemed to be suspicious of everybody's story, that was part of his job, after all. But maybe he was right about the fishermen. When Jack called the other day, he'd mentioned one of them visiting his yard—a Tony Silva from New Bedford. This Tony Silva had acted suspiciously, according to Jack. Had Silva been looking for something, and if so, what?

She called the Carver Creek boatyard and learned from Jack that Tony Silva didn't have a telephone. "I don't think they have the money for a phone, but I do have his address." Mary copied it down as he read it off.

"Are you and John both going into the private eye business now, collecting evidence, working with the law, and all that undercover stuff?"

It occurred to Mary that her only connection with the law at the moment was in trying to get her husband arrested for murder. She decided not to mention that detail. "I'm just doing some research while John is away for a few days."

"You're not planning to visit Silva by yourself, are you?"

That was exactly what she planned to do. Mary settled on a little whitish lie. "This is just research, Jack."

"Good 'cause his house is in a pretty rough neighborhood, and I'm guessing he's the one who stole your boat."

It didn't occur to Mary, until she'd hung up that she could be mindlessly putting herself in danger, the same way John was. My, how easy it was to start down that slippery slope. She firmly set the thought aside. The whole thing was probably a waste of time, but sitting around doing nothing was worse.

Mary left Wendy with her mother and borrowed Janet's car in the bargain.

It took several stops for directions, but at last Mary found herself in front of a rundown, two-decker tenement. It was probably just her imagination, but she felt unseen eyes appraising her from the shadows. Mary held her purse close as she hurried to the door.

The man who answered her knock was husky, with dark curly hair, graying at the temples, and brown eyes set in a prematurely weathered face. Having determined that he was the right Tony Silva, Mary put on her best salesperson smile and introduced herself as an old friend of the Cummings family. Silva's eyes narrowed at the name, and he shifted his weight as if to shut the door in her face.

"Who's there, Tony?" A woman appeared in the tiny hallway behind him. There was barely room for the two of them. She was darker skinned than Tony, with straight black hair and facial bones that suggested Mashpee Indian blood.

Mary repeated her introduction, noting much the same expression on the woman's face as she glanced at her husband's rigid back. "I'm Maria," she said at last. "You'd better come in."

The living room occupied most of the front end of the apartment, yet it was barely large enough to accommodate two upholstered chairs, an overstuffed sofa, and a coffee table. A crucifix hung over the sofa. Besides the door through which they'd entered, the back wall contained an archway leading to a Pullman-sized kitchen/dinette. The house and furniture had seen better days, but everything had a spotless, frequently scrubbed look. Maria motioned her guest to the sofa while she took one of the chairs.

Tony lowered himself painfully into the other chair. "I can't tell you anything that isn't already in the newspapers."

"We've had nothing but bad luck since it happened," the woman added. "First the motor stopped running in the boat. Then Tony hurt his back getting it out. He hasn't been able to go fishing all week." She looked at her visitor as though hoping for some words of consolation, or at least understanding.

Mary, thinking that *Abracadabra* seemed to be bringing bad luck to a lot of people, starting with the Commodore, nodded vaguely before plunging ahead.

"You can imagine how upset Mrs. Cummings is by her husband's death," she said, "and I was wondering if you noticed anything at all, even something too minor to be of interest to the police, that might help Mrs. Cummings deal with what happened."

Mary's heart leaped as Tony's eyes flicked towards Maria.

"How do we know you really are a friend of the Cummings and not just another reporter?" Tony asked suspiciously.

Mary's fingers trembled with excitement as she pulled her driver's license from the wallet in her purse and handed it to him. "Here's my driver's license. You can see my address is on High Street in Wissonet. We live almost next door to the Cummings. I've known the family all my life."

Maria got up without a word and left the room, her feet scuffing faintly on the worn linoleum as she passed through the narrow archway into the kitchen.

"It's her brother, Al Valero," Tony explained. "He's a little strange in the head." He looked up as his wife returned with something in her hand.

"People think my brother is dumb because he talks funny, but he's not stupid," Maria said. "He means well. It's just that he was wounded in the war and doesn't think like most people any more." She perched tentatively on the edge of the sofa next to Mary.

"I guess this is what you came for." She leaned over and placed a round, gold pendant with a broken chain in Mary's palm. Mary didn't dare take more than a quick glance at it—a simple disc, about the size of a silver dollar, with the words "Valere Veritas" circling its face, and a triangle filling the middle. Mary cupped the pendant in her hand and looked up.

"Like Maria says, Al means well, but he doesn't always know what's right. We just didn't want him to get in trouble with the police again, and they keep coming back, asking more questions." He shifted in his chair, wincing with pain as he did. "I knew the boat was in Carver Creek, so I went there to put the medal back, but the boat was out on a mooring. Then we were going to mail it to Mrs. Cummings, but we didn't know the address." Tony shrugged helplessly, grimacing again.

"It's the words," Maria said, leaning forward and pointing. "Al's got sharp eyes and can read some—his name anyway." Maria's chipped fingernail pointed to the word "Valere." She leaned back, waving her hand uncertainly. "Valero, Valare. You can see how he might think it was his name."

She studied Mary's face, searching for a glimmer of understanding. "His name," she repeated, "on the neck of a dead man. It seemed like a bad thing to him, a sign, so he took his knife, cut the chain, and took the medal without thinking."

"Al is awful quick with a knife," Tony muttered.

Maria frowned at Tony briefly before going on. "Father O'Mally—he's our parish priest—had shown Al some pictures of magic symbols and things a few years ago, and he told Al they were bad. I think that's what made him take it."

"He gave it to Maria when she talked to him about it," Tony said, "but we just didn't know how to get rid of the thing without getting Al into trouble. "You see, he killed a man once." Tony stared into space. "He has a temper sometimes."

"It would be a big load off our minds if you could just give it to Mrs. Cummings and explain what happened without saying anything about Al," Maria said. "He didn't mean any harm."

Mary looked at the pair of anxious faces. "I understand. Tell Al he doesn't need to worry. It will mean a lot to Mrs. Cummings to have this back."

In the stress of the moment, a question leaped unbidden from her mouth. "How was your brother able to see the pendant?"

Tony shifted uncomfortably in his chair. "Well, the body was floating right in front of our faces when we opened the hatch. You couldn't miss the pendant, since he didn't have any clothes on."

* * *

Mary pulled over to the side of the road as soon as she reached the main highway. She hadn't dared to examine the pendant in front of the Silvas, but she couldn't wait any longer.

It had little in the way of beauty to commend it as a piece of jewelry—just a simple, gold disk on a broken gold chain. Looking more closely, she saw an eye atop the triangle, surrounded by the inscription, "Ab Valare Veritas." Her Latin was sketchy at best, but she was pretty sure "Ab" meant "from" and "Veritas" meant "truth," but she was less sure about "Valare." Did it mean "courage?" No, it wasn't that simple. "strength" or "power" was closer. What did the words mean? "Strength from Truth?" "Power from Truth?" Perhaps both. Or perhaps neither.

Mary turned the pendant over. Facing her was a horned goat's head superimposed on an upside-down pentagram.

Beneath the pentagram was engraved a tiny, upside-down cross.

Chapter 28

Wissonet, August 13

A scorching early afternoon sun and temperatures over 100 degrees had made it easy to persuade Mary's mother to spend a few hours babysitting Wendy at the town beach. The same weather that had filled Wissonet's beaches had left Wissonet's library empty of patrons. Mary found Fred Ogilvy alone in the reading room, his nose buried in the *New York Times*.

"Ah, there you are," he said as she approached, "Shall we adjourn to the basement where it's cooler?"

Mabel Sturtevant looked up with disapproval at Fred's words. "You're not taking her down to the archives, are you?"

"Why not? That's what the Historical Society is there for."

Mabel opened her mouth to protest, but snapped it shut with an audible click as Mary and Fred swept by her desk to the cast iron, spiral-staircase at the back of the building.

The basement to the right of the stairs was filled with musty shelves containing outdated periodicals, seldom used reference books, and other miscellany that didn't fit anywhere else. The wall to the left contained a door with the neatly lettered words "Wissonet Historical Society."

Fred produced a key, unlocked the door with a flourish, and

ushered Mary inside. Shelves containing a welter of books, and cartons of papers, took up most of the space. An oak table, encircled by a half dozen straight-backed wooden chairs, stood near the door. A tiny desk hid in the corner under a pile of papers.

"I had no idea there was so much room in here."

"Yes," Fred said absentmindedly, "I suppose it's a measure of an architect's skill to make a space seem larger than it really is.

"We're fortunate that the town fathers had the foresight to set aside a place for the creation of an Historical Society when the library was built. Much of the town's past would have been lost otherwise. As you may know," he went on, "Henry Merton was instrumental in setting up the Historical Society in 1886. In fact, he donated most of his family papers to the society and served as president for some fifty-five years."

He bustled over to the desk, pulled an envelope from his pocket, and added it to the chaos. "I do my bit as well by clipping articles of local interest from the area newspapers."

Fred had always been short, and the passing years, an expanding waistline, and a gradual loss of hair, gave him a somewhat gnomish appearance. He looked at her like an inquisitive owl. "Perhaps you can tell me exactly what you are looking for, so I have a clearer idea of how I can help."

"That's the trouble. I'm not really sure what I'm looking for. I'd like to know more about Ruth and Prudence Cummings, if there are some newspaper articles or letters from that time."

"Ah." Fred's glasses were perched half-way down his nose, and he eyed Mary with a hint of disapproval over the top of them. "A lot of people have asked about Ruth Cummings over the years. Unfortunately, we don't have much material on her or her daughter, Prudence."

"I suppose people ask about the witchcraft legend?"

"Yes," he replied. "I suppose it's irresistible, but I really can't help with town folklore of that sort—we just don't have any material on the subject. There was a collection of newspaper clippings going back to the early 1800's at one time..." Fred looked wistful. "Unfortunately, my predecessor didn't take proper care of them, and newsprint being what it is, they all disintegrated." Fred snorted disapprovingly. "He threw them out just before I took over. 'Tidying up the place for me,' he said." A faint strangling noise rattled in the amateur historian's throat.

He tore his mind away from the newspaper catastrophe with a visible effort. "We do have an undated letter from Ruth to her daughter, probably written shortly after Prudence married, and a number of letters from John Merton," he said. "As you know, he was Prudence's husband."

And Henry's grandfather, Mary thought. "I understand Prudence committed suicide."

"Oh my, no," Fred replied in a shocked voice. "I can't imagine where you heard that. She died giving birth to Amos Merton. John was devastated, as you can imagine. He wrote two very poignant letters on the subject." He pulled a loose-leaf notebook from a shelf. "I've transcribed many of the old letters to protect the originals and make them easier to read." He thumbed through the pages.

"Then why isn't Prudence buried in the cemetery?"

"Eh?" Fred pried himself out of the notebook and stared at Mary over his glasses.

"I couldn't find her gravestone when I looked the other day. John Merton's second wife, Elsie Barton, is there, but not Prudence."

"Yes, that is peculiar. I'm afraid it's one of those little

mysteries that pop up now and then."

"Is there a private family cemetery?"

"Not that I know of. We have a list of all the area cemeteries, if you'd like to check." Fred poked ineffectually at the papers covering the desk. "Why don't you ask Henry Merton about Prudence? He'd probably know where she is buried."

Mary nodded. "What happened to Jeremiah Dutton?"

Fred was spending a great deal of time staring at Mary over the top of his glasses and he did so once again. "Jeremiah Dutton? Why, he was struck by lightning while repairing his barn roof. Jeremiah was one of Wissonet's most influential citizens in the early 1800's. He was First Selectman, and Deacon in the local church for many years."

"How do you know he was struck by lightning? Was there a newspaper report?"

"Ah," Fred said happily. "Better than that, we have a copy of a letter from John Merton to his son, Amos, mentioning the event. Henry Merton gave it to us."

Mary turned to the notebook. "Are most of these letters from John Merton?"

"Yes, he was a very prolific writer. A copy of the letter from Ruth Cummings to Prudence is in the back if you'd like to see it." Fred reached over Mary's arm and turned to the place. "It's the only letter we have from Ruth. Dianne Cummings found it when she cleaned out the house after the Commodore's father died."

Mary felt a shiver go up her spine as she looked at the page. Even with Fred's typewritten copy, Ruth's words seemed to leap off the page.

It was a short letter. "My precious daughter," it began. Ruth's words echoed with a desperate loneliness. One sentence caught her eye, "Though we cannot see each other, you have my love and my talisman to keep you safe." Safe from what?

Fred broke into Mary's reverie. "Would you like to look at the original? It's just that the paper is quite brittle, so we try not to handle it too much."

"No." Mary recoiled at the idea. For some reason the typewritten copy was as close as she wanted to get to Ruth Cummings. "Why would Ruth write to Prudence?"

"People wrote a lot more frequently in those days," Fred informed her.

"Yes, but why didn't Ruth just go and visit? Was she in bad health?"

"I don't believe so," Fred replied. "She wasn't all that old—only in her early fifties when she died. She was a very handsome woman, according to various letters I've read. The term 'raven-haired beauty,' comes to mind."

Fred gave Mary a resigned look. "The common myth that witches—if there is such a thing as witches—are old and ugly is not true. Many of the so called Salem witches were in their thirties and forties, for example, and I believe there were even two pre-teenagers." Fred snorted in disgust.

They spent almost an hour going through stacks of documents with little to show for their efforts.

Fred turned abruptly as they were about to leave. "Oh, I almost forgot the Register." He fished a leather-bound book from under the papers infesting the desk. "We ask everybody doing research here to sign the Register and mention what subject they were researching. It's a silly little custom, but the Register is a bit of history itself, in a way."

Mary signed her name, noting the book was only half filled. "Do you get many people coming to you?"

"Not really, I'm sorry to say. Most people come in to learn

more about family members in town or look at some of the old town meeting records. A few high school students come in to do papers on town history." Fred turned the pages. "Now here's a contemporary of yours. Jeff Barton did a high-school report on the lumber schooners of Wissonet harbor." Fred glanced reflexively at the appropriate row of shelving. "We have quite a bit of material on the lumber trade, as a matter of fact."

Mary remembered a worn lumber schooner from Maine had ghosted into Wissonet harbor just last month, tying up to one of the ancient granite piers, her deck piled high with boards to feed the post-war building boom in southern Massachusetts.

Mary relieved Fred of the Register and began scanning the pages. Most of the names were familiar. In 1931, she found Commodore Cummings's neatly printed name, with the entry "family history." Mary's eye caught another name as well. In 1930, the signature of Dianne Harkness reported that she was researching the "Cummings family." Could she have been doing some research on her future husband?

"See what I mean about the Register? Fascinating, isn't it?" Fred's voice brought Mary back to the present.

"When did you become president?"

Fred gazed at the ceiling, looking for all the world as though he expected to find the date written up there somewhere. "I believe it was 1941," he said.

So, many of the entries would be before Fred's time. Mary skipped ahead. "I see Loretta Clayton has been here researching the Leary house."

"Yes. Having bought the house from Mildred Leary after her husband died, Loretta was curious about the history of the place. She was curious about a great many other things as well, now that I think about it. She is a very inquisitive person."

Mary suspected that Fred didn't know the half of it. "Do

you have much information on the houses in town?"

"We're very much hit-or-miss on that subject. We have some old photographs of the Leary house because it's an historic building, and there are some recent newspaper clippings because of poor Ralph Leary's death."

"I'm afraid I haven't been very helpful," Fred said as he returned the Register to its hiding place on the desk.

"There is one more thing," Mary said as she took the Commodore's pendant from her pocket. "I wonder if you'd look at this and tell me what you think."

Fred took an oversized magnifying glass from the desk and sat at the table, poring over the pendant like a near-sighted, rotund version of Sherlock Holmes. "Jewelry isn't my forte, I'm afraid, nor is Latin. I'm not sure, but I think Valere means "strong," or "healthy."

"Truth from strength? Strength from truth?"

"Possibly," he mused. "Of course, you've seen the symbol—the eye over the pyramid."

"It does look familiar."

"It should look familiar, young lady, since it's the Great Seal, which can be found on the back of a one dollar bill, as well as a great many other places."

He went on pedantically. "The phrase, "Annuit Coepotis" over the eye means "favor our undertakings," and can be traced to the Roman poet, Virgil. The eye itself is commonly thought of as the eye of God. Of course, Freemasons refer to it as the Eye of Providence."

He glanced at Mary disapprovingly. "But I suppose you're more interested in witches and all that occult foolishness."

"Yes."

Fred harrumphed. "The same image is also referred to as the Eye of Horus and is an ancient Egyptian symbol of protection personified by the Goddess, Wadjet. The eye of Ra is a similar protection symbol related to the God, Ra."

"Protection as in Ruth's letter?"

"Perhaps," Fred murmured, turning the pendant over. "Let's look at the other side...Oh my, this is a bit darker." He moved it under the magnifying glass, muttering to himself. "The engraving has very fine detail, and it's a bit worn..."

He straightened up and put away his magnifier. "This is a satanic revenge symbol," he said briskly. "The horned goat skull, the inverted pentagram and cross; they cry vengeance." He carefully put the pendant back on the table. "I suppose," he mused, "it could be meant to represent the two sides of life: light and dark. Protection from evil and evil itself. An odd piece to wear around one's neck."

"Do you think this might be the talisman Ruth mentioned in her letter?" Mary said again.

Fred poked gingerly at the gold disk as though it might be too hot to touch. "I'm not in a position to conjecture on that possibility." Mary had repaired the chain's broken link with a few loops of thread, and Fred picked up the amulet by its chain and returned it to her.

* * *

"Why do you want to know about Prudence Merton?"

Mary didn't know the answer to Henry's question, except that Prudence seemed like a loose end, one more hangnail on the town's historical cuticle.

"I happened to be walking through the cemetery the other day, and I noticed that she wasn't there."

Mary and Wendy had found Henry at his favorite fishing spot on the end of the town pier, where he sat in a canvas folding chair. There weren't any lumber schooners tied up here today, or most other days, so it was it a peaceful spot. The wind had died, making the heat even more oppressive. The radio mentioned a storm passing off to the south, and a fringe of hazy cloud streaked the horizon. Perhaps it would bring rain, and, with luck, cooler weather.

Henry looked askance at Mary. "You just happened to be walking through the cemetery? I didn't know the real estate business was that bad."

"We're selling the Waller house, so I was down that way."

"Ah." Henry reeled in his line. The bait was gone. "Well, she's in there. Grandpa is right on top of her." He took a chunk of quahog from a pail beside him and baited the hook. "Pardon my putting it that way, but that's how old John had it in his will. He was more fond of Prudence, my grandmother, than he was of his second wife."

"Then why isn't her name on the stone?"

"Did you look at it?"

Mary took a firm grip on her patience. "Of course I looked at it."

"Then you know it isn't an upright stone; it's a flat one." Henry flipped the line out. "Grandpa wanted her name on the stone along with his, and it is." Henry grinned up at Mary like a mischievous gargoyle. "On the underside where nobody can see."

"But why?"

"Didn't you say you'd looked at the stone?" Henry groused. "John died young, in an accident, in 1823." He paused, and Mary feared for a moment that she was going to be treated to a long-winded story about John Merton's demise. "His second wife, Elsie Barton, outlived him, and she buried him. She did it just like he wanted—the letter of the law—except she turned the stone over, so Prudence's name is nowhere in sight, and Elsie's name ended up being on top."

"Then Prudence didn't commit suicide?"

Henry jigged the line. "Suicide? You're full of crazy ideas. Hell no, she couldn't be buried in the church cemetery if she'd killed herself."

"Was she a witch?"

Henry's eyes narrowed as he looked up at Mary. "Ruth Cummings was the only real witch. The rest are just humbugs, playing at witching," he said sharply.

Mary leaned close to Henry's ear so Wendy wouldn't hear. "Playing?" she hissed. "That may be, but somebody painted an upside-down cross on our door. In blood." She took Wendy's hand and stalked away.

Mary and Wendy made their way over the pier's storm-tossed granite blocks. Half way across, she glanced back and saw Henry watching them, a haunted look on his face.

* * *

Henry Merton had excellent eyesight for a man whose age was measured in three digits, at least by his reckoning. He'd recognized the Cummings amulet easily enough, but what he didn't understand was why this sprout of a child would be wearing it, or what that might mean.

The fact of the matter was that Henry knew very little about witchcraft and cared even less. Until now.

On the bright side, he suspected that the town's so-called witches didn't know much about their chosen vocation either. Even so, he suspected the Wissonet Witches wouldn't take kindly to young Mary Gooden wearing the amulet.

On the dark side, it occurred to him that things could be

getting badly out of control, and he sat for a long time, mulling the problem over like a toothless dog eying an overripe bone.

* * *

The New Bedford library was an imposing granite structure across from the town hall. Mary sat at a desk on the library's top floor, where microfilm records of ancient newspapers whirred hypnotically through the machine in front of her. She had persuaded her long-suffering mother to take Wendy for two more hours, telling her that she was researching some old deeds for Phil Cantor.

It had become clear to her that what was missing from the Wissonet Historical Society was more important than what was there. Not sure what she was looking for, and strangely afraid of what she might find, Mary knew only that a secret festered at Wissonet's core, it had to do with Ruth Cummings, and it threatened to engulf her.

Chapter 29

Maine, August 13

The morning's trip to Bristol had been helpful for Hibbert's boat-to-be, in that a builder there was willing to offer a quote. One more quote and John figured he could go home with a clear conscience, declaring the trip a success—except for *Abracadabra*, and the men who had tried to kill him.

He also learned in Bristol that Barrick Cove, next on his list, happened to be the home of a small boatbuilding shop with a good reputation. John pointed the Ford's steaming nose up the coast towards Barrick Cove with mixed feelings. On the one hand, the attack in Yarmouth had turned the Commodore's murder into something far more personal; on the other hand, he was beginning to get homesick. He would call Mary this evening.

It was mid-afternoon before John reached the village of Payton Harbor, his ears ringing and his muscles vibrating from long hours on the increasingly indifferent roads whose imperfections were magnified by the Ford's antiquated suspension system.

The local general store had a view of Payton Harbor and John could see Barrick Island, with a bank of fog behind it, a mile or so beyond the harbor's rocky entrance. Inside the store, he purchased a quart of motor oil and learned that a boat went out to the island "about" every two hours, and would be leaving "soon enough."

"Stand by them boxes," the wizened proprietor said, "and someone will be along to take 'em over."

John did as he was told and discovered a large-scale chart of Barrick Cove tacked to the wall. Flyblown and yellowed with age, the chart had been hand-drawn in ink by someone with considerable drafting skill. In the lower right corner, almost obscured by a thumbtack, were the neatly inked initials "T.B." A faded note at the bottom of the sheet proclaimed William Barrick to be owner of the island's boat shop, as well as the island itself. Presumably, he was a descendant of the original settler whose immortality the place's name proclaimed.

Having nothing better to do, John studied the map. Barrick Cove lay on the seaward side of the island and was actually sandwiched between Barrick Island and a small sliver of land, referred to as "Hogback Isld." on the chart. The resulting channel partially closed off an indentation in Barrick Island's flank, marked "Barrick Cove." Access to the cove was through a narrow channel between the two islands. The northern tip of Hog Island ended in a jumble of rocks, ominously named the Devil's Kitchen. Looking closely at the smudged paper, John discovered that some of the larger rocks bore names like the Devil's Oven, Devil's Kettle, and a long spine of rock marking the channel's edge labeled the Devil's Sideboard. The southern end of Hogback Island angled in to nearly touch its neighbor, leaving a narrow gap that was heavily starred and marked with the word "Rky." A snug harbor, if you could find your way in.

The promised ferry arrived after a while, in the form of *Alice May*, a battered work boat. John boarded, along with three other passengers, and an assortment of boxes.

Wisps of fog were creeping across the water and dimming the afternoon sun as they headed out towards Barrick Island. Two girls in their late teens lounged against the transom, surreptitiously eyeing John and trading whispered jokes. A grizzled, gray-haired man in bib-overalls sat on a wooden crate, his head drooping onto his chest, apparently asleep. A youth stood at the helm, a tangle of long, dark hair crawling from beneath his greasy cap, and the mangled ruins of a long-dead cigarette drooping from his mouth.

John watched in fascination as they rounded the northern tip of Barrick Island. This was the rockiest piece of shoreline he'd ever seen. To the right, the northern tip of Barrick Island dropped in a thirty-foot cliff down to the water. The ebbing tide was almost low, exposing the Devil's Kitchen in all its monolithic glory. The chart in Payton Harbor's store didn't begin to do justice to what John was seeing. Boulders the size of buses jutted out of the water, with an occasional swell washing over them. The Devil's Sideboard, the size of a railroad boxcar, marked one side of the channel, while Barrick Island's cliff-face marked the other. The Devil's Oven, Kettle, and Skillet lay in a jumble at the mouth of the channel.

It seemed to John as though a titanic axe had chopped off the face of Barrick Island and tossed the rubble to one side, leaving only a narrow gap in between. He felt sorry for any unwary boat trying to pass through that treacherous maze at high tide. No wonder the dark humor in naming the place.

Alice May turned into the channel, with only a few yards to spare.

A line of rocks ran from the Devil's Kitchen to the tip of Hogback Island, a razorback of living rock thrust up out of the sea. A few scraggly trees and patches of grass clung desperately to the top of the island, their roots clawing for a foothold in the granite.

"Pretty rocky around here," John said, looking at the welter of rocks as they slid by the rail.

"Yup," the helmsman replied. After a long pause that led John to assume the conversation was over, the youth added, "Not bad once you know the channel, though. And so long as you to stay out of there." He nodded towards the Devil's Kitchen. "A lot of people get balled up real bad in there."

The old man stirred from his reverie. "You got that right, Jimmy." His surprisingly powerful bass voice made John jump.

"Must be hard on people who don't know the area," John said.

"They're the ones who usually get in trouble," Jimmy agreed.

The old man gave an almost imperceptible nod and his head started to droop back onto his chest.

The cliff angled to the right, forming the upper end of Barrick Cove. The island itself consisted of a hundred acres or so of rocky soil, covered by fir and spruce. Here and there patches of land had been cleared in an attempt to farm the marginal ground.

The village of Barrick Cove was a place in obvious decline. Fishing, lobstering, and hard-scrabble farming were getting less viable, and John could see the once prosperous houses falling into decay. A dozen houses and a small boatyard huddled around a shallow indentation in the shoreline. Most of the cove was framed by the space between Barrick and Hogback islands, a bit less than three-hundred yards wide at the upper end where the village sat and tapering down to a narrow tidal channel at the southern end where the islands nearly touched.

John looked down the length of the cove to the south, perhaps half a mile.

Anchored off a tiny inlet about two-hundred yards to the south of town lay a black-hulled boat that looked very much like *Abracadabra*. There was no way to read the name off her transom at this distance, of course, and John didn't dare show too much curiosity. Still...

"That boat been here long?" John said indicating the black sloop.

Jimmy peered down the harbor and shrugged. "I don't remember for sure, but I think it came in a couple of days ago. It wintered over here last year." He looked some more. "Whoever brought it in must have left, 'cause there's no skiff."

"You take any strangers over to the mainland?" the old man thundered helpfully, thereby saving John the need to ask.

"Not me," Jimmy replied, "but Junior or Willard could have."

In truth, John hadn't really expected to find *Abracadabra*, but it appeared that he had done just that. He'd have to call Riley. There probably wasn't any phone service here, which meant he'd have to wait until he got back to the mainland. Apparently, his attacker had gotten away, but just knowing where the boat was would give Riley a start at unraveling whatever was going on.

In any case, John wasn't about to waste the trip. "I've been told that Junior is a good builder. Is he pretty busy?"

"There was some war work, but things have been slow since then," Jimmy replied.

"He gets by." The words boomed forth from the lowered head.

John gave another start. The old man was a menace. Just when you thought he was unconscious, or worse, that great rumbling voice burst out like a thunderclap.

"Sure, he always gets by," Jimmy agreed, with a hint of

sarcasm.

They pulled up to a lopsided wooden dock.

"I'll be out here again in a couple of hours," Jimmy said. "Last trip of the day. You'll want to be here then, unless Junior can give you a ride, or you're planning to spend the night," Jimmy said.

"That's fine. I'm just going up to see him about getting a boat built," John said.

"Well, good. Grab that box and take up with you. Save me a trip."

Junior Barrick was a gaunt, stringy man who looked to be in his early seventies, with thinning gray hair and deep-set blue eyes.

The loquacious boatbuilder informed John that in addition to being a descendant of the notorious Thadeous Barrick, who acquired the island through a shady land deal in 1817, he was also the one and only, boatbuilder in Barrick Cove.

"I can build her all, from top to toe," Junior boasted, as he and his two assistants greeted John at the big, open doors of the work shed. After a tour of the yard, John had to admit that Junior's boast wasn't such a far-fetched claim.

There were great piles of lumber: spar-grade spruce, knot-free fir, oak, and cedar, all carefully stacked to dry. The collection of machinery was equally impressive: a large thickness planer, a monstrous bandsaw, a well equipped machine shop, and a small forge out back for making ironwork. Junior even had an old bathtub—much of its porcelain coating spalled off by the heat—set up on bricks in order to melt lead for pouring keels. The facilities would have turned Sam Barton green with envy. A wall in Junior's office was covered with snapshots of various boats he'd built over the years. All in all, Junior's shop lived up to its reputation.

"Being on an island, we have to be able to do more for ourselves," Junior explained. "It ain't so easy to go runnin' to the store. Show me some drawings and I'll give you a quote."

Perhaps, John thought, he'd found another potential builder for Hibbert's boat after all. He handed Junior a bulky manilla envelope containing a set of preliminary plans. "My address is on the front."

A subtle change came over Junior's face as he scanned the address. John tensed.

They were standing in the middle of the spacious boat shed, where his two assistants, a hulking, muscular man named Ted, and a smaller individual called Willard, were fitting a new plank to a lobster boat.

"I'll send you a quote in a few days, Mr. Wendell, but there's someone I want you to meet before you go."

Ted ambled over.

"I do have to catch the boat back."

"Don't worry about that," Junior replied. "Willard can run you back to the mainland later on."

Ted wrapped a paw around John's forearm.

"I knew we should have hid the damn boat until we got everything sorted out," Junior muttered.

"Gonna take some fancy sorting," Ted commented.

"I don't think we can let you go back to the mainland for a while," Junior said to John. "We don't want to bring you harm, but us folks have to make a living, and you've got us into an awful snarl."

"Let's just take a little walk," Ted added, tightening his grip on John's arm.

John glanced at Ted and tried to remember what the beefy petty officer had taught him years ago. Planting his leg behind Ted's knee, John ducked, turned, and threw his weight against the larger man. Caught by surprise, Ted fell backwards over John's leg. As it happened, John's bad leg wasn't up to the task and he fell himself, his full weight driving his other knee into Ted's unsuspecting midriff.

John had just scrambled clear of Ted's thrashing arms when he saw Willard swinging what looked like an oversized shillelagh at his head. John dropped to the floor as the club swished past his ear.

At this point Junior entered the fray. "That's my best slick, you damn fool!" he yelled at Willard.

With an agility that belied his years, Junior snatched the big two-handed chisel out of Willard's grasp.

John took advantage of the distraction and scuttled to the back of the shop.

He scolded himself for getting into this mess unprepared. It hadn't occurred to John that Junior would recognize his name, and might even be involved in the Commodore's murder and *Abracadabra's* disappearance. Mary had been right: last week's concussion must have dulled his thinking far more than he'd realized.

Sadly, he didn't have much time to brood over the situation because Ted's preoccupation with the effort of retching and inhaling at the same time was sure to pass soon, and he would come seeking revenge. Meanwhile, Willard had rearmed himself with a husky oak club, and Junior, having put his precious slick away, was clearly more dangerous than he appeared. Worst of all, there was no way out except through the front of the building.

At the same time, John felt a wild exhilaration, a release of the frustration that had consumed him since Yarmouth.

A large, cast iron wood stove stood in the back corner, its pipe running up to the roof. Beside it was a pile of stovewood, waiting in readiness for the fall.

Willard and his club advanced, apparently unconcerned about John and the woodpile. Willard wasn't too bright, John concluded as he picked up a piece of firewood and hurled it sidearm at the advancing figure. Two more pieces followed in quick succession.

Willard dropped his stick with a bellow of pain, and staggered back out of range.

Unfortunately, Ted was beginning to breathe again, albeit noisily. Worse, he was starting to get up—a very bad sign. John darted for the other side of the building. With the work boat between him and the two men, John had a clear run for the door.

But where was Junior?

John sprinted for the rectangle of light. He was almost in the clear when Junior made an appearance, stepping into John's path with a double-barreled shotgun in his hands.

Chapter 30

Barrick Cove, August 13

The faded wallpaper, battered wainscoting, and elegant fireplace told of a long-lost gentility. A pair of windows looked out on what had once been the back yard, where wisps of fog crept through the overgrown tangle of brush and pressed against the glass.

The furniture consisted of a horsehair sofa, whose mildewed scent filled the air, a small table, and the straight-backed chair John was tied to with lengths of pot warp. He shifted in an effort to ease the pain where the rope was cutting off the circulation to his hands and feet.

A feeble, low wattage bulb in a wall sconce alternately dimmed and brightened in response to the vagaries of Junior's generator. It was fully dark outside when he heard the bolt being drawn back from the door.

She was a large woman, and she carried the all-too-familiar shotgun in her right hand. A sleeveless cotton-print dress, covered by a stained apron, looked like scant protection against the cold dampness that was seeping into the room. She stood in the doorway to study her captive.

He noted the yellowed teeth and shrewd brown eyes staring at him. Mostly, he noted the shotgun, an ancient double-barreled 12-gauge. At least the external hammers weren't cocked. It would take her a few extra seconds to pull them back and blow him to bits.

"What are you doing here?" Her voice had the husky undertone of a life-long smoker.

"I'm a yacht designer, and I'm looking for someone who'd be interested in building a boat for my client. Look, I don't know what this is all about, but—"

The shotgun waved irritably. "You people give me the pip, coming in here with all your money and big schemes, making trouble for us. You came in here when they put the law on booze and wanted power boats to run the stuff. Easy money, and lots of it. And lots of trouble too. They were good, honest hard-working people in these parts 'til the likes of you came around. We were just pullin' out of it, getting back to an honest living, and now you come in again with more of your crooked ideas."

John remained silent. In a way, perhaps she was right, and he had brought trouble to this place—though it had brought trouble to him in the bargain.

She stepped back. "Are you the one who did in Commodore Cummings? I bet you know more than you want to say."

"I don't know much of anything, and that's why I came here, to find out who killed him."

She eyed him suspiciously. "Are you the law?" The shotgun's muzzle twitched.

"No, I'm just a friend who is trying to find out what happened."

"A friend?" She paused, as though deciding whether to believe him. "I thought he was all right, but I don't care for his wife much."

"Dianne has been up here, too?"

The woman scowled. "Thinks she's too good for the likes of us. Didn't like that we don't have any telephone, or electricity either, except when Junior runs the light plant down at the shop."

It sounded as though Dianne had left, if she'd been here at all. What would keep her here anyway, especially if she didn't like the place? John nodded sympathetically in hopes she would tell him more. His shoulders were beginning to cramp from having his arms tied behind him.

"We don't hold with killing people, not even strangers," she went on, "but you got yourself into a big snarl by coming here."

"And yet here I am," John said, tugging at the pot warp.

The woman looked at him appraisingly. "I'm thinking that what you know is going to get you killed for sure." She heaved a wheezy sigh. "And if we don't do you in, someone else will."

"I told you, I don't know anything." John worked his shoulders, trying to ease the cramps.

"So you say," she muttered half to herself. "Doesn't matter, anyhow. You're still big trouble for us just being here."

She stared at him, thinking, for what seemed like a long time. Finally she said, "You won't be here long the way them fools tied you up." She propped the shotgun against the sofa, stepped behind John, and fiddled with the knots. He could feel them loosening, along with the pain of pins and needles as blood began returning to his hands. "There, that should keep you."

She stepped back. "A smart fella could've undone the knots them fools tied, and snuck out the window behind you in a flash." She picked up the shotgun. "A smart fella could've climbed down the pitch out back to the creek at the bottom, and followed it 'til he came to the water. He could have found the skiff that's tied up there, and he could've taken it and rowed down the south channel." She shrugged. "If he'd been able to get loose. Which he would the way them fools tied those knots."

She paused and eyed him dubiously. "You know which is south? It's the other channel from the one you came in."

John nodded.

"It's about half-tide, so there's enough water for the skiff if you watch out for rocks. Stay close to the island 'til you get to the end then row cross-wind to the mainland. Don't go into Payton. Head down-coast about three miles to Wilke's Cove. The railway line runs through town. If you don't get lazy you can make the morning train."

She took the end of a loaf of bread out of the pocket of her apron and tossed it onto the table, where it clattered stalely on the scarred surface. "In case you get loose and are hungry."

"Thank you." John said. "Are you going to get into trouble for this?"

She laughed, a mixture of incredulity and scorn on her face. "Nobody messes with me. Besides, they're the ones tied you up with them loose knots." With those words of wisdom, she left the room and closed the door.

It only took John a few minutes to free himself and turn to the window. Being worn and loose, it opened easily. The window had no sash weights, but the inevitable stick lay on the sill. He used it as a prop.

John clambered out the window and into a wall of white where the visibility wasn't more than a yard or two. The dampness was suffocating, and the circulation returning to his hands and feet made him unsteady.

The pitch, when it came, was more like a cliff and John barely avoided falling over it. A trickle of a brook lay at the bottom, and he followed it until the narrow cut finally widened out to tidal mud. This, he realized, must be the head of the little inlet where *Abracadabra* was moored. A small dock, nothing more than a plank and a row of stakes, loomed out of the fog. John hurried forward.

There was no skiff to be found.

Now what? His absence would be discovered soon, and he was quite sure they could hunt him down on their own island. He followed the shore towards the mouth of the inlet, which he remembered as being no more than twenty feet wide where it opened into the harbor. If the fog was thick enough, he might be able to swim out to *Abracadabra* and sail her out of the harbor without being seen. He could hear the low rumble of Junior's generating plant coming from the boat shed. With luck, the noise would cover any sound he might make while raising *Abracadabra's* sail.

The difficulty lay in the fact that the south channel was too shallow for *Abracadabra*. He'd have to go out the way *Alice May* came in, pass directly in front of the dock, and hope the fog would hide him. Even then, navigating that narrow, rock infested channel at night in the fog was an almost impossible task. Could he swim the mile or so to the mainland? No, he'd never get that far in this cold water. He could look for another skiff, but where? In any case, he had to get off the island. And soon.

John tried to remember the scene as it had appeared that afternoon. If this was *Abracadabra's* inlet, then she couldn't be far away.

John removed his clothes and wrapped them in his coat. The mud-caked shoes went on top. If he was right, *Abracadabra* would be directly in front of where he stood—not more than thirty feet or so. Only a short swim. If he was wrong, he could end up going around in circles, lost in the fog.

John waded through a muddy, slippery world that barely existed beyond his outstretched hand. At last the ooze turned into ledge.

He sensed, rather than saw, the opening. There was a feeling of space, a breath of wind, and the murmur of voices in the distance. He caught himself just in time as the ledge in front of him dropped away to deep water.

He eased into the icy water, holding the bundle of clothes overhead. The ledge dropped from under his feet and he nearly fell before pushing off.

The fog engulfed him. With the shore gone, he couldn't be sure if he was going in the right direction, or even in a straight line. The breeze and the voices were nowhere to be found with his head at water level, and he had only the fog's suffocating isolation—along with the growing cold. John counted strokes as he paddled awkwardly trying to estimate distance while also trying to keep his clothes above water.

He couldn't find the boat.

He wasn't entirely sure he could find the shore again, either. None too warm when he entered the water, John's legs were getting numb, and the bundle of clothing was getting heavier by the second. *Abracadabra* was toying with him, luring him on, always just beyond reach, waiting patiently for him to drown.

The boat's black hull gave her away in the end—a faint smudge of darkness showing at the corner of his vision.

Fortunately, *Abracadabra* was built low to the water and John managed to climb aboard fairly easily, with only a couple of scratches on his left leg. The fog seemed marginally thinner as he stood in the tiny cockpit and he could feel the breeze again, chilling his skin as he got dressed. He could see a faint glow of light through the fog—probably from the open boatshop doors. The sound of voices and the rumble of Junior's light plant were strangely comforting after the oppressive isolation of the water.

The cabin hatch was closed, but the wash boards had been removed, leaving an opening through which John was able to stick his head. He felt along the bulkhead to where he remembered a coat-hook being located, usually with the Commodore's coat on it. There was no coat.

He turned his attention to the problem of raising the sail without making too much noise. A few tentative tugs on the lines cleated to the cabin top didn't produce any loud squeaking, and he was soon raising the mainsail. He knew from experience that *Abracadabra* would sail well enough without the jib, and he dared not risk raising it as well. He took a long time, dreading each creak and rattle as the sail went up.

Finally, he dropped the anchor line, and a light wind pushed *Abracadabra* noiselessly through the fog. Unless he had misjudged the wind direction, Hog Island's rocky shore was less than two-hundred yards ahead. He would sail as close as he dared to the island and follow it up to the channel. The problem was to find the island before running into it. John scoured his brain trying to remember the details of the trip in. Were there rocks along this part of Hog Island? A glow of light from Junior's shop was all he had for reference, but how far away was it? He needed to get close to Hog Island before turning towards the channel. The light was abeam now. If only the fog would lift enough to see where he was.

Perhaps *Abracadabra* betrayed him, or perhaps some malevolent force had read his mind, because at that moment an errant wind shift, picking up drier air from aloft, split the curtain of fog and lay Barrick Cove bare in the moonlight.

John had misjudged the wind direction. *Abracadabra* wasn't

approaching Hog Island, but was practically in the middle of the harbor, almost directly opposite, and perilously close to the dock, where Junior and two other men were sitting—probably discussing their visitor's fate. The wind shift that lifted the fog also caught *Abracadabra*'s sail aback. The boom swung in, then whipped out again with a crash as she announced her presence for all to see.

Chapter 31

Barrick Cove, August 13

Faces stared out from the dock, mirroring John's surprise and consternation. The fog descended as quickly as it had lifted, muffling angry shouts and tramping feet. There had been three workboats; one tied up at the dock and two others moored close by. How long would it take them to cast off and cover the hundred yards to where he lay?

At least he'd seen where Hog Island was before the fog closed in again. John changed course, turning away from the island and closer to the dock. They'd probably expect him to head away from them, in which case they might go right by in their rush across the harbor. With luck, he might skirt the shore of Barrick Island until he came to the cliff edge marking the north end of the harbor and follow it to the opening of the channel.

The amount of yelling and splashing suggested that all three boats were going to join the hunt. John could hear the growl of starters as *Abracadabra* gathered way on her new course.

An engine came to life with a roar that sounded right alongside. He resisted the temptation to steer away from the noise, knowing he had only the wind to guide him.

The sound came closer and closer—a mechanical banshee

howl that seemed to be only a few feet away. John stared into the gray wall surrounding him, waiting for the first glimpse of a knife-edge bow slicing out of the fog and into *Abracadabra's* side. Instead, the noise shifted suddenly astern and a wave swept under him. He listened in horror as the wake shook the sail and rigging with a loud clatter. Would they hear *Abracadabra's* cries over the roar of their engine?

The first boat continued on as the second and third opened their throttles.

There was a faint sound up ahead—the whisper of an echo reflecting the cacophony of engines. John peered over the bow, where somewhere very near, a wall of spruce-clad granite awaited. It appeared with a shocking swiftness only feet from *Abracadabra's* bow. He pushed the tiller over and the boat responded eagerly. Swinging parallel to the shore, John stayed just close enough to see a faint smudge of the shoreline through the fog.

Soon, that shoreline would lead him to the clutter of boulders making up the channel, and the Devil's Kitchen. At that point he'd have to turn back into the fog, where he would need a miracle to find his way through the channel to open water.

His pursuers were now almost directly upwind and John could hear them clearly and see the dim glow of spotlights as they yelled to each other over the roar of their engines. Deceptive as the sounds were, he was certain that the hunt was centered near Hog Island, across from the dock.

It wouldn't be long, though, before the search moved to the channel he was groping towards.

He took a last look at the smudge of shoreline, hauled in the sail and aimed for a spot in the fog where the center of the channel should be. John counted off the seconds to himself to estimate his progress. He was now moving towards his pursuers and they towards him. It was not a comfortable feeling.

A sudden crash and series of oaths came over the water, suggesting one of his pursuers had found Hog island the hard way. It was reassuring to know that Junior's friends weren't immune to rocks. As he listened, John realized that the closer boat's engine was gradually shifting to the left. One of the hunters must be close to the tip of Hog island and turning into the channel. If they were skirting the shoreline to avoid running aground, then *Abracadabra* must be near the Devil's Sideboard. John mentally crossed his fingers and swung the tiller to enter what he hoped was the channel.

One of the hunters was passing through the channel and moving ahead of him, and its wake rolled under *Abracadabra's* keel as it passed, bringing a sigh of relief from John. The wake meant the Devil's Kitchen wasn't between him and them, so he must still be in the channel. He tried to hear the lapping of water against granite, but the engine noise was too loud.

Suddenly, John realized the wake rocking *Abracadabra* had stopped. Something stood between him and his pursuer. He must be out of the channel and into the rocks of the Devil's Kitchen. John frantically pushed the tiller, trying to reverse direction, but it was too late. *Abracadabra* struck with a resounding crash that nearly drove the bow under water and shook the mast like a soda straw.

There was instant silence as the hunters shut down their engines to listen.

"He's in the Kitchen!"

"Get the sonofabitch!"

The engines started up again, more cautiously now as they closed in for the kill.

John jumped onto the stern in hopes of rocking free of the

rocks. Incredibly, *Abracadabra* responded, spinning on her heels. He ignored his instinct to flee and headed towards the oncoming engines. If he was right, the Devil's Sideboard must now lie between him and the oncoming boats. If he could find the strip of granite, he might be able to follow it out on the Devil's Kitchen side while they followed it on the channel side. If there was enough water on this side—and if they didn't decide to follow him in here.

There were lots of if's, but few choices.

The tide was higher than when he'd come in, and the Devil's Sideboard was now so low and black as to be almost invisible. *Abracadabra* grazed the slick granite as her bow swung around. John followed the low shadow, keeping just close enough to see it, yet far enough away to remain, he hoped, unseen by the boats that were moving back and forth, apparently thinking that he was still impaled on a rock. Behind him, the questing searchlights swept back and forth, vainly trying to pierce the murk. The sounds gradually faded and finally the Devil's Kitchen disappeared astern.

He was free of the channel, with nothing but the Atlantic Ocean ahead.

But where to go? The woman had warned him not to go back to Payton Harbor, and even if it was safe to land at one of the neighboring harbors, it was doubtful that he could get there before one of Junior's boats arrived to head him off. In any case, John was in no mood to revisit that rock-infested coastline in the fog and dark.

The best solution was to sail directly out to sea. If the wind held through the night, *Abracadabra* would be well into the Gulf of Maine by the time the fog lifted in the morning. There would be time in the daylight to see what provisions might be on board and decide where to go next.

Having settled on a plan of action, John made himself as comfortable as possible. Comfort was a relative term, since the cockpit wasn't much bigger than an oversized bathtub—a similarity that was enhanced by the presence of a drain at the forward end. The only thing needed to complete the picture was a pair of faucets and perhaps a shower head.

Turn-of-the-century yachtsmen were a hardy lot, and one was expected to sit on the floor, seats being an optional luxury in such a small boat. As a result, John was reduced to propping his feet against one side of the cockpit, and leaning his back against the opposite corner. He tied the end of the main sheet to the tiller and looped it around a cleat behind him. A minor adjustment or two on the line and *Abracadabra* settled onto her course. With the wind broad on her beam and *Abracadabra's* sail stretched out like the wing of some gigantic raven, she sailed herself, rolling along in the gentle swell.

The questing growl of boat engines was barely audible astern.

Once he was satisfied that the boat would sail herself indefinitely and the danger was past, John realized how hungry and tired he was. He dragged the bread out of his coat pocket, broke off chunks of the water-soaked loaf, and ate them greedily.

Finally, he settled back and closed his eyes.

John hadn't slept well the last few nights, and the gentle motion of the boat soon had him fading off to sleep. Tomorrow, after all, was another day and he would need his rest.

Perhaps it was wishful thinking, but John dreamed of luxuriating in a hot, steamy bathtub. Faucets spewed water, constantly filling the tub to a deliciously scalding temperature.

Even in his dream, John realized that he'd uncovered

Abracadabra's secret.

Meanwhile, two eyes watched his nodding head from the blackness of the cabin. There would be a time of reckoning in the morning.

Chapter 32

Payton Harbor, August 13

John was still navigating the perils of the Devil's Kitchen when Paul Thibedeau parked his state police cruiser next to the battered Model A Ford with Massachusetts plates. "Well, well," he said to himself, "long way from home." Thibedeau got out, peered into the Ford and touched the radiator, determining that the vehicle had been there for a while. He kept a hand near his revolver as he entered Payton Harbor's general store.

It didn't pay to take chances with a hardened criminal.

"Know who belongs to that old heap outside?"

"Sure do." The proprietor rubbed the glistening top of his head as an aid to memory refreshment. "Young feller was in this afternoon. Went out to Barrick."

"He still out there?"

"He didn't come back with Jimmy, and I don't imagine Junior's likely to bring him in before morning, what with this fog." The proprietor leaned over the counter in eager anticipation. A stranger being pursued by the cops was always a welcome diversion. Especially a stranger from Massachusetts. "You want him for something?"

"Not me, but the Massachusetts police are looking for him. Something about a murder. They think he may be dangerous."

"You don't say?" The proprietor rubbed his head again. "You're not planning on going out there tonight in this pea soup, are you?"

"Hell no."

"Good, 'cause I doubt if you'd be able to get anybody to take you out, anyhow."

Thibedeau shrugged. "Catching this guy isn't my lookout. I'm just going to call the Massachusetts police and let them worry about it."

"Junior's got a shortwave rig on the island if you want to talk to him." The shopkeeper turned on the war surplus radio, and glanced at the wall clock. "We'd better call him pretty quick, though, 'cause he shuts down the power plant out there around ten o'clock."

"I don't think we need to—"

"You said this guy might be dangerous and the shortwave will be all warmed up in a second," the shopkeeper said helpfully. "Can't hurt to let them know about that feller, just in case he goes berserk with a hatchet, or something."

A woman's voice responded quickly to the shopkeeper's call. "Gladys, this is Fred at the store. The state police are here, looking for that out-of-state string bean Jimmy took out this afternoon. He still out there? It turns out he's wanted for murder, or something, down to Massachusetts, over."

Thibedeau's fingers twitched hungrily at the microphone, but the shopkeeper wasn't about to let go of it.

"Not any more, he ain't," Gladys replied. "The crazy sonofabitch stole a sailboat right out of the harbor and took off. Junior and a couple of others are out looking for him now, over." Her voice, tinny over the speaker, sounded scornful.

"He stole a sailboat in this fog?" Thibedeau said.

"In this fog?" the shopkeeper echoed into the ether,

thinking about the rocky gauntlet guarding the island. "How big a boat was it, over?"

"About 26 feet. Junior's had it in before. Anyhow, I figure the fool's bound to run up on a rock pretty quick, over."

"Guess I'd better call it in and see what they want to do down in Massachusetts," Thibedeau said, "though I imagine they'll have to wait until tomorrow."

Chapter 33

Gulf of Maine, August 14

John had slept with his head on his chest and as a result he woke up with a sore neck. The welcome smell of coffee greeted his nostrils. Sadly, he was also greeted by the unwelcome sight of Dianne Cummings, who was sitting on the end of a berth with the after end of the hatch coaming coming up to her waist as she leaned out of the opening. He should have known she'd be here.

Still worse, Dianne held a .38 caliber revolver in her hand. "Good morning, dear," she said with a smile. "No need to get up. I made some coffee for us to drink while we talk."

A small, one-burner alcohol camp stove hung from a gimbal just inside the cabin hatch, and a steaming, two-cup coffee pot sat on it. Dianne filled a pair of enamel mugs and slid one towards John.

"I suppose you've been hiding in the cabin all night," John said. "The sun is coming up, and it looks like a nice day; why don't you come out and join me in the cockpit?" In fact, the fog had lifted overnight and the sun was shining in his eyes, making it hard to see Dianne's face clearly. He smiled invitingly.

"Nice try," she replied. "But I wouldn't trust having you that close. I must say I never dreamed that you'd be able to get out of there in the fog. I was scared to death when you ran onto that rock."

"You were scared? Why? Why didn't you raise the alarm when I climbed on board?"

"It's a long story, but I'm glad you escaped. For once you did something helpful, even if you didn't mean to." She studied John, her eyes wide and her head cocked to one side like a cat eyeing a mouse. A well-armed cat. "What are we going to do with you though? You've been nothing but a headache since you turned up in Yarmouth. Is it safe to have you on board the boat?"

"Why not? After all, we both escaped from those people." Dianne, sitting at the opening to the cabin, was only six feet away, and John thought about making a grab for the pistol, but she looked too competent with it. And much too alert. Besides, his muscles were stiff. Had he really slept all night jammed in this corner? He must have been a lot more tired than he'd realized.

"Where were you planning to go?" she asked.

"Out to sea, anywhere away from Barrick Cove, then down the coast, maybe to Camden."

"I can't even see the land now," she said.

John glanced over his shoulder and realized she was right. *Abracadabra* had covered a good distance overnight.

"We could steal away to Nova Scotia," Dianne mused.

"But you just left Nova Scotia."

"You're right, and thanks to your meddling, I'll have to wait a few more days for the police to calm down before it will be safe to go back." She scowled. "You were supposed to be dead. How did you get away?"

"Your associates in Yarmouth weren't very competent." John took a sip of the coffee. It tasted awful, but at least it was wet, and he was parched. "Do you have anything to eat down there?"

"That rat, Junior Barrick, has kept me bottled up on the damn boat in his godawful harbor for three days. I finished the last of the food yesterday. The man was trying to starve me out."

"So that's why there was no skiff. He wouldn't let you go ashore."

"I wouldn't trust him enough to go ashore."

John was beginning to understand her dilemma. Dianne and Junior needed each other, even though the need was based on mutual distrust. "How about some sugar, then?" He leaned forward, holding out the mug.

"Sit back where you were," Dianne commanded as she slid a small Mason jar of sugar across the cockpit. Dianne was clearly too wary to let him get close. "You've caused a lot of trouble," she said, "and you'll have to be dealt with, even if you did get us out of Junior's clutches last night." She spoke like a school teacher dealing with a difficult pupil.

"Why don't you trust Junior?" The longer he kept Dianne talking, the better his chances of catching her unawares, and the longer he'd stay alive.

"He's a double-crossing snake," she groused.

Pieces of the puzzle were starting to fall into place. "But a necessary snake," he said. The sugar wasn't exactly a meal, but it was better than nothing. He added a generous helping to his mug.

"I wonder how much you know," Dianne said pensively. "How did you figure it out?"

Keep her talking, John said to himself. "At first I thought Lieutenant Riley was right and Sam Barton was behind all this—up to his old smuggling tricks," he said. "He had a lot of connections in Canada during prohibition, and when the boat turned up in Yarmouth, it seemed to make sense. But then I saw Junior's bathtub, and realized it had to be him and not Sam."

"And that's all it took?"

"Not quite. The fact that Junior recognized my name on the plans meant he was probably involved in what you were up to."

John took another swallow of coffee. Not even the extra sugar got rid of the bad taste. Frowning, he put the mug down. "It would be easy for Junior to put a few gold bars into the mold while he was pouring a new keel."

Dianne's eyes narrowed.

John went on. "Since private citizens aren't allowed to own gold, except for jewelry, you must have been sneaking it out of the jewelry company a little bit at a time, right under the federal inspectors' noses."

Dianne smiled. "A little bit every day is easy for a company our size, and before you know it, a couple of years, there you are."

"I suppose the plan was for the Commodore to sail *Abracadabra* up to Junior's yard, and you'd follow in your Cadillac filled with the gold. Then Junior would poor a new keel with the gold bars in it. Then you'd sail to Nova Scotia—"

"The customs officials there are less strict about checking for smuggled gold, so the plan was to load the boat onto a steamer as deck cargo to France," Dianne said, clearly proud of their scheme.

"But then the Commodore was killed, which must have put a crimp in your plan."

Dianne's cheeks flushed with rage. "Mike Hartwell is a double-crossing rat," she hissed. "He will pay for his treachery."

"He already has," John commented.

"What do you mean?"

"You wouldn't know about it, but Mike was murdered while you were sailing around the Gulf of Maine. It looks like there's more than one double-crossing rat out there."

Dianne digested this news for a moment, and then shrugged. "A minor inconvenience in the end." She waved the gun at John. "You, on the other hand, have been a pest for the last time."

"How much gold are we talking about?" John said, hoping to deflect her mind from him.

"There's over a thousand pounds of gold underneath us," she boasted. "Fifteen thousand Troy ounces. Do you know what that's worth?" Dianne's cheeks were flushed.

"At thirty-five dollars an ounce, that would be over $500,000." John was staggered by the sum.

"Thirty-five dollars an ounce is the legal price in this country," she crowed. "Our contact in France can get three times that much on the European black market."

"We? Who else is in on this besides you, the Commodore, and Junior?"

Dianne ignored the question. "You may not know everything, but you still know too much."

"I'm harmless. You should be more worried about what Lieutenant Riley knows, not to mention whoever else is trying to double-cross you."

"Enough of this talk. Unfortunately, it's too soon to go back to Nova Scotia, but there are lots of little coves along the Maine coast where nobody will notice the boat for a few days. I can look at the charts for a good spot." She nodded to herself. "Yes, we'll have to turn around."

John didn't give her time to think about things. "Okay, Maine it is. Jibe-ho!" he said, pushing the tiller hard over.

With her short keel and big rudder, *Abracadabra* was quick on her feet, and she spun on her heels with dizzying speed.

"Not so fast—" Dianne began, but too many things were happening too quickly for her to keep up. The boom scythed across the cockpit, forcing her to duck, while the sun suddenly shone full in her eyes as the boat swung around, and John threw the mug of scalding coffee in her face.

He leaped for Dianne's gun-arm, but his bad leg had been cramped all night and it refused to respond quickly enough. The gun went off, and the bullet plowed a furrow across his upper arm as Dianne fell back into the cabin, knocking over the camp stove in the process. The gun went off again as they struggled, with John half in the cabin and half in the cockpit. Meanwhile, alcohol from the upset stove spread a flaming puddle across Dianne's sleeping bag. Suddenly, the gun went off a third time as John fought to wrench it out of her hand. Her head jerked and she became still.

John dragged her limp body into the cockpit, and snatched a pair of life preservers and a small saucepan out of the rapidly spreading flames.

The bullet had entered under Dianne's chin and left a jagged wound on the top of her head.

There was no question about her being dead.

Oblivious to his wounded arm, he sat back, hypnotized by the flames leaping at him from the cabin, frozen by memories of fire and death, the cries of men trapped in the flames.

There was a dull thud, and a ball of fire erupted as a gallon can of stove alcohol went up, sending a column of fire and smoke out of the companionway.

This was way beyond the capabilities of a saucepan, and John slid in the washboards and closed the hatch to seal off and slow the fire.

Abracadabra was old, and the flames hungrily devoured the many layers of paint and varnish in the cabin. A pillar of oily black smoke rose into the sky as the dying boat labored towards shore.

It would only be a matter of time before the flames ate through the hull and deck, sending *Abracadabra* to the bottom. How close to shore could he nurse the doomed boat before she sank? Would gasses trapped in the cabin explode? Which was worse, burning to death, or drowning in the water?

What was it Henry had said about people having three lives? This was the second time he'd faced death by fire. Would there be a third?

John put on one of the life preservers and strapped the other one around Dianne. She looked very dead, but he couldn't bring himself to let her go down with the boat. Only then did he notice the blood dripping from his sleeve and the pain in his arm. He tore off the sleeve of Dianne's shirt, and used his teeth and good hand to tie a serviceable bandage over his shirtsleeve.

The bandage might not be much, but John figured it would do until the Navy Corpsmen arrived.

Paint on the foredeck was blistering from the heat, and steam was hissing from the planking at the bow. *Abracadabra* was slowly sinking as the fire ate through the hull, making it a race between burning to death and drowning, and the finish line was drawing near.

* * *

A glint of light on the horizon caught John's attention—a Japanese torpedo bomber, looking for a target. Soon, the Kate skimmed by just above the waves, low enough for John to see the pilot staring at him as the plane roared past.

Except suddenly it wasn't a Kate at all. Not even close. It was a PBY Catalina flying boat, looking for the *Dunn's* survivors, circling to check the wave conditions before landing. The great, whale-like hull, suspended beneath the wing with its twin engines, made for an ungainly looking aircraft, well-suited to its "Goony Bird" nickname.

Abracadabra was barely afloat now, with water nearly up to the rail. The fire had burned through the foredeck, and was licking at the mast and sail.

The PBY landed and taxied over to *Abracadabra*. As the plane swung around, its prop blast caught what was left of *Abracadabra*'s sail and heeled her rail under.

With a sudden rush, the boat vanished like a magician's closing trick, leaving John to splutter in the icy water.

"Grab my hand," the bosun said, reaching into the oil-slicked waves. But it was Riley's hand that John grabbed and Riley who pulled him aboard the rubber dinghy. And the PBY wasn't really a Navy Catalina, but a Coast Guard PBM Mariner.

The world spun for a panic-filled moment as John struggled to snatch reality from the kaleidoscope of images, real and imagined.

"Is that Dianne?" Riley asked, nodding at the corpse.

John looked at the body floating in its war-surplus Mae West. His empty stomach was churning. It should be Dianne. It must be Dianne, or else he was losing his mind, and was somewhere else an ocean away and a lifetime ago.

"She's dead," John said.

Riley sighed. "You're really racking them up, Wendell."

"She's the only one I've killed, and it was self-defense." He was quite sure that was true.

The dinghy's bobbing was churning John's empty stomach.

"You look like hell," Riley said

"Get me out of this damn raft and onto the plane. I didn't realize it at first, but Dianne must have put something in the coffee, because you looked like a Japanese torpedo plane for a while."

"A Japanese what?"

"How did you find me?"

"Lucky thing you set fire to the boat, so we could spot the smoke. Even luckier thing, your loving spouse found the murder weapon—your wrench, by the way—in her flower bed, and turned you in for killing Mike Hartwell. We put out an APB the day before yesterday, and the Maine state police spotted your car last night."

"My wrench?"

"Remind me never to get on the wrong side of your wife."

John looked at the bits of *Abracadabra* that hadn't sunk as they floated on the waves. "How deep is the water here?" he asked the Coastguard bosun's mate, who was paddling the raft.

"Three-hundred feet, maybe more," was the reply. "It drops off fast out here."

"How hard would it be to go down and get the boat?" Riley inquired.

"Pretty damn hard," the bosun's mate replied. "The Brits dove on a ship at about 500-feet last year, and that was a record, but it was a full-sized ship and they knew right where it was. Trouble is, here you're talking about finding a little wooden sailboat that's burned half to hell."

"There goes the only evidence we had," Riley grumbled, as he stared into the water.

"There goes half a ton of gold," John murmured.

Riley gave John a disgusted look. "You're the worst thing that's happened to my life in thirty years on the force."

Chapter 34

Gulf of Maine, August 14

The flying boat lumbered south towards its Coast Guard base in Salem, Massachusetts. John and Riley were seated in a tiny compartment behind the navigator's station, while Dianne's body lay in the sick bay, located below them in the spacious hull of the aircraft. His wounded arm bandaged, wearing dry clothes, and wrapped in a blanket, John had finally stopped shivering.

Riley eyed his would-be prisoner. "So, does this thing still look like a Japanese torpedo plane? Are you ready to tell me what really happened, or isn't the war over yet?"

"What is reality, Joe?" John replied, using Riley's given name for the first time. "Twenty minutes ago, I knew for a fact that this was a Japanese torpedo plane. Did that make it real?"

"You had a couple of screws loose twenty minutes ago."

"The trouble is that some people in Wissonet have their own reality, their own facts. And they know they're real."

Riley scowled. "I haven't spent God knows how many hours flying around in this thing—which is an even worse plane than it is a boat—just to get into some crazy philosophical discussion with you. I'm a cop, not an oriental guru. Reality is about facts, and I deal in facts; it's as simple as that."

John was disappointed, but not surprised, by Riley's scornful reaction. John was becoming convinced that there was more involved in the murders than just gold smuggling, and he doubted that Riley would ever fully unravel the mystery, or find the killer, while burdened with his present attitude.

Everybody has their own version of reality and will defend it above all others. John had thought about this a lot lately, and he knew that Mary and their relationship was his reality. It was her unflagging determination that dragged him from his post-war shadows into the light. Reality was her smile, the sound of her voice, the taste of her lips, the smell of her hair, the familiar shape of her body when they embraced.

But now the shadows were being pulled back out of their caves, destroying his reality. Henry's bucket, the firecrackers, Len's groceries, Edith's casserole, the planted wrench, and even Dianne's drugged coffee. Was he being paranoid, or were some of the acts intentional, an effort to undermine his credibility, or his confidence in his own sanity?

How could he explain it all in a way that Riley could grasp when he didn't understand it himself?

In end, John didn't try, sticking to the facts as he knew them. Even so, it took him almost an hour to tell what had happened, starting from the time he arrived in Barrick Cove.

"So Dianne Cummings thought Mike Hartwell had killed her husband?" Riley said when John was finished.

"All I can say is she called him a double-crossing rat, and didn't know he was dead. The trouble is that I don't see why Mike would kill the Commodore, and if he did, surely he could come up with a better alibi than engine trouble."

Having no answers, they surrendered themselves to the roar of the two big, Wright Cyclone engines just over their heads.

"How am I going to get my car back?" John asked Riley

after a while.

"The only reason you're getting it back at all is because I persuaded them that piece of junk is a crime scene."

"A crime scene?"

"Damn right. I told them it contains evidence that we need in our investigation."

"What evidence?"

"The murder weapon was in there, and who knows what else we might find. Anyway, the Maine police loaded your car on a flat-bed truck last night, headed for Salem. With any luck, it'll be waiting for you when we get there."

"Wouldn't it have been simpler to put me ashore in Maine so I could drive it home myself?"

Riley looked at John incredulously. "Do you have any idea how much trouble you're in with the Maine state police? It's a good thing you were in international waters when you blew that poor woman's brains out. You set foot in Maine and we'll be in the middle of a jurisdictional hassle for weeks."

"Am I under arrest, then?"

Riley favored John with another of his patented scowls. "For your information, I was up most of last night persuading the Coast Guard to send out a plane to look for you, not to mention letting me ride along. It wasn't easy to convince them that you're a criminal mastermind, either. You're damn lucky that I'm such an easygoing guy, seeing as how you don't even remember whether you or the emperor of Japan killed Hartwell."

"Are my fingerprints on the wrench?"

"That's a problem. In her attempt to frame you for the murder, your loving wife was kind enough to give me a drinking glass with your prints on it, and they match a partial print on the jaws of the wrench. Unfortunately, the killer seems to have wiped the handle clean."

Riley shrugged. "I gather your next door neighbor borrowed the wrench, too. If he'd killed Hartwell, he might have wiped off his prints before dropping it in your flower bed for you to pick up.

"The question is, if you had killed Hartwell in some kind of trance, would you have bothered to wipe the handle clean before dropping it in your own flower bed? Much as I hate to say it, there are still too many unanswered questions for me to arrest you."

"I didn't know that gold smuggling was such a big thing," John said, in a effort to distract his companion.

Riley shook his head. "I should have known you'd figure it out."

"It wasn't hard, once I spotted Junior's bathtub."

Riley rubbed his forehead as though in pain. "Do I really have to ask about Junior Barrick's bathing habits?"

"It's the bathtub he uses to melt lead when he's pouring a keel."

"The guy melts lead in his bathtub? You're a great source of weird information, Wendell."

"What about the gold smuggling business?" John persisted.

Riley couldn't resist the chance to educate his companion, suspect or not. "The customs service estimates that some fifty million dollars worth of gold was smuggled out of the country last year. So long as most of the gold in the world is in this country, and the government keeps the price fixed at $35 an ounce, people are going to smuggle it out, especially where there's such a big demand in the rest of the world. Actually, the half-ton of gold you just sank isn't all that much."

"But how do people get it out of the country?" John inquired.

"I'm not sure it's a good idea to be giving you pointers, but you did tell me about Junior's bathtub, so what the hell. A lot of it goes out in cars. People load the gas tank with gold bars, hide them in the upholstery, glue sheets of gold inside the bodywork, all kinds of places. Sometimes they have to put on heavy-duty springs to carry the extra weight.

"Once the gold is hidden in it, you have the car shipped overseas—France is a popular spot. The thing is, the customs people are getting a lot more thorough about checking cars leaving the country. That's why this boat business is so smart."

"I suppose the government suspected the Commodore's murder was about gold smuggling from the start."

Riley shrugged. "Dianne Cummings was right. Jewelry manufacturing takes a lot of gold, so it isn't hard to siphon some off: fudge the books, or maybe add a few impurities to the jewelry to cut down on the purity. And it's not hard to buy up used jewelry, melt it down, and under-report the gold content."

"What about the men who tried to kill me in Yarmouth?"

"Your friend, Inspector Walters, has been busy up in Nova Scotia. He asked around, and discovered the boat was headed to a yacht broker by the name of Lester Harkness outside Yarmouth. Apparently Harkness exports boats to Europe—"

"Harkness? That's—"

"Dianne's brother."

"I did hear that the Commodore was planning to sell *Abracadabra*," John said.

"He was going to sell it all right, keel and all. "There's a demand for pleasure boats over there, with the war over, so Harkness crates up boats and has them shipped as deck cargo. customs inspectors aren't as strict in Canada about gold smuggling as they are in this country, and who's going to melt down a boat's keel to check for gold?

"The only trouble with their scheme was that it had too many moving parts, too many people getting a cut, too many chances for a double-cross. The gold may be worth millions in Europe, but the money gets divided up at least three ways, not counting any accomplice they probably had working inside Cummings Jewelry."

"Mildred Leary is in charge of procurement," John suggested.

"Do I tell you how to design boats?" Riley demanded.

"Dianne did accuse Junior of being greedy."

"He probably got unhappy when Dianne brought the boat back without his cut," Riley said. "Maybe he demanded more money."

"Why don't you arrest Junior and ask him?"

"Arrest him for what? For having a bathtub? Thanks to you, we don't have any evidence on him, or Harkness. They're a pair of choir boys to hear them talk—don't know anything about anything. All Junior will say is that you and Dianne stole the boat out of the harbor."

"You know a lot about gold smuggling, Lieutenant," John commented. "I'm guessing that it's one of your specialties, and that's why someone with your seniority was assigned to this case. The Commodore's murder must have been just the chance you needed to really dig into their shenanigans."

"We've been keeping an eye on Cummings Jewelry for a couple of years. They have to submit a requisition to the government for every shipment of gold they want to buy from the mint, and the amount they were asking for seemed to be little high. I figured they might be planning to sneak a car-load of gold out of the country in their Caddy, but not a whole boatload."

"Okay, now it's your turn," Riley said. "You're a boat

expert: how would you hide half-a-ton of gold in the boat's keel?"

"I've been thinking about that, and it would be tricky. Gold is a lot heavier than lead—"

"1200 pounds per cubic foot," Riley said.

"You're the gold expert. Anyway, lead is only 700 pounds per cubic foot, so you couldn't just drop a bunch of gold bars into the mold while you were pouring the keel—it would end up being much too heavy. You'd have to add something lighter than lead to make it come out right."

"Like what?"

"Maybe sash weights. Cast iron only weighs about 450 pounds per cubic foot. Fortunately, lead melts at a much lower temperature than gold or cast iron, so they can be recovered pretty easily later."

"You know a lot about this stuff."

"Yacht designers have to know how much things weigh."

Riley looked at John speculatively. "Be easy for a yacht designer like you to figure out how many sash weights it would take."

John wondered if his companion was serious. "I've heard rumors that Cummings Jewelry wasn't doing well."

"Stop spending so much time thinking about *my* case." Riley leaned forward in his seat. "I want to keep a lid on this for a while, until we can finish sorting things out. As far as the public is concerned, Dianne and the boat were lost at sea. As far as the public is concerned, you had nothing to do with the smuggling or Dianne's death."

"I certainly won't say anything," John said, relieved to think his reputation wouldn't take yet another hit in Wissonet. At least not right away.

"I'm still wondering about the timing on all this," Riley said.

"Timing?"

"We know the boat was stolen from Carver Creek on Wednesday evening, and you found the boat in Yarmouth on Sunday evening. What happened in the four days between?"

"I've been thinking about that, too."

"Of course you have," Riley said dryly.

John went on, undeterred. "I've looked at the charts, and it's about two-hundred-and-fifty miles from Carver Creek to Yarmouth as the crow flies. The wind has been blowing out of the south for a week or more, which is fairly typical for this time of year, so *Abracadabra* had a fair wind—"

"What does all that mean in English?"

"It means the boat could probably cover a hundred miles a day under those conditions, so she could have made it to Yarmouth in two to three days."

"Okay, suppose Dianne wasn't a crow and she stopped in Barrick Cove on the way to Yarmouth?"

"It's roughly two-hundred miles from Carver Creek to Barrick Cove, and probably another hundred and fifty miles from there to Yarmouth—"

"You've been doing your homework."

"Those people tried to kill me, dammit."

"Just remember, I'll lock you up for obstruction of justice if you keep meddling in my investigation."

"Do you want my advice, or not?"

"Advice, yes, meddling, no."

Riley ignored John's you-don't-get-one-without-the-other look and said, "So, Dianne Cummings could do that in about three and a half days, and have half a day left over in Barrick Cove to put on the new keel."

"Not possible, Lieutenant. Even assuming that *Abracadabra*

was stored at Junior's yard last winter to give him a chance to make a mold of the old keel and free up the bolts so it would come off easily when the time came, they'd still have to bring up the gold, pour the new keel, let it cool enough to work with, and bolt it on. I'd guess at least two days to do the job. There's only one answer that works: they must have swapped keels this spring before the Commodore brought the boat down to Wissonet. Storing the boat up there last winter would have given Junior plenty of time to get the old keel off, and get everything ready for the new one. Dianne and the Commodore must have driven up the Caddy full of gold in the spring and supervised Junior, to keep him honest, while he poured the new keel and installed it. Then the Commodore sailed home. It would explain why it took him so long to bring the boat down to Wissonet this spring."

"You mean he's been sailing around all summer with a keel full of gold? Suppose the boat had run into something and sank?

"Easy come, easy go?"

"And I thought you yachting people were crazy before," Riley marveled.

"I don't see any other explanation that works."

"Do you realize what you're saying?"

"Yes. Whoever killed the Commodore and tried to sink *Abracadabra* couldn't have known the keel was filled with gold, which rules out Dianne and Junior."

"And at least one of your two witches, Mildred and Edith, since it looks like one of them was helping sneak the gold out of Cummings Jewelry," Riley said. "On the other hand, there's no reason for Mike Hartwell to know about the gold, which makes him a prime suspect."

"Which means Dianne could be right about Mike being the killer," John replied, "but, if so, what was his motive, and who killed him?"

Chapter 35

Wissonet, August 14

John got home in time for a late supper, and Mary waited until Wendy was in bed before confronting him. Sadly, the child had better than average perceptiveness when it came to sensing parental tension, and she reacted to that tension in the worst possible way. As a result, Mary had built up a good head of steam by the time her troublesome daughter was safely in bed and she was seated on the front porch with her even more troublesome husband.

"What in heaven's name did you think you were doing up there?" she exploded. "Couldn't you have told me what you were up to?"

"I did tell you," John said defensively. "I went up to find a builder for Hibbert's boat, and I found one in Bristol who will give me a quote."

"And you just left out the part where you were going to look for *Abracadabra*, and maybe get yourself killed?"

"I didn't want to worry you, and I didn't think it would be a problem."

"Not a problem! You nearly died up there! Couldn't you have just left it to Riley?"

"What makes you think he'd have paid any attention to my

theory? Hell, you had to frame me for murder to get him moving."

"I did not frame you! I kept you from drowning!" Mary took a deep breath. "Would you rather I had left your bloody wrench in my flower bed?"

"I was mad, okay? Do you have any idea what it's like to be sealed up in goddam barrel—"

"Hogshead," Mary snarled.

John glared at his wife. His eyes suddenly narrowed.

"What are you looking at," she demanded, "and don't try to derail me."

"Where did you get that pendant you're wearing?"

"Pendant?" Mary reached for her throat in confusion.

"Technically speaking, it's an amulet." She temporized. Why was she wearing it? Try as she might, she couldn't remember putting it on.

"An amulet?"

"Amulets have symbols—incantations—on them." She must have slipped it on absentmindedly without thinking, but when?

"Incantations?"

"We're supposed to be talking about you and *Abracadabra.*" She swatted viciously at a passing mosquito.

"It looks familiar," John persisted.

"It belonged to the Commodore," she said in frustration. "It was on his body. I was going to give it to Dianne, before you killed her." Mary fingered the amulet. Why in the world did she put the damn thing on, anyway?

"How did you get it?"

"Somebody found it and gave it to me," she muttered sullenly.

"Which somebody?" John said, alarmed. "Did one of the

fishermen give it to you? Did you talk to one of them? You *are* going to give it to Riley, aren't you?"

"Of course," she replied airily.

"Has anybody else seen you wearing it?"

Mary's mind churned. She'd changed to a fresh blouse around the middle of the day, before going to the library. "I showed it to Fred Oglivy to have him look at the inscription, but I don't think anybody else saw it," she said uncertainly. Had she put it on without thinking when she left the library? She'd obviously put it on this morning without noticing. What had possessed her? She snatched the amulet off and dropped it in her lap.

John picked up the disk and squinted at it in the fading light. "I remember the Commodore wearing it once in a while when we were racing. He used to say the 'all-seeing eye' was a good luck symbol. I never saw the back side, though." He returned the bauble to her lap. "So, why were you wearing it tonight?"

"I don't know why I wore it all, except that it seems to stir up vague memories, childhood memories, that I can't quite put my finger on."

The setting sun had loosed shadows that were creeping up the lawn towards them. John gave her a crooked smile. "So, you have forgotten memories that you can't remember, and I have remembered memories that I can't forget. We make quite pair."

Mary smiled in spite of herself. "Maybe we should share what we've been doing the last two days, since it looks like we've both been meddling in Riley's case," Mary suggested.

It was dark by the time they were done.

"And Riley promised to keep your part in Dianne's death a secret?"

"Until the investigation is over."

"So we don't have to worry about a lynch mob arriving on

our doorstep for a few more days, then," Mary said.

"What about that little trinket you managed to get your hands on?"

"I don't think it has anything to do with the Commodore's murder," Mary said uncertainly, "but I did come across something else interesting."

"What?"

"Apparently, Henry hasn't been completely honest about Ruth Cummings and the town legend."

"I'm not surprised, but why do you say that?"

"It's what I found in the New Bedford library. I ended up spending all afternoon in there," Mary replied. "You remember the story of Elijah and Ruth Cummings, how Ruth was left to fend for herself after the 1812 war, and how she nearly starved? Well, I found Ruth Cummings's obituary in the New Bedford paper and it seems that our esteemed sorceress engaged in a profession even older than witchcraft. The paper referred to her as a 'woman of notorious ill-repute.'"

"Not exactly a glowing eulogy. And I thought she was supposed to be a recluse out there on Marsh Point."

"That depends on what you mean by recluse," Mary said primly.

"Running a one-woman bordello does not qualify in my book."

"There's more," Mary said. "Ruth didn't die in her bed."

"She was burned at the stake?"

"Nothing that glamorous. According to one of the newspaper articles, she was hung from an oak tree in her front yard by a lynch mob—the paper called it a 'group of irate citizens'—for poisoning and robbing a traveler."

"A customer who waved around too much cash, I suppose," John said. "Prostitution, witchcraft, and murder.

Ruth was a busy woman."

"We only have the amulet and Henry's word for the witchcraft, though she could have been one, secretly."

"Okay, let me get this straight," John said. "If Prudence married Henry's grandfather, it must have been before Ruth was exposed as a witch or a killer."

Mary nodded, and John watched her pick up the amulet, turning it over and over in her hand. "Ruth gave this to Prudence for protection," she said. "We know that from her letter to Prudence. It was the best Ruth could do for her daughter." Mary ran her fingers absentmindedly over the engraving. "But it wasn't good enough in the end. I think Prudence was hounded into committing suicide after Ruth was lynched."

"Why do you say that?"

"First, she's not buried in the graveyard. Oh, Henry had one of his tales about the headstone being turned over so her name doesn't show, but that doesn't feel right."

"I hope you're not planning a midnight foray to dig up the Merton gravestone."

"Don't be silly; it's much too heavy for me to move by myself."

John sighed.

"Besides," she went on, "I couldn't find anything in the church records about Prudence, and there's no obituary in the papers. According to Henry, Prudence was John Merton's favorite wife."

"Not surprising for Henry to want his grandmother to be John's favorite wife."

"Yes. Surely John Merton would have put something in the paper when Prudence died, which takes me back to the question of why Ruth give the amulet to Prudence. What or who would

Prudence need protection from?"

"The same irate citizens who lynched Ruth?"

"Exactly. Protection from them and their rumors. Guilt by association. If Ruth was a prostitute and murderer, why not her daughter? After all, she had lived with Ruth before marrying John Merton. I can't help wondering what a fine upstanding gentleman like John Merton would do if his wife was accused of being a witch."

"Put the damn amulet down," John said. "It's giving you too many ideas."

Mary answered her own question. "He'd certainly stop her from seeing her mother, and probably disown her, in the end," she said bitterly.

"He had to live in town, after all." John added, shaking his head. "And the amulet?"

"It must have been important to Prudence, and my guess is that she found a way to see that it got back to Jonathan as a family heirloom when he returned, perhaps in her will. And there's more."

"I was afraid you'd say that," John grumbled.

"While I was looking through the obituaries, I found four people who died within a year after Jonathan returned home. The first was Jeremiah Dutton, First Selectman, church Deacon, and probable leader of the lynch mob."

"Is he the same Jeremiah who was careless enough to sit on his barn roof during a thunderstorm?" John asked.

"I couldn't find anything on the thunderstorm business in the newspaper. My guess is that Jonathan took his revenge on Jeremiah in a more down-to-earth way. There also was the minister of the church, another selectman, and the town constable, all dead of 'unknown causes' within a year of Jonathan's return."

"Vengeance run amok," John murmured.

"I think Jonathan sent the amulet to Ruth while he was still away as a promise that he would wreak vengeance on her persecutors."

"Which he apparently did." John watched Mary fiddling absentmindedly with the amulet. "Are you sure you're not making up history, like Henry did?"

"Maybe, but it feels true, and it answers a lot of questions." Mary put the amulet back in her lap. "Mainly, it explains why Henry might want to change history to paint his ancestors in a better light. Imagine how he must have felt about his great-grandmother being a witch, and his grandfather disavowing his grandmother."

"I wonder about the skeletons out on Marsh Point," John said. "Do you suppose they were Ruth and Prudence, and maybe an out-of-town customer or two who happened to be carrying too much money?"

A rabbit came out of the underbrush at the edge of the field to nibble on some clover. Mary watched for a moment, wondering how an animal as cute and timid as a rabbit could suddenly become associated with bloody crosses and vengeance symbols in her mind. Would a rabbit's sinister aura ever go away for her? How would her mother react to Ruth Cummings's activities? "I don't think we should mention the bordello business, or the lynching, or Prudence's suicide, or Jonathan's revenge, to people in town."

"God no," John said fervently, "We're in enough trouble as it is." He scratched his leg absentmindedly.

"What's wrong with your leg?" Mary asked.

"My leg?" He rolled up his trousers to look. Several red, inflamed scratches ran down the inside of his left leg. "I must have scratched it while I was dealing with Dianne."

"You need to clean those up and put iodine on them; they look infected," she said.

John looked thoughtful. "Or maybe it was the tussle I had with Junior's gorilla, Tiny Ted-what's-his-name."

* * *

Just then, Sam Barton called, sounding impatient. "Set your alarm clock; I've got some work for you," he said abruptly.

"What kind of work, and how early?"

"Five o'clock. A yacht broker named Quigly up in Hingham has a customer who wants to buy a boat and needs to have it changed from a gaff rig to a Marconi rig. You do the design work and I'll do the modifications."

John couldn't remember when he'd last had a decent night's sleep. He groaned. "Five o'clock? I just got back—" he caught himself. Riley wanted the details of Dianne's death kept quiet for now. "Why not have the job done in Hingham?"

"Why should I look a gift horse in the mouth? Anyway, Quigly said the customer wanted somebody named John Wendell to redesign the rig on his boat, and do I know who this Wendell person is? Should I have told him I never heard of you?"

"What's this customer's name?"

"All I have is the broker's name, Bruce Quigly."

"You don't know who the customer is?"

"What difference does it make?"

"I just like to know who I'm working for and where he got my name," John said stubbornly. The job was straightforward enough. A customer wanted the boat's old-fashioned gaff rig replaced with a modern sail plan. It was a common enough alteration that often did wonders.

"You want to know who you're working for? You're working for money," Sam informed him. "What more do you need to know? Obviously somebody got the crazy idea that you know something about boats. You should be thankful there are people out there who have heard of you and don't hate your guts. Did you suddenly strike it rich that you don't need some honest work?"

"It's just that I'm uncomfortable doing work for someone I haven't even met." The job would earn John a modest fee and Sam would get a week or so of work doing the modifications. It was just the sort of short-term project Sam appeared to be looking for.

"Look, there's supposed to be storm passing off the coast tomorrow afternoon, and half the people in town want their boats out of the water, so I need to get back early before everybody has a fit. Anyway, I don't have time to argue with you about it. Do you want the job or not?"

"Yes, of course."

"You know what your problem is?" Sam went on, "You don't know how to run a business. If someone comes and offers you work, you don't give him the third-degree. You know what you do? You say 'yes, sir Mr. Barton, sir. I'll have my worthless, pig-headed, trouble making carcass on my front doorstep at five o'clock tomorrow morning, sir.' That's what you say, dammit. And don't forget that I want to get back early, so don't keep me waiting."

Chapter 36

Wissonet, August 15

Sam's pickup truck, its weathered black bodywork checkerboarded with sheet metal patches, pulled into the driveway a few minutes after five the next morning.

"Henry wasn't in yet, so I had to leave him a note and let him know where we're going," Sam explained.

"You look like a wreck," John commented as he slid onto the seat, dodging a hole in the upholstery.

"There's a bunch of Nervous Nellies who seem to think a hurricane is out there in spite of the weather forecast of just rain. I was up all night, helping people haul their boats."

"Is Henry okay? That's pretty hard work for a man his age."

The truck whined tiredly as Sam backed out the driveway. "He'll be fine as soon he gets over this Cummings business. You know how he is when anything bad happens in town—he treats it like a personal insult."

They rumbled up the back roads towards Hingham. Once again, the morning air was hot and humid in spite of the early hour and cloudy skies.

Bruce Quigly, a small, ferret-faced man in a loud Hawaiian shirt and tan Bermuda shorts, was waiting for them at the entrance to the boatyard where John's would-be patient waited.

"Let's go look at the boat before it starts to rain," Quigly said when the introductions were complete. He set a brisk, knobby-kneed pace as he led them towards the back of the yard.

Sea Song lay in a weed-infested corner of the yard. She was big, and she was old, but mostly she was a wreck. Years of neglect had left peeling paint and decayed wood. Streaks of rust ran down the planking where fastenings were in the final stages of dissolution. Seams between the planks were rough and cracked. In places, loose caulking hung down like pale, Medusan snakes.

Sam gazed at the wreck in awe. "Jesus, somebody paid for this thing?"

Quigly had the grace to look uncomfortable. "Well, the buyer hasn't actually finalized the purchase yet." He wilted under the skeptical eyes of his visitors and added hastily, "It's an earnest offer, though. He sent a deposit by Western Union, plus he's given me money to pay for your trip up here."

"Has the boat been surveyed?" John asked doubtfully. "Does he know if it's seaworthy?"

Sam barely suppressed a laugh.

"The buyer understands that some work is needed, along with the modifications: caulking and a few new fastenings. That sort of thing."

* * *

Monday normally was a workday for Mary, but Phil had chosen to take the day off and gave Mary the day off as well. Mary reveled in the chance to enjoy a late breakfast and savor the prospect of a peaceful morning. On a quiet day like this, she was able to think that things really would get back to normal someday, and her feelings about Wissonet would eventually become less sinister. Wendy, surrounded by a collection of toys, was amusing herself on the kitchen floor, while eyeing Nat's ample form as the cat sprawled on one of the chairs.

Mary turned on the kitchen radio, and WBZ bloomed as the set warmed up. It was aggravating that Boston should come in so much better than the New Bedford stations. She carefully adjusted the dial until New Bedford came through the static. She was tempted to take the carpet sweeper to the living room rug and listen to the local news on the big RCA console, which had better reception, but there was a stack of dishes on the drainboard to deal with first. The weather forecast finally came through, talking about a tropical storm passing by out to sea, well south of Cape Cod.

Spatters of oversized raindrops were pockmarking the driveway as Mary glanced out the window to see Edith's car pull in behind the Ford.

For some unknown reason, Edith was dressed in what Mary considered almost normal clothes. In this case almost normal was in the form of a white, low-cut dress with a full skirt and a lavish quantity of lace. Wendy greeted Edith by tossing her stuffed rabbit into the air, much to Nat's horror. "Bunny is flying to the moon," Wendy said gleefully.

"Bunny will need to get into her spaceship to do that," Edith replied with a smile. "Any coffee left?" she asked Mary. "Sit. I'll get it," she added as Mary turned towards the stove. "Do you suppose we ought to set out a cup for Loretta? She seems to practically live over here."

"No need," Mary said. "She and Ed are away for a few days."

Edith brought over two steaming cups and sat at the table. "Oh, I forgot they're visiting Loretta's mother," she said.

"That's all right, you can be the first to wish me a happy birthday. Just don't ask how old I am."

"So that's why the dress; you look very festive." Mary toasted Edith with her cup. "Happy birthday, Edith. Funny, I thought it was in March sometime. Are you doing anything special to celebrate?"

"I'm going out to a party, later," Edith said vaguely as they sipped their coffee. A gust of wind rattled the house. "That storm may be coming closer than they thought."

"At least the rain should cool things off."

"I hope John doesn't get caught in any nasty weather," Edith said.

"How did you know he's away?"

"Word gets around," Edith said in a sing-song voice, mimicking Loretta.

Suddenly, Mary felt a wave of dizziness. She looked up to see Edith's face melt like a Dali painting. Black toad-like eyes bulged from a grotesquely swollen forehead. Her enormous mouth, framed by drooping rubbery lips, opened to emit a deep rumbling voice like someone dragging their thumb on a Victrola turntable.

"You look a little tired," the Edith-monster said. "Why don't you put your head down and rest for a while until you feel better."

Long, hideously deformed fingers reached across space, catching Mary as she collapsed. She wanted to scream, but all voluntary control had escaped her.

"You rest for a while, dear," Edith crooned as she leaned close to Mary's ear. "Wendy and I are going for a little drive. Don't worry, I'll take good care of her. Your daughter is very special." Edith straightened up. "You know where we'll be. Come and find us when you feel better. Come alone."

She turned to the small form playing on the floor. "Wendy dear, your mommy is taking a little nap. How would you like to go for a ride with aunt Edith? You and Bunny can take a trip in my space ship."

Chapter 37

Hingham, August 15

In Hingham, twenty miles to the north of Wissonet, a few tentative raindrops were beginning to fall, driving Sam and Quigly to seek shelter in the open boat shed doorway. John stayed beside *Sea Song* and absentmindedly ran his fingers over the roughened seams, while his mind wandered aimlessly. The vessel was a forty-foot ketch that must have been a handsome boat in her heyday. John suspected the Commodore would have liked the boat as a bigger, more comfortable replacement for *Abracadabra,* assuming *Sea Song* could be rebuilt.

The Commodore was a traditionalist though, and he'd probably want to keep *Sea Song*'s original gaff rig, just like *Abracadabra*'s.

John paused. Or would he? After all, he was willing to loot the family business and sacrifice his beloved *Abracadabra* in order to work his gold smuggling scheme.

John could understand how the Commodore might have no enthusiasm for running Cummings Jewelry, as Ed Clayton had said, but *Abracadabra* was different. The Commodore loved that boat in the special way so many boat owners develop a deep affection for their vessels—one more reason why poor, neglected *Sea Song,* seemed so forlorn. Someone had loved her and cared for her, once. He patted the boat's side sympathetically, and suddenly remembered how he'd scraped his leg—not from struggling with Dianne, or Junior's hulking employee. He'd gotten it from *Abracadabra's* planking when he climbed aboard in Barrick Cove—planking that should have been glassy smooth.

So, the Commodore had found a way to cling to tradition and smuggle gold at the same time. Which suggested that tradition, and all that it meant, lived on in Wissonet as well. Suddenly, it all made sense.

John turned abruptly and descended on Sam and the gaudy yacht broker. "I need to make a phone call," he said.

"A phone call?" Quigly echoed.

The last few minutes had transformed *Sea Song's* repair and modification into serious money, and Sam wasn't happy to be interrupted. "Can't it wait a few minutes, for crying out loud?"

"No."

"You can use the phone in the yard's office," Quigly suggested, pointing the way.

There was no answer when John called home. There was no answer when he called his mother-in-law's house, either. A call to Cantor Realty confirmed that it was closed for the day.

None of that necessarily meant anything sinister. She was probably just out running an errand. Still, he couldn't shake a growing sense of dread. He went outside, where it was beginning to rain in earnest.

"We have to get back to Wissonet," John said to Sam.

"The sooner you start paying attention, the sooner we can leave."

"We have to leave *now*." John turned towards the truck.

"But—" Quigly began.

Sam grabbed John's arm, spinning him around. "We have

business to attend to first."

"It's the fifteenth of August, Sam. It's not over."

"What the hell are you talking about?"

"Mary doesn't answer the phone." The urgency in John's voice stopped Sam short.

"I'll call you later today," Sam told Quigly as John led him to the truck.

"Okay, tell me what the hell is going on." Sam demanded as he started the engine.

"This isn't just about gold smuggling. It's about Marsh Point, Ruth Cummings and the town legend."

"The town legend?" Sam snorted derisively. "Nobody takes that fairy tale seriously, except Henry, and maybe the town witches."

"The killer takes it seriously. I think Riley has been spending so much time thinking about the gold smuggling that he hasn't paid enough attention to the big question, namely who killed the Commodore and Mike, and why."

"I thought the murders were a double-cross of some kind—probably because Mike was trying to muscle in on the gold smuggling."

The Commodore's gold smuggling scheme was common knowledge by now, but true to his word, Riley and the police had been deliberately vague about Dianne's death, saying only that she had "been lost at sea, along with a substantial amount of gold," and keeping John's role in the tragedy quiet. At least while the investigation continued.

John shook his head. "The gold is only part of it. It's more than just that. I think we've been set up. *Sea Song* was just a decoy. Somebody wanted to get us out of town."

The truck's gears ground harshly as Sam pulled out of the lot. "Get *us* out of town? Why would anybody want to do that?"

John answered with a question of his own. "Why did you happen to be outside our house on the night Mike attacked Mary? And don't tell me it was a coincidence, and you just happened to be walking by."

Sam heaved an impatient sigh. "Mary was there, alone, and Mike was drunk. You know how much he resents that you 'took her away' from him and moved into town."

"Don't you see?" John said impatiently. "The killer knows that you've been watching out for Mary when I wasn't around. And the killer wants her to be alone today."

He turned to face Sam. "But Mike being drunk wasn't the only reason you were watching him, was it? There was more, wasn't there?"

The transmission ground harshly as Sam missed third gear. "What the hell are you talking about?"

"Do you remember back when Mary was thirteen or fourteen and she hung out with the Commodore, Dianne, and Mike?"

"That was way before your time, and they'd broken up long before you came along."

"Yes, but I've heard rumors, and Mary has said a few things over the years." John watched as Sam's jaw muscles began working. "Apparently they used to call themselves the Four Musketeers?"

Sam wrestled with the wheel as a gust of wind caught the truck cross-wise. "They were pretty close for a while," he conceded.

"Then something happened, and they broke up. Something in Ruth Cummings's house."

"I don't know where you're going with this," Sam said, "but you're nuts. It was just four kids having a lark in an old, abandoned, and supposedly haunted house. They probably started telling each other ghost stories and scared themselves witless. The gold smuggling business still makes a lot more sense to me as a motive for murder than your legend nonsense."

Maybe Sam was right, and it was just about the gold. Maybe it was nothing more than ghost stories—the sort of thing kids love to frighten each other with. But still...

"Looking at *Sea Song*, I realized that there were two *Abracadabras*," John said. "That's why they tried to kill me in Yarmouth. They were afraid I'd recognize the phony *Abracadabra* and get suspicious about why there were two boats. The Commodore must have kept his boat in Barrick Cove last winter so Junior could fix up another Manchester 17 to make it look like *Abracadabra*."

Sam was quiet for a while before saying, "There was nothing wrong with Mike's boat. He filled the tank the afternoon before the Commodore was killed, and he filled it up again the next morning, after you and Riley left. He must have gone somewhere."

John looked incredulous. "You didn't think to tell Riley that Mike's alibi had a big hole in it? Don't you see what that could mean? At the very least he probably helped the killer."

"It wasn't much of an alibi to start with," Sam muttered. "Riley's a cop, isn't he? It's his job to check Mike's alibi, isn't it? How was I supposed to know the damn fool would end up getting himself killed? Serves him right for killing the Commodore."

"I don't think Mike killed him. Somebody else did. Mike probably helped by loaning his boat to the killer, maybe not knowing why, at first. If everything had gone as the killer planned, the Commodore and *Abracadabra* would have vanished, and everybody would have assumed he'd been lost at sea—no murder, just an accident.

"But that didn't happen. The body turned up, and suddenly it was a murder investigation with Mike holding the key to who did it. The killer may have decided that Mike needed to be silenced. Or more likely, Mike tried a little blackmail, and got himself killed for his trouble." John fidgeted in his seat. "Can't you go any faster?"

"Faster? It's raining like hell. Besides, I still don't see why we're in such a rush."

John's reply came from the question that still gnawed at him. A question that led him back to Mary. "The Commodore was wearing a gold pendant when he was killed."

Sam swerved to get around a fallen branch. "A gold pendant? The size of a silver dollar? With some kind of writing on it?"

"Yes," John said. "He was wearing it when he died, and now Mary has it."

It was quiet for a while except for the rush of wind and the monotonous slap of the windshield wipers as they fought a losing battle with the rain. Sam broke the silence. "Mary has it?"

"Don't ask how."

"That pendant dates back to Ruth Cummings," Sam said. "It's a family piece. I remember the Commodore's father used to wear it once in a while."

"And I remember the Commodore wore it, too."

Sam's knuckles were white on the steering wheel. "She shouldn't have it. It belongs in the family."

"There aren't any Cummings left, Sam."

"Then it should go to some next of kin." Sam stole a quick glance at John. "How long has she had it?"

"A couple of days."

"How many people have seen her with it?"

"I asked her that, and she's not sure."

"She's not sure? How can she not be sure?" Sam's obvious horror wasn't reassuring. "Does she know what trouble she could stir up if the wrong people see her with it?"

"That's what bothers me. She seems to have a strange attitude about the thing. She calls it an amulet."

"An amulet?" Sam concentrated on his driving, which was becoming more challenging by the minute.

After a while he said. "Look, you know I don't believe in witches, or ghosts, or any of that foolishness," he said slowly, "but you're right that something happened to those kids out there that scared the bejesus out of them. Like I said, probably just some kind of mass hysteria—"

"Don't you see?" John interrupted, "it doesn't matter what it was, or wasn't, and it doesn't matter what you or I believe. It's what other people believe to be real that counts."

Sam was driving faster, now.

"What does it mean to be related to the Cummings, Sam? Dianne and the Commodore are dead and the gold is gone. What else is left?"

"Mary is the last of the four musketeers," Sam murmured.

"It all comes down to her. She's the fulfillment of the legend."

Sam Barton accelerated the battered truck dangerously fast down the rain and wind swept road.

* * *

It wasn't too bad as long as she didn't move. Mary tried lifting her head at first, only to have the kitchen spin around her and the walls bulge in and out with the thud of her heartbeat. Mary groaned, fighting back waves of nausea as she slowly eased herself to a sitting position. How long had she been unconscious? The sagging wall clock, looking like something out of a Dali painting, said it had been almost an hour. After a while—what seemed like a long while—the room settled down.

A sudden gust shook the house like a petulant child with a rag doll, and rain pelted against the windows. Mary looked around. Where was Wendy? She started to get up to look for her. It was a bad mistake. She slumped back in the chair until the room stopped spinning.

Then she remembered Edith's words.

Slowly, slowly, she got to her feet. Her body seemed like a marionette that she was trying to control through tangled strings. She took a few tottering steps, caught the doorjamb as it slid by, only to find that the dining room was transformed into a garish fun-house. The colors were luminous, and even the shape of the room itself was changed, with the ceiling and floor coming together in one corner.

Many years ago, a fireplace had occupied one wall, before it was plastered over leaving only a vestigial strip of mantle that jutted through the wallpaper and provided Mary with a handy shelf for her flower arrangements.

And also the amulet. Somehow, Mary knew it was important to take it with her as a bargaining chip, if nothing else. She dropped it into her pocket.

The door leading to the front hall looked impossibly small, but Mary leaned against the wall and doggedly followed it to the hall.

The front hall was endless, stretching off to a tiny front door in the distance. The floor bulged and shifted under her feet like something alive as she made her way towards the living room. Mary barely noticed the crash behind her as another gust of wind blew one of the porch chairs through the diningroom window.

She propped herself against the living room door and picked up the telephone ear-piece. It felt burning hot, and she dropped it with a cry as the aroma of singed flesh filled her nostrils. Mary sobbed with frustration. What had Edith put in her coffee? She forced herself to try again but, turning the crank, she realized the line was dead.

Getting to the car was a problem. Even though the street-side of the house was sheltered from the worst of the wind, Mary stumbled as a gust eddied around the corner and pushed her off the porch step into the mud. She lay there for a while, with the blood-warm rain soaking her clothes while she waited for the world to stop pulsating.

She made it to the car at last by crawling through the mud, vowing all the way that Edith Whitten would live to regret this day.

Chapter 38

Wissonet, August 15

While Mary was sprawled, unconscious, on her kitchen table, Edith and Wendy were on their way to Marsh Point. Many toddlers would have been frightened by the wind, rain, leaves, and twigs that were assaulting Edith's Buick, but Wendy found the experience exciting as she sat in the front seat, talking happily while she and Edith drove the short distance to the Point.

Edith had introduced Wendy to the spacious trunk of her car a week before. Lined with a quilt and supplied with an assortment of toys, it made an appealing cave-like playpen, which Edith called a space ship. She also fixed the trunk's glass-domed courtesy light so it stayed lit with the trunk lid closed.

Edith parked in a brush choked cul-de-sac, just beyond the Oglivy's driveway and out of sight of the road, and put Wendy in the trunk where she settled in contentedly with her assortment of toys.

"I'll shut the lid of your spaceship now," Edith said, "while you take off to the moon. Stay here and Aunt Edith will be back soon." With that, the trunk lid closed.

* * *

Sam swerved through a cornfield to avoid a fallen tree. Stalks whipped against the sides of the truck, making a counterpoint to the rain pounding on the roof.

John was getting frantic with their slow progress, in spite of Sam's reckless speed. It was almost eleven o'clock, and they still had a way to go. Not that Sam was sparing the horses. If anything, he was going recklessly fast considering the debris that littered the road.

"We should stop and call the police," John said.

"You want to get that over-upholstered Irish flat-foot involved in this, after all the trouble he's stirred up already? Leave the cops out of it. We can take care of things ourselves."

"We can take care of things ourselves? People are being killed—real people! This isn't just some crazy witchcraft legend; this is my family, and the police can get to our house a lot quicker than we can."

"For Christ's sake, be sensible," Sam said. "Look around. There are wires down all over the place here, and things are bound to be worse further south. We'll waste a lot of time just trying to find a phone that works, and what are you going to tell the cops when you do get through? That a bunch of would-be witches are threatening your family? They'll never take you seriously. Besides, they've got enough problems already with this storm, and there's no guarantee they can even get to Wissonet."

Sam turned to John. "Look, I'm as worried about Mary and Wendy as you are, but I've known Mary all her life; she's smart and she can take care of herself. Besides, we'll be there in half an hour."

More and bigger branches were beginning to litter the road.

For a long time Sam was silent, seemingly intent on his driving.

"It's too bad you don't have a radio in this thing," John said. "At least we could get a weather forecast." The wind was building steadily, and it was starting to rain even harder.

"I never needed a radio before and I don't need one now. Besides, you don't have a radio in your car," Sam pointed out.

"My car is eighteen years old, for crying out loud. It barely has a speedometer."

"Your car barely needs a speedometer," Sam retorted, dodging another tree branch.

* * *

Getting the Ford started and backed onto the street took a force of will that left Mary panting and dizzy. Once clear of the house, the boxy vehicle became a plaything for blasts of wind that swept across the street, and time after time the car was blown onto a sidewalk or a lawn.

Mary wondered at the way her mind seemed to be clearing, while her connection to the reality around her remained so distorted. How much of the trees' mad swaying and the car's erratic swerving was due to the wind, and how much was due to the concoction Edith had put in her coffee? Was it the same stuff that Dianne had used to spike John's coffee on *Abracadabra*? Was the drug some kind of secret witchcraft recipe, passed down through the generations from Ruth Cummings?

The wind howled, a great ceaseless roar overlaid with a high, keening scream. Torrents of rain lashed at the Ford and blasted through cracks in the bodywork. A huge tree fell just behind her, silent in the tumult, and a limb brushed the rear of the car, flicking the aged vehicle onto the Wilson's lawn.

Mary, barely able to see through the laboring windshield wipers and unsure if she could believe what little she did see, jerked the wheel. The front fender bounced off a tottering phone pole as she regained the pavement.

Three blocks from her house, and Mary was lost. The road was already paved with leaves, and now it ended in a wall of brush. A downed tree? She forged ahead, aimed for what looked like a thin spot in the foliage, and plunged into the heaving greenery. Branches scraped and tore at the roof and sides as the tires fought for traction. Mary emerged, having lost the road and one rear window, and found herself nose-to-nose with the side of the Bondi's garage. She turned down the driveway while a wide-eyed Stan Bondi watched from his kitchen window as the battered apparition ricocheted off his porch and faded from view.

Mary might be feeling stronger as she neared her rendezvous with Edith, but her trusty steed was not. Between the Wilson's phone pole, the Bondi's porch, and other minor collisions Mary hadn't even noticed, the old Ford had taken a beating. Its front fenders were both deformed in a way that made steering difficult, while the interior smelled of antifreeze and hot oil in spite of the wind whistling through the broken windows and the rapidly disintegrating roof. A loud, grinding noise suggested that the engine was devouring itself, but Mary pressed on regardless, bouncing over branches and flinging the car headlong at fallen trees to force a way through to Marsh Point.

She finally came to a place two hundred yards beyond the Oglivy's house where a huge tree blocked the way. Mary got out and staggered around the tree and down the sandy track to where an overgrown wall of briers blocked the path that once led to the Cummings homestead.

Except the path wasn't overgrown any more. Somebody had recently hacked a path through the jungly growth in what must have been a superhuman effort.

A great wall of wind howled over the treetops, while capricious eddies reached down to push her from unexpected directions. Below the roar of the wind, Mary could hear the rumble of surf and feel the ground tremble as each wave beat itself into oblivion on the sand.

She stood for a moment, buffeted by wind and memory, before starting down the narrow path, intent on finding Wendy and settling accounts with Edith. Loose strands of catbrier, whipped by the wind, lashed at her face like barbed snakes as she passed. Finally, she came to the clearing and the house, her hands and face whipped and bloody.

Next to her, at the clearing's edge, an ancient oak tree writhed and twisted in the gale as though in agony.

It was thirteen years since she had last been here, and the two-room building seemed smaller than she remembered it.

The front of the house looked strangely like a face: the front door was propped open like a gaping mouth; the boarded-up windows looked like a pair of blinded eyes gazing sightlessly out over the tiny clearing.

Through the doorway, Mary could see the massive stone fireplace that dominated the back wall.

A raging fire was burning on the hearth.

To Mary's eyes, the place looked unchanged from her childhood visit. Except for the fire.

Maybe it was Edith's psychedelic potion, or even the amulet in her pocket, but as she stood there, memories were suddenly turned loose. True or false, they bubbled relentlessly to the surface, carrying her to a place she feared to go, yet had to revisit for Wendy's sake.

Chapter 39

Wissonet, Thirteen Years Earlier

The Commodore was called Pudge, a descriptive term, during Mary's childhood. It often occurred to her in later years that people in town hardly ever called him by his real name, just "Pudge" and later, "the Commodore," almost as though he had no identity of his own.

Pudge was in his mid-twenties then, and dating Dianne. He didn't usually associate with Mary and Mike, who were, after all, a mere thirteen years of age. When it came to sailing, however, he made an exception, since the young pair were a willing and obedient crew who offered a hero worship that Pudge absorbed like a sponge.

As a result of this relationship, Pudge, Mary, Mike, and Dianne had been out sailing one afternoon in Pudge's Beetle Cat when they were caught off Marsh Point in one of the unexpected summer squalls that occasionally sweep across Buzzards Bay. Through a combination of luck and good seamanship, Pudge managed to shoot through the narrow entrance into the cove at the tip of Marsh Point, thereby avoiding the humiliation of being blown onto the beach.

In retrospect, the beach would have been preferable.

Pudge brought an anchor part way up the sandy slope to

keep the boat from drifting off, and they stood on the beach, cold and wet. The cove sheltered them from the wind, but a cold rain soon had the youngsters shivering.

In those days, the roof of Ruth's cottage was still visible through a low screen of young brush and briers, and it seemed to beckon them with the promise of shelter.

"Let's go into the house," Mike said between chattering teeth. "At least it'll be dry."

They looked at Pudge—it was his parents' house after all—but he seemed oddly hesitant, as though torn between conflicting emotions. Mary could understand his dilemma. After all, his parents had made it well known in town that nobody was to break into, or even play near, Ruth's house.

Such was the power of the Cummings legend among the town's youth that few came here at all. None had ever dared to enter.

"You aren't afraid of an empty old house are you?" Mike teased Pudge.

Mike didn't wait for an answer, but shouldered his way through the undergrowth while the others followed.

Ruth Cummings's house was a small, one-storey, center chimney cape, which sat at the edge of a small, weed-choked clearing.

Mike ran up to the building and began pulling on one of the boards that covered the door. Pudge reluctantly joined in. The first board was the hardest, but once it was free they were able to use it as a lever to pry off the others. The weathered planks came off one by one, the square-cut nails screeching noisily as they tore from the door frame.

The old house exhaled a cool, musty breath as they opened the door. The four entered the cottage in a tight group, instinctively huddling together, none of them willing to show fear. A great stillness muted the sounds of wind and rain outside. It was dark with the windows boarded up, but their eyes gradually adjusted, and they began to make out the main room, dominated by a huge stone fireplace. A steep staircase, almost a ladder, reached up to a loft.

The youngsters' attention, however, was drawn to a narrow door beside the fireplace which led to a tiny closet of a bedroom tucked beside the chimney.

According to legend, Ruth Cummings had died in that bedroom, and for all the shivering youngsters knew, her bones still lay in there.

Aside from a coating of dust, the accumulation of a century, the sparsely furnished house looked as though it might have recently been abandoned. A rough wooden table, surrounded by four high-backed, rush-bottom chairs filled the middle of the room. Two dust-covered dishes and a pewter candlestick, its candle mostly gnawed away by mice, sat on the table. A small, wooden sea chest stood against one wall, and a cast iron kettle hung from a wrought iron crane in the fireplace. Another pewter candlestick, its candle surprisingly intact, sat on the mantelpiece.

"Hey, a candle," Mike exclaimed. "I've got some matches."

"No. We can just stay by the door until the rain stops," Pudge said. He was too late, though, because Mike had already pulled a box of Rosebud matches from his pocket. They were damp, and it took several tries before one lit with a sullen flame. He stood tip-toe on the worn hearth, touched the match to the mantle candle, and the room was bathed in a dim, sputtering light.

A mahogany, high-backed rocking chair stood beside the table, its beauty and craftsmanship in sharp contrast to the crudeness of the other furnishings. According to Pudge, the rocker had been a wedding gift from Ruth's husband, and she'd clung to it when all else was sacrificed during the lean times. It sat now in dusty splendor, hypnotizing Mary with the beauty of its delicately turned spindles and elegantly shaped arms.

Mike noticed her reaction. "Do you like the rocking chair, Mare?"

He wiped his rain-soaked hands over the dusty seat bottom and arms, revealing the reddish brown of the wood. The finish glistened in the flickering candlelight.

"Why don't you try the chair there, Mare?" Mike was delighted with his poetic efforts.

"Hey, leave that stuff alone." Once again, Pudge was too late.

As though drawn by a magnet, Mary sat down.

She rocked experimentally. It was the perfect size, since she was big for her age and Ruth had been a small woman.

"You want me to rock the chair for you, Mare?" Mike said.

"Don't you dare rock the chair." Mary could resort to rhyming too.

"I think we should wait outside," Dianne said nervously.

"The rain is starting to let up," Pudge lied.

Mary ignored them all, rocking gently. Her senses seemed to become oddly acute, expanding, encompassing the entire room. She could see the room in her mind's eye, without looking. Without leaving the chair, she could climb the staircase to the loft with its low pallet bed and tiny table. She could even go through the narrow door to the back room, seeing what waited for her in the darkness…

"Ouch!" Mary was back with the others. Something, perhaps a splinter from the chair, had scratched her arm, leaving a row of tiny blood droplets to mark the injury. It was a minor scratch and she instinctively licked the blood away. The skin on her arm looked strangely wrinkled in the wavering candlelight, and she saw liver spots on the back of her hand, as though it belonged to someone twice her age.

She looked up and saw Mike open his mouth to ask what was wrong.

The words never formed. Instead, Mike's jaw dropped, his eyes bulged, and he staggered back in horror. Dianne screamed. Pudge ran for the door.

Mary wasn't sure what happened after that, except that everything seemed terribly, terribly wrong.

Pudge was long gone, but Mike and Dianne seemed frozen in place. Mary lurched out of the chair, consumed by the urgent need to get to the bedroom before it was too late.

The entire house spun around her as she tried to stand, her legs refused to obey, and she fell to the floor.

Mike grabbed her arm and struggled to pull her away as she crawled towards the bedroom door. Dianne joined him, taking the other arm. Mary had never felt such fury as the two dragged her out of the building.

They laid her on the ground in the cold, soaking rain and stood around her uncertainly until the rage passed.

Chapter 40

Wissonet, August 15

Wissonet Harbor came into view as Sam and John turned onto High Street. Sam stopped the truck and gazed downhill to the water.

Vast, white-capped waves rolled down the harbor, tearing at the few boats that still clung to their moorings. The wreckage of others littered the shore.

"Lord Almighty." Sam stared in awe. "The storm was supposed to go out to sea. Do you know how many people will be yelling for my hide because I haven't saved their damn boats? I just hope Henry didn't do anything stupid and kill himself out there." He accelerated noisily up the road.

The house door was unlocked, but it took both of them to force it open against the wind. A blast of rain-filled air whistled down the hall in greeting.

"Porch chair blew through your window," Sam yelled. Rain, leaves, furniture, and assorted debris filled the living room.

There was no sign of Mary or Wendy.

"She may have left a note in the kitchen," John said.

There was no note, just Henry Merton huddled at the table. A few wisps of his white hair whipped wildly in the gale that whistled through the room.

Two long strides took John to the old man. He put a hand on Henry's shoulder. His shirt was soaked.

"Where are they?" John yelled against the howling wind.

Henry looked up, and John recoiled, unprepared for the bloodshot eyes, the gray, ruined face staring up at him. Henry looked old enough to have remembered George Washington.

"I saw Sam's note, and realized Ruth died today and Mary was alone. I came right over, but I was too late."

"Today's the fifteenth," Sam said, impatiently. "There's nothing in your fool legend that says Ruth Cummings died on the fifteenth."

"She died on August fifteenth," John said. "The date is in Ezra Waller's diary."

"Ezra Waller's diary?" Sam said.

"I've killed them all." Henry's eyes pleaded forgiveness.

Sam slumped in the doorway like a tire gone flat.

"There was so much evil," Henry went on, his voice barely audible above the storm. "I was just trying to give people something good. A history they could be proud of."

A crash shook the house to its foundation, drawing Henry's grief-stricken gaze to the window, where Wissonet was being systematically torn apart.

Henry flared. "Goddamn it, Ruth was no more a witch then I am!"

Sam took a step forward, but John was there first. He grabbed Henry by the shoulders, dragged him out of the chair, and shook him. It was like rattling a bag of twigs.

"Where are they? Why didn't you go after them?" John yelled.

"Leave the old man alone!" Sam pulled them apart and Henry collapsed back in his chair. "He barely managed to get this far, for chrissake. And you know damn well where they are."

"It's come full circle," Henry moaned, his voice—the words of a dying old man—nearly lost in the wind that whistled through the house. "Mary has the talisman; I saw it yesterday. It's come full circle."

But John and Sam were already running for the door and didn't wait to hear the rest.

Sam's truck didn't get them far. A huge maple tree blocked the road in front of the Wilson's house, forcing them to retrace their path. In the end they detoured through half-a-dozen side streets and back yards before arriving at the turn off to Marsh Point. Here their luck ran out, for a whole stand of trees had come down across the road. They sat, looking at the destruction while the wind rocked the truck like a child playing with a toy boat before sinking it in the bathtub.

"We'll have to walk from here," John said.

They came to the wrecked Model A, caught in another tangle of trees a few yards further along.

"What made them come out here in this storm?" Sam said.

"Nothing good," John replied.

Chapter 41

Wissonet, August 15

Mary stood in the clearing, gasping for breath. Were John's flashbacks as vivid and all-consuming as what she'd just experienced? The difference, of course, was that his were based on actual events, while hers were the result of Edith's hallucinogenic coffee.

It wasn't a comforting thought.

Mary approached the house warily.

Edith appeared in the doorway. "You're late," she scolded.

"Where is Wendy?" Mary screamed into Edith's face.

"She's safe, for now," Edith replied serenely.

Fury overwhelmed Mary. She was younger than Edith; she would wring the truth out of the bitch if it meant strangling her to death. What she failed to anticipate was Edith's blinding speed, strength, and arms the length of telephone poles.

Edith threw Mary to the ground, leaving her stunned and gasping for breath. Before she could recover, Edith picked her up like a rag doll and dropped her onto the rocking chair, wrapped a rope around her waist, and tied her tightly enough to make breathing difficult. It occurred to her that John had also been lashed to a chair recently. Were she and her husband fated to share common experiences? For some reason that Mary didn't want to think about, Edith had left her right arm free.

Edith pushed the rocker up to the table so Mary was facing the fire. A knife, and a bowl of something that smelled like brandy sat on the table, just out of reach. The heat in the room was stifling.

"You want to kill me, don't you?" Edith crooned when she was done. "But you're weak as a kitten. Did you know the ancient Mayans gave hallucinogenic drugs to people before they were sacrificed? Any sudden movement or physical activity, makes you fantasize. Stay calm and you're fine. Isn't it intriguing?"

The room slowly stopped spinning.

"Do you know why you're here?" Edith said.

"I'm here to find Wendy!" Edith was right. She was a lot weaker than she'd realized and struggling only made it worse.

"No, dear, you're here to correct a great wrong. Isn't it ironic that your whole life has come together to bring you to this moment? And to think it all began when you and the others broke into this house. From then on your life was preordained."

"None of this was preordained!"

"Oh, but it was. Why else would we have this storm today, on Ruth's birthday, of all days?" Edith paused, nodding. "Or more correctly, August fifteenth is her deathday."

Mary swore under her breath. Why hadn't she remembered the August fifteenth date from Ezra Waller's diary? Would she have made the connection in time to prevent this madness if she had remembered?

"Yes, she died on this day exactly 130 years ago," Edith went on, her faced flushed with excitement. "Do you know what that number symbolizes? The one stands for new beginnings, the three is for creativity, and the zero is for wholeness. Can't you see how it has all come together to this moment?"

Edith picked up the knife. It looked razor-sharp. "Today will be a new beginning. Today I will claim her legacy. You touched the rabbit's foot, didn't you? You touched the blood. You put yourself in my power. You see that, don't you?"

"I don't see anything of the kind! This is all a crazy fantasy! Tell me where Wendy is!" Mary paused, gasping for breath.

"I wouldn't dream of hurting little Wendy. After all, she's blood of your blood. But you should never have married John and brought him into town. He nearly ruined everything, but he'll pay a special price. He will die knowing that his family's blood is on his hands."

"Henry made up the town legend out of thin air!" Mary screamed. "Ruth Cummings was no witch! She was a prostitute and a murderer!"

"Liar!" Edith bellowed in fury as the knife slashed out.

* * *

Wendy played happily in her rocket ship for what seemed like a very long time. There were loud wind noises and occasional lurches, all of which made her space voyage seem more realistic. Like any small child, however, boredom eventually set in. She pulled aside the quilt to explore the grimy floor mat beneath it. That provided some diversion, as did the partial dismantling of the courtesy light, but eventually even the gritty corners of the trunk became boring. Suddenly, a terrific crash rocked the car, bouncing Wendy into the air and springing the trunk lid partway open. It certainly felt as though she'd landed on the moon.

Wendy peered out the crack and discovered that the moon looked very much like Marsh Point.

She pushed the lid open the rest of the way and climbed out

to find the wind had turned savage, and the trees were heaving and twisting overhead.

Upended by a gust, she sat with a jolt and Bunny slipped from her grasp. Something had gone very wrong, and Aunt Edith hadn't come back. She tried to stand and grab Bunny, who was caught in a tendril of brier, but the wind pushed her over like a giant hand.

Wendy was forced to crawl on all fours to rescue her intrepid companion, while blasts of wind threatened to send her tumbling. She had no choice but to keep the wind at her back.

She didn't know where she was going, or whether her mother had woken up from her nap yet.

Then she spotted a low opening in the brush and catbrier—a hidey-hole. Bunny clutched firmly in one hand, Wendy crawled into the opening. Aunt Mildred lived in there; she would take her home.

*　*　*

The storm had laid waste to the brush hiding Edith's cul-de-sac by the time John and Sam got there, and Sam was first to spot the rear end of her car, barely visible beneath a maze of branches. A tree had landed just behind the steering wheel, crushing the roof and flattening the entire car down on its springs. "I'll check the back," he said, leaving John to peer through the shattered side windows.

The trunk was partially open and Sam saw toys scattered on the floor. He shuddered. Did Edith really shut Wendy in the trunk, in this storm? Who would do a thing like that? Disgusted, he slammed the lid.

"Anybody inside the car?" Sam asked.

"No. How about the back?"

"Nothing." Sam approached John, shouting in his ear to be heard. "I'm going to look around here for a while and see if I can find anything. You go on down and check Ruth's cottage."

"What's to find here?"

"Why the hell can't you just do what you're told for once in your life!" Sam demanded. "Taste the rain, for Christ's sake!"

John licked moisture off his hand, and tasted salt. He could feel the ground tremble under him as huge waves beat against the sand.

"See what I mean?" Sam shouted. "Parts of Marsh Point flood in a good line storm, and this is a lot worse. If spray is coming this far inland, we're likely to have waves breaking over the beach any minute. The whole place will be under water when that happens. Get moving!"

* * *

John found the Model A, abandoned where a tree had fallen to block the way two hundred yards beyond Edith's Plymouth. Mary and Wendy had apparently made it this far. He hurried on, staggering against the gale, until he came to a newly-cut path leading towards Ruth's cottage.

* * *

The ground was alive, its heartbeat throbbing with incalculable power. Mary could feel its slow beat through the chair as Edith stood across the table with her back to the fire and held Mary's wounded arm in a vise-like grip over the bowl, watching her blood trickle into the liquid.

Edith's rage seemed to be spent for the moment as she stood, silhouetted against the roar of the fireplace. The gale pulled hungrily at the fire as it whipped over the chimney top, sucking the flames high. Edith must have used the ancient, powder-dry logs from the wood box to feed the fire.

"You're smart but not wise, Mary Gooden," Edith said, watching the blood dripping. "Your life was forfeit the day you and your little friends broke into this house. I'm here to take back what you stole."

"I didn't steal anything!"

"You stole everything!" Edith seemed fascinated by Mary's blood as it mingled with the brandy. "But you weren't pretending. You really didn't remember. I suppose none of the others told you that you were possessed that day, but they told me. It wasn't until years later when I'd studied the old ways, Ruth's ways, and learned them better than anybody else, that I knew what happened—that you'd stolen the Power that should be mine. And now I'll have it back."

Mary realized that it had been a bad mistake to challenge Edith's version of reality. The town legend was all too alive in her captor's twisted mind.

But there was another way.

"I have something you want," Mary said.

Edith tore her gaze away from the dribbling blood. "You do have something I want, and I'll have it back, soon enough."

Mary took advantage of Edith's momentary distraction, snatched her arm away, and pulled the amulet out of her shirt pocket. She held it up for Edith to see. Blood running down her arm stained the gold. "I'll swap Ruth's amulet for Wendy. A simple trade. You can have it as soon as I know where Wendy is and that she's safe."

"There's blood on it," Edith said, aghast.

"My blood," Mary replied, having no idea what the significance might be.

"Take it away!" Edith held up her hands as though warding off a blow.

Mary paused, baffled by her tormentor's reaction. This wasn't what she had expected or hoped for.

"Take it away!" Edith screamed again. "Throw it in the fire!"

Confusion gave way to clarity. Mary had gotten it backwards. She couldn't tempt Edith into revealing Wendy's location with the amulet; she could only terrify her. Indeed, Mary had inadvertently held up the goat's-head side of the amulet facing outward. To Edith's twisted mind, what Mary held in her hand was the Commodore's spirit. A vengeful spirit seeking out his killer.

A deeper understanding hit her like a blow. She knew now why Edith had killed the Commodore and left the Amulet around his neck. She knew now why it was so vital in Edith's mind to sink *Abracadabra*. To her, the Commodore wasn't just the last Cummings—he was a warlock. A warlock who's power lived on in both the amulet and the boat. That's what Dianne had meant with her "so much evil" comment. The Commodore had been keeping a lid on Edith's excesses.

Mary held the amulet up towards Edith like a shield. "As soon as I know where Wendy is, and that she'll be safe, the amulet will go into the fire."

Mary jabbed the amulet at Edith's cringing face for emphasis. "Tell me where she is!"

Edith seemed to regain her composure. She smiled. "So, you stole the amulet, too. It has no power if you stole it."

"Think, Edith. The Commodore was wearing the amulet when you killed him. How could I possibly have stolen it? No, it was a gift, a freewill offering." A gift to her, at least, Mary thought. "The Eye of Horus sees the Commodore's killer, and the amulet seeks vengeance." Mary had no idea in the world what she was babbling about—the words just seemed to pop into her head and out of her mouth. In any case, they had the desired effect as Edith took a step back.

"Tell me where she is!" Mary jabbed the amulet at Edith again.

"She's in the trunk of my car. You must have driven right by it." Edith seemed to be having trouble breathing.

"The trunk of your car?"

"She's played in there before and she likes it. We've made a game of it. It's her space ship."

"One more question and this goes in the fire," Mary said, hoping the flames were hot enough to melt gold. "You saw Phil Cantor walking around here and assumed the Commodore was going to sell Marsh Point, didn't you?"

What is it, Mary thought bleakly, that makes a person create a myth out of something they see and kill two people as a result of it? For that matter, how many other deaths had the Ruth Cummings legend left in its wake?

"You wanted to stop him from selling Ruth's house," Mary went on, "so you borrowed Mike's boat to go to Onset. And I suppose you bribed Mike to help you steal and sink *Abracadabra*, too. I suspect it was easy to catch the Commodore unawares and stab him, since you two were probably having an affair."

"You're smart, Mary Gooden. Of course I killed the Commodore. And I killed Mike too when he tried to blackmail me over using his boat."

The knife was next to the bowl, almost within reach. If she could distract Edith for a few seconds, she could make a grab for it and cut herself free. "Why leave the wrench in my flower bed?"

"Don't be a fool. I did it for you. I didn't care if the police got it or not. I just wanted you to find it and wonder if your husband was a killer. I wanted you to live in doubt."

"And I suppose the firecrackers were to torment John—another way to play with our minds?"

"He deserved it for his meddling. Now, get rid of that thing!"

Mary started to toss the gory bauble into the fire, turned at the last instant and threw it at Edith's face. She missed, and the amulet tangled in the lace at the neck of Edith's gown.

"NO!" Edith screamed, staggering back, clawing at her dress, just as Mary managed to heave herself across the table and grab for the knife. She overshot and the rocker's high back caught Edith across the chest, driving her into the fire, along with one of the rush-bottom chairs.

Edith fell onto the blazing logs, tried frantically to rise and untangle herself from the burning chair. The knife and the bowl of brandy fell onto the hearth stones. The bowl's contents burst into flames, licking the floor at Edith's feet with fire.

In an instant, flames began to lick hungrily at the building's powder dry wood, as though the house wanted to die.

The exertion of propelling herself forward had left Mary dizzy and weak. She lay sprawled across the table, her free arm trapped under her, and the rocker's suddenly massive weight on her back. The room spun around her while she lay trapped, unable to get her feet under her to push away from the table, unable to escape Edith's screams as she thrashed in the flames.

* * *

Where could Wendy be? Sam had trouble believing that a toddler could get far in this wind. Hell, he could hardly stay on his own feet. Sam walked—staggered would be a more accurate term—back down the road with the brush and briers writhing all around him.

It was pure luck that he spotted Wendy huddled amongst the undergrowth beside the path.

"Uncle Sam!" she said as he picked her up.

"You've had quite a morning, little Wendy," Sam replied. "I think we'd better find your mommy and daddy, now."

* * *

John followed Edith's path and arrived in the clearing to find a scene of chaos. Saplings and briers flailed madly in the wind. A massive oak at the clearing's edge, its branches stripped bare of leaves, twisted and tore at the ground as though in its death throes.

John only needed seconds to take it all in—seconds that seemed like minutes—before his attention was drawn to the house itself.

The cottage door was filled with flame, and screams cut through the howling wind.

Once again he was on the bridge of the *Dunn* amid cries of agony.

He had cheated death by fire twice now. Was Henry right? Was this time going to be fate's revenge?

A flaming apparition moved by the doorway as he sprinted across the clearing, ignoring the pain as he willed his bad leg to drive him forward, knowing that it was too late, that he had failed again, failed to save his own family.

Running into the building, he almost welcomed the fire that engulfed him.

Flames seared his hands and arms as he grabbed Mary and the chair, and ran for the door.

The screams finally stopped while John was cutting Mary loose. He looked up and saw something sprawled in the flames erupting through the door, its limbs slowly contracting in the heat.

Mary turned away, noticed the rocking chair, its polished mahogany glistening in the rain.

"Get that thing away from me!" she yelled. "For God's sake, throw it in the fire!"

* * *

"I was scared, Uncle Sam," Wendy said in a trembling voice. Her arms were wrapped around his neck like a starving boa constrictor.

"You were very brave, little Wendy," Sam replied, holding her to his chest so she couldn't see the burning cottage with its shriveling corpse. He looked over her shoulder to where the child's parents were silhouetted against the flames, clinging to each other. "You must get that from your mommy and daddy."

Sam didn't dare to wait long, however.

"Stop standing around you two, we need to get out of here!" he said as a sudden stillness descended on them. "The eye of the storm is right over us, and things will get a lot worse in a few minutes, once it passes off."

Chapter 42

Wissonet, August 22

A week of bright sun and cooler weather had followed the hurricane, and Mary was still recovering from the battering she'd received on Marsh Point. Thanks to Edith, Mary's right arm had required fourteen stitches. The fire had frizzled her hair, and both arms were red and sore from the burns she'd suffered. John's hands and arms were burned as well, not to mention the bullet wound to his arm. It was a miracle their injuries hadn't been worse.

Wissonet had suffered far more. National Guard troops were still patrolling the streets, keeping outsiders away, while work crews struggled to clear the main roads of fallen trees and the wreckage of assorted boats and houses. Most of the side streets were still impassable, and nobody could even guess when electricity would return.

Details of the "Cummings Gold Smuggling Scheme," and the deaths of Dianne, Mike, and the Commodore, as well as John's part in the sordid affair, got only passing mention in the newspapers, thanks to wall-to-wall coverage of the hurricane's devastation along the east coast.

Edith Whitten's body hadn't been found, and it was assumed that she accidentally drowned in the storm, like so many others. Mary didn't try to explain that Edith had killed the Commodore in the mistaken belief that he was planning to sell Ruth's house, or mention what had really happened on Marsh Point, lest she'd be called crazy. Or worse, that some present-day Henry Merton would turn the reality into another fantasy.

Henry's death was mention in the news, but not the Ruth Cummings legend, which went to show how little the larger world cared about Henry's carefully built creation. After all, the townspeople had more urgent things to worry about.

The Claytons had been over regularly since the storm, helping John and Mary with the myriad chores that were still too hard to do with their burns.

Of course, the much welcomed help came with the less welcome questions, as Loretta used the time to gather details of the Wendells' adventures. She sat at the kitchen table this morning with Mary and John, drinking coffee which she'd brewed over an alcohol camp stove. Once again, the questions began. "I know you've explained it already, but I still haven't got this witchcraft business straight. Was Ruth Cummings really sealed up in her bedroom?"

Mary gave John a meaningful look and buried her face in her coffee cup.

"I seriously doubt it," John said. "She was probably buried somewhere next to the house."

"You mean she's one of the skeletons out there?"

"That would be my guess. Henry Merton wanted a more palatable, or a more exotic, explanation for why Ruth wasn't buried in the church graveyard, other than her being a woman of ill-repute, and possible serial killer, so he invented the idea of her being a witch instead. The witchcraft story must have appealed to him, and being an incurable storyteller, he couldn't resist embellishing it over the years. And since he was by far the oldest resident in town, nobody challenged his version of history. Why bother when the Wissonet Witch legend was so much fun?"

"According to the obituary, Henry was one-hundred-and-one years old," Loretta said, "so he probably did remember Abraham Lincoln."

"He was a remarkable man," Mary murmured.

"It's kind of romantic, in a way," Loretta went on, "Witches, covens, secret rituals, and the like." She sipped her coffee. "And to think Henry made the whole thing up all by himself."

"Not all by himself," Mary said. "The town played its part by going along, without bothering to question Henry's version of history."

John nodded. "As the town historian, it was easy for Henry to create the legend: throw out some of the old newspapers, tell a few tall stories, maybe forge a few letters, and presto, an intriguing new history was born. The whole thing was harmless enough, and even kind of fun for Henry—until people like Edith started taking it too seriously.

"Henry must have realized the witchcraft business was getting out of hand when Mary started asking him questions while she was walking around with Ruth's amulet. And when he read Sam's note on the morning of the hurricane, recognized the August fifteenth date, and that Mary was alone, he sensed trouble. By the time he got to the house Mary was on her way to meet Edith."

"Why did Edith lure you out to Marsh Point?" Loretta said. "And why did she drug you, tie you up, and try to burn you to death? What was her game plan, anyway? Was it one of her witchcraft things?"

Mary had hoped not to get sucked into that discussion.

Fortunately, Riley was happy with the theory that the Commodore's death was part of a gold smuggling double-cross gone wrong, Mike's murder was drug-related, and Edith accidently drowned in the storm. Since they were all dead, only she and John could contest Riley's theory.

Neither of them was about to do that.

She and John had talked things over and ultimately come up with a rational story, which might even be what really happened, up to a point. They knew, of course, that they were copying Henry's lamentable practice of rewriting history, but it seemed worthwhile in this case.

"When we were young," Mary said, "four of us broke into Ruth's house to get out of the rain." She took another swallow of coffee. "We had very active imaginations at that age, and the place was supposed to be haunted." She shrugged. "And we fooled ourselves into believing that something terrifying happened that didn't. For some reason, Edith thought I had gotten some kind of magical power from Ruth Cummings that day, and she wanted to claim it."

"With a knife," John added.

"So, it was some kind of attempted sacrifice?"

"Luckily, Mary managed to get away from her in the storm," John said, hoping their neighbor wouldn't want too many more details.

Loretta shuddered. "Was Mildred a witch, too?"

"What does it take to be a witch?" Mary said. "I talked to Mildred the other day, and according to her, she and Edith had read some books on witchcraft, and practiced a few spells and incantations. For Mildred, it was just a kind of game, but it became much more than that for Edith. Apparently, it got to the point where she would go out to Marsh Point at night and hold rituals with small animals that Rufus caught in the woods.

"Edith's growing obsession finally scared Mildred to the point where she tried to warn me one day when I was picking raspberries out on the Point." She watched Wendy prowling after Nat. "If only I'd taken time to understand what she was trying to say, and she'd dared to be more blunt, this might not have happened," Mary said, holding up her injured arm.

"The police couldn't build a case against Mildred for her role in smuggling gold out of the company," John said. "She was too good at cooking the books."

"Did you know Mildred is moving away?" Loretta said.

"The last of the witches," John commented.

Loretta took another swallow of coffee. "I feel sorry for poor Henry, in a way. Nurturing the town legend was what kept him going all those years, and then it all came crashing down around his ears."

"Literally as well as figuratively," John said. "It was too much for his heart."

"You found his body right here in the kitchen?"

"Yes," John said. "A massive heart attack. Mary and I found him sprawled across the table."

Loretta slid her chair back a few feet.

Mary sighed. "If only I hadn't read Ezra Waller's old diaries and started poking through the old newspapers, Henry might still be alive."

"Nonsense," Loretta said stoutly. "It wasn't your fault, unless you conjured up the hurricane. The truth about Ruth was bound to come out sooner or later, Henry or no Henry."

"If you want to think about 'if only's,'" John said, "think about Phil Cantor. If Edith hadn't learned that Phil had been walking around Marsh Point and leaped to the conclusion that the Commodore was planning to sell Ruth's house, none of this would have happened, and nobody would have been killed."

Loretta glanced at Mary. "I don't suppose you've been out to Marsh Point since?"

Mary didn't answer.

"Sorry," Loretta said softly. "My big mouth. If it's any comfort, there's nothing left to go back to. The whole end of Marsh Point is gone. The cottage, the little cove—even the marsh almost back to the Oglivy's house—was all washed away. All that's left is the fireplace hearth and part of the chimney."

"Perhaps that's a good thing," John said.

Mary wondered if the fire had melted the gold, or if the amulet had been washed out to sea by the retreating storm surge.

Maybe the amulet was still there, she thought, buried in the sand, lying in wait for some unfortunate beachcomber to stumble over it.

Loretta droned on with her litany of town gossip, and Mary's mind began to wander as she watched Nat prowl over to his food bowl, while Wendy looked on with predatory interest. Mary surreptitiously slid her foot under the table and rested it on John's sneaker. He looked over with a smile and she gave a tiny nod at Wendy. Yes, she thought, it might have a few dark corners, but this was her world and her reality, and for now the sun was shining.

CPSIA information can be obtained
at www.ICGtesting.com
Printed in the USA
BVHW071752060321
601780BV00001B/29